THE SEASCAPE RETREAT

MEGAN SQUIRES

"Friendships between women, as any woman will tell you, are built of a thousand small kindnesses... swapped back and forth and over again."

- Michelle Obama

CHAPTER ONE

*I*t was the second time that week that the persistent beep had plummeted into a prolonged and monotonous tone, as though someone's hand had fallen asleep on a piano key.

"Time of death, 6:23 P.M."

The emergency surgery was an extreme risk from the get-go. Tabitha Parker had anticipated this outcome, though she'd hoped for a vastly different one. She had been relentless in her lifesaving efforts, putting her years of education and hours of trauma surgeries to the best and most practical use. But the intraoperative death was unavoidable. That's what the peer review would determine in the following days. Had any of her surgical colleagues been in her shoes, they would've been met with the same grim ending.

That mild comfort expanded within her as she shucked off her gown and scrubbed, and that reassurance continued to bolster Tabitha when she delivered the news to the family. Tabitha wouldn't allow herself to feel guilt. Empathy, certainly. But not guilt. Tabitha was the best in her field, not only at Seascape Shores General, but in all of Southern California's level one trauma centers combined. If she couldn't save her patient, no one could.

Two hours later, after finishing the necessary paperwork and changing from her scrubs into a blue silk blouse and fitted jeans, she slipped her purse over her shoulder and headed to the parking garage, now lit with lamps that buzzed like the bugs that swarmed around them. It took her five full minutes to locate her BMW i8 Coupe on the physician parking floor. Morning, afternoon, and night had lapsed since the start of her shift and the memory of parking her vehicle was fuzzy. Even fuzzier was her ability to recall her last real meal. Her stomach growled a muted rumble as she reached for the door handle to slide into the luxury vehicle.

Tabitha paused before starting up both the car and her personal cell phone. She knew the second she turned her phone on, an onslaught of texts and voicemails would trill and continue throughout the duration of her short drive home. She was tempted to leave the phone off until morning, but the plumber was supposed to call with tomorrow's timeframe for the dishwasher repair. She'd grown weary of hand washing her dishes and even though she currently lived alone, she'd accumulated quite a dirtied stack in the sink basin, clean plates and cups the lowest on her list of priorities.

As she suspected, alert after alert pinged. She could ignore most of them, all except those from her sister, Camille. That was one person who wouldn't offer Tabitha any grace when it came to her quest for solitude.

Brewster's. 9:30. I've already got us a table.

Before backing out of the parking space, Tabitha fired off a quick reply: ***Already headed home for the night. Tired. Thanks for the invite, though.***

Camille was composing her next text practically before Tabitha had even clicked send.

It's not an invite, it's an order. I know you're not used to being bossed around at the hospital, but in this family, I'm still your older sister. I should have some authority. ;)

If the growl of her stomach hadn't been so impeccably timed, she would've protested. But she had to eat and mozzarella sticks and marinara sauce from Brewster's sounded much more appetizing than the prepackaged dinner she had waiting in the freezer at home.

I'll be there in ten, she typed back, startled when her other phone—the one she used when she was on call—rang within her purse.

She withdrew the cell and wedged it between her jaw and shoulder as she pulled out of the garage and onto 12th Avenue. For a Thursday night, the streets were uncharacteristically congested, the echo of honking cars and screeching brakes bouncing off the high-rise buildings like an earsplitting game of pinball.

"Hello?"

"Dr. Parker, it's Chief Houston. I know you just finished your shift, but I want to sync up with you soon. Can we carve out some time to chat when you come in on Saturday?"

"Of course. Absolutely. I'll plan to be in early."

"Fantastic. I'm putting it on my calendar right now. And good work today. We can't save them all, but you certainly did everything humanly possible, and that's all we can ever ask. Enjoy your day off and I'll see you Saturday."

Everything humanly possible. Tabitha replayed the words in her head up until the moment she angled her car into the dimly lit lot of Brewster's, right next to Camille's silver sedan.

Wasn't that the entire problem? For as accomplished as she was in her area of expertise, for as skillful as her hands had become in her surgeries, and for as steadfast as her steel-hard emotions remained, at the end of the day, she was only human.

To Tabitha, it almost seemed unfair.

CHAPTER TWO

*H*er sister had ordered a cabernet and that clued Camille Todd into the fact that it had been a rough week, likely involving more than one flat-lining patient. If Tabitha had saved every life wheeled through her operating room doors, she would've ordered a soda, possibly a lemonade. If she'd lost only one, a pinot grigio or something equally light. The week that Tabitha had four patients perish under her care, she'd ordered a late harvest zinfandel, followed by a tawny port.

The alcohol content of Tabitha's drink choice directly reflected her work week. Apparently, this one had been middle of the road, but when you were an attending trauma surgeon, that still involved what the average layperson would consider overwhelming amounts of stress.

Camille never really understood how her sister could do it—cope with loss over and over again.

Expect it, even. It likely explained her blasé reaction to the divorce papers Ben had served her four years earlier. Tabitha's flat-lined marriage warranted a merlot that day. That was it; just a medium-alcohol-content glass of red wine.

Still, Camille didn't judge her younger sister. They all coped differently and in unique ways. Camille was still learning to cope with her own failed marriage and the fact that a woman half her age now shared her ex-husband's home, affection, and most recently, his last name.

"You'll bounce back. That's what we do," Tabitha had told her when news of Mark's affair hit the papers. As a state senator, he spent much of his time commuting to Sacramento. And along with racking up travel miles, he also acquired a collection of women clamoring to keep him company while away from his San Diego home. Camille had always suspected things would end this way. Mark was out of her league, both in looks and ambition. But they had been high school sweethearts and, at one point, started off on level ground.

While Mark's aspirations expanded into the political arena, Camille was content to stay out of the limelight. She was never fond of the small talk required while parading around on his arm during functions that involved copious amounts of schmoozing. Feigning interest in boring laws was not her forte. She put up with it, at best. But she wouldn't put up with his infidelity. She knew many women in her position turned a blind eye to their husband's adultery, but Camille couldn't do that. She deserved nothing less than the faithfulness she had given Mark throughout their twenty-five-year marriage. He'd made his bed elsewhere, so that's where he would remain.

"For someone who didn't want to go out tonight, you really seem to be enjoying those cheese sticks, sis," Camille shouted over the steady white noise chatter surrounding the two women in the establishment.

Tabitha swatted her sister's hand away when she tried to steal one of the appetizers from the basket. "Hands off. They're all mine."

"Not even one?"

"Nope. After a seven-hour surgery, I think I'm entitled to my own order of fried cheese."

Camille couldn't fathom the hours her sister put in at the hospital. Looking at her, one would never guess she'd been up long enough to see the sunrise two times over. Her chocolate-brown hair looked recently styled and even though Camille knew she wore little to no makeup, her dark eyelashes and permanently rouged cheeks made her appear youthful and vibrant. Tabitha was beautiful in an effortless, natural way, and at forty-four years of age, she didn't look a day over thirty-five. One would think the stresses of her job would lead to premature aging, but if anything, Tabitha seemed to age in reverse.

Camille sipped her lemon drop martini, licking the sugar crystals off the rim. "Tomorrow's your day off, right? I want to go see that new Chris Hemsworth movie."

"Can't. I've got the plumber coming over." Tabitha bit into an end of a mozzarella stick and pulled it, a melted string of cheese suspending in the air between her mouth and fingers.

"What time? We can work around it."

"He gave me a one to five o'clock window. Anything after that won't be matinee pricing."

"Tab, I know your salary. You can afford to pay full price." Her sister was strange in the things she was frugal about. She drove a luxury vehicle and lived in an extremely affluent area of town. But she wouldn't pay full price for an oil change or a flight and Camille knew she had chosen the cheese sticks tonight because they were on the half-off menu. She certainly had her quirks. "Better yet, I'll buy your ticket for you."

"I don't want to waste a perfectly good afternoon in a movie theater. If I'm going to give up two hours on my only day off, it should at least be spent doing something worthwhile."

"Then let's go to Edie's art show at The Dock. I feel bad that we haven't gone yet, and this is the last week her photographs will be on display. Some best friends we are, right?"

"Edie'll forgive us. She knows we're busy."

That was true. Edie would forgive them. Too easily, in fact. But busyness wasn't an excuse Camille felt comfortable giving. She wasn't busy in the way Tabitha was, saving lives and teaching residents at the hospital to become tomorrow's best and brightest surgeons. Camille busied herself with an unfulfilling, nine-to-five receptionist job at the Swanson Accounting Firm located two blocks from her modest rental townhome. The measure of busyness in her life crested and ebbed with the tax seasons.

"I think we should go and support her," she said again. "I'll pick you up at 5:30 and we can hit that taco truck on 6th before we head over. I'm craving some barbacoa street tacos, extra cilantro."

"Did you know I operated on a guy that was *literally* hit by a food truck last week?" Tabitha twirled coagulated cheese around her finger. "Perforated bowel and ruptured spleen. He won't be eating street tacos anytime soon, that's for sure."

"You need to get out more, Tab."

"Going out is what lands many of my patients in my operating room. Most traumatic injuries occur outside the home."

"Well, I think we should take our chances. I'll be there at 5:30. You better be ready."

CHAPTER THREE

*E*die Lancaster taped the brown craft paper into place and turned the wrapped canvas over on the counter. This was her third sale of the day and even though she kept reminding herself that she wasn't in it for the money, it certainly felt good to be rewarded in that way.

"I trust this will look just wonderful in your home. You'll have to send me a picture once you decide where to hang it."

"I already know exactly where it will go," the older woman said as she reached out to take the artwork from Edie's hands. "In the foyer, just above the sideboard table. I've been in three times this week to admire and measure it, just to make sure it'll fit. You have a real gift with that lens, dear. Thank you for sharing it with the rest of us."

"You'll have to thank the owner for taking a chance on me and letting me showcase my work in his studio. He's the only reason my photographs are hanging on these walls."

"Well, if that's the reason, I think I just might thank him." The woman ran her fingers through her silver hair that stopped just short of her shoulders. If Edie's grays had been that beautiful and not the wiry, scraggly kind that seemed to spring up out of nowhere in between salon visits, she would've gone gray gracefully. Her red tresses had started out God-given, but over the years, they'd needed help from a bottle to maintain their luster.

The woman squinted at her as she asked, "Do you happen to have his business card?"

"I do. Right here." Scanning the counter, Edie located the stack of cards that listed Cal Burton's phone number and email address. She handed one to her latest customer. "He's really good about returning messages."

And he was. In fact, Edie felt bad about the amount of last-minute questions she had fired Cal's way right before the opening of her art installment. To her surprise, he'd answered each within minutes, as though her inquiring texts weren't the nuisances she'd assumed them to be.

"Thank you again for the canvas. I can't wait to get this thing home."

Edie offered a genuine smile. She had doubted her talents at first, never imagining anyone would pay good money for one of her photographs.

The opportunity to sell her work came seemingly

out of nowhere. Three weeks earlier, she'd had her macro lens fixed on her camera and the viewfinder up to her eye, attempting to capture the intricate beauty of the hummingbird stopping for a drink from the feeder hanging outside The Dock's front door. She'd been so engrossed in getting the shot that she'd almost dropped her camera to the ground when the shop owner broke into her deep concentration.

"His name is Hank."

The camera fell away from her face and she was suddenly staring at a man—tall, tanned, and a significant bit younger than her forty-five years. He had the effortlessly relaxed look of a surfer, his dirty-blond hair worn longer than the businessmen her age who kept their professional styles trimmed, neat, and altogether boring. The flecks of paint on his hands were still wet, and when he went to cross his arms over his chest as he leaned in the doorframe, a smudge of teal spread over his forearm.

"Hank?" Edie had asked, clueless.

He nudged his chin toward her tiny, fluttering photography subject. "The hummingbird. I call him Hank. He comes by here everyday right around this time."

"I'm sorry," Edie had stammered, feeling like she'd somehow overstepped. "I didn't know he was yours."

"He's not mine…" His pause indicated his search for her name.

"Edie." She slung her camera strap over her

shoulder and jutted out a hand, not even caring about the paint on his.

"Cal Burton." He'd taken her hand and given it a cordial shake. "I own the art studio, but not the bird." He'd offered an arresting, lopsided grin as he leaned forward a touch and said in a lower voice, "He's all yours to photograph."

A blush had betrayed her, and she pulled her camera back up to her face to cover it.

"Mind if I take a look at what you've got?"

"My photographs? Oh, it's just a hobby. Nothing special."

"Just because it's a hobby doesn't mean it's not a talent. I saw how intently focused you were through that lens. I'm sure your work is better than you think."

He'd spent the following five minutes scrolling through the images on the back of her camera and when he'd handed it back, he'd said, "That's not talent." Edie's heart didn't have a chance to fully nose-dive before he added, "It's a *gift*. Listen, I'm thinking about opening the gallery up to other artists to showcase their work from time to time. I'd be honored if you'd be the first." He'd disappeared within the studio for a moment before returning with a business card slipped between his index and third fingers. "Shoot me a text if it's something you'd ever be interested in." Grinning again, he'd added, "It would make both Hank and I very happy."

Edie had originally worried she wouldn't have enough work for an art show, but over the years, she'd amassed an impressive portfolio. Widowed at twenty-eight with a six-year-old daughter to care for, she'd been stuck in her grief for as long as she could remember. She'd viewed her surroundings through the lens of heartache until one day, she made herself take a closer look at the life all around her. The world continued to turn, evolve, and thrive even without her late husband, Evan, in it. That reality struck a chord deep inside. She owed it to Evan to explore and cherish that existing beauty, and her camera gave her the perfect avenue to do exactly that.

This opportunity to showcase her work at The Dock was just the cherry on top.

"Hey, Mom."

Edie pushed her elbows off the cash-wrap counter and snapped from her reverie, her attention drawn to the entrance with her college-aged daughter now walking through it. "Hannah! I didn't know you'd be stopping by." She rushed over to pull her into a long overdue hug.

"We brought you dinner." Hannah held up a grease-dotted bag and swung it like a pendulum.

Behind her, Casey, Hannah's lifelong friend and—as of last year—boyfriend, moved her out of the way to step into Edie's arms. "Don't hog all the hugs, Hannah. Save some for me."

"I've got plenty to go around." Edie squeezed Casey and grinned. "You two must be able to read my mind because I'm starving and this smells wonderful."

"Tano's Taco Truck." Dropping onto a metal

barstool, Hannah reached deep into the bag to pull out a handful of street tacos. She passed two to her mom and two to Casey. "We ran into Camille there, actually. She says she's on her way over to check out your showcase. Should be here any minute."

Edie peeled the foil wrapper and lifted the steak taco to her mouth. It was every bit as delicious as its aroma had promised. "That's sweet, but she doesn't need to do that. She's seen all of my stuff already. It's not like they look any different hanging on these walls."

"She's a good friend," Casey said, then added, "My mother could take some pointers."

"Don't you say that." Edie's brow pulled tight at the accusation. Tabitha Parker was an incredible woman with an unparalleled skill, intellect, and drive to be the best in her profession. That inevitably meant sacrifice in other areas of her life, to the detriment of several of her friendships. But Tabitha's friendship with Edie wasn't one to lose. The women had met as young mothers in a toddler playgroup and a busy season in life couldn't jeopardize the close relationship built over the many years. "Your mother is a great woman, Casey. *And* a great friend."

Lifting his mouth into a conciliatory smile, Casey shrugged. "For an art show, these walls look pretty empty." He changed the subject, which seemed to be his MO when it came to discussions mentioning his mother. "Is that a good thing?"

"That's a very good thing." Sliding the curtain to

the backroom studio aside, Cal stepped into the gallery. As usual, he had a smattering of bold-colored paints across his white t-shirt and his hair was disheveled like he'd just rolled out of bed. He'd look out of place anywhere else, but at The Dock, he fit perfectly. "There was no question in my mind that Edie would sell out. She's remarkable."

"I haven't exactly sold out." Edie didn't know why she couldn't just accept the compliment. Something about Cal made her nervous in a way she hadn't been in years.

"You will. I'm sure of it. And once you do, you'll have to get back out there and take more pictures so this gallery looks like a gallery again and not a boring, bare-walled box."

"Mom, I know macro is your thing, but you should try some landscapes. Beach ones," Hannah chimed in as she crumpled the foil in her hand and tossed it back into the bag now discarded on the floor. "I mean, we do live just minutes from the ocean. You've got a pretty incredible photography subject right outside your door. You should take advantage of that."

"I think the fact that everyone around here can literally walk outside and see the ocean with their own eyes is the reason I shouldn't do that."

"Not everyone sees things the way you do, Edie." Cal hunched over the counter and shook his head to toss a lock of hair that had fallen across his brow. "I'm with Hannah. In fact, I'm giving you that as your next assignment: Edie takes on the ocean."

"That sounds intimidating," she admitted, not sure if it was her feelings about the project or the man assigning it that intimidated her more.

"Nah." Cal winked confidently, then spun around to retreat to his paint studio. Before he disappeared, he called out over his shoulder, "You've totally got this, Edie. I believe in you."

CHAPTER FOUR

"*A* sabbatical?"

"It's an idea we've been tossing around for a few years now, but we've only recently implemented an actual program that our physicians can benefit from. We think you would be the best attending surgeon to test it out. Most deserving, certainly."

Tabitha smoothed her hands down her medical coat and rolled out her shoulders. The office chair was stiff, the leather taut and unused like she was the first to ever sit in it. "Like a learning fellowship?"

Chief Houston's wide mouth pinched in the corner, as though trying to keep from disclosing something Tabitha wasn't privy to. He paused, then said, "No. More like a time of rest and rejuvenation. There's a place—local, in fact—that specializes in these sorts of retreats for professionals."

"What sorts of retreats?" Tabitha's voice roughened. "What sorts of retreats, Chief?"

"Tabitha, we've noted some things related to your performance lately. Fatigue. A couple significant slip-ups. And the numbers…"

"I'm a trauma surgeon. The fatality count will always appear skewed. You, of all people, know that."

"Yes, I do know that. But I also know that you can't keep going at the rate you have been throughout your career here at Seascape Shores General. You're going to burn out and we need you at your best. Our staff. Your patients. We all need you."

The insult cut into her more sharply than any scalpel ever could. "I am at my best. I'd argue that I'm at the top of my game."

"If that's the case, then we want to keep you there. And the easiest way to do that is to make sure you're taking care of yourself mentally and physically. Emotionally, too. Listen, I know this isn't your first choice—"

"Do I have a choice?"

She could see Chief Houston's Adam's apple bob in his throat with a constricted, labored swallow. "We *highly* suggest you go on this retreat."

"I see."

"Tabitha, there's no risk here. Your job will be waiting for you as soon as you return. I'm extremely confident this month away will bring you back at a level you didn't even know you could achieve. It's a win-win all around."

Tabitha's eyes flashed. "A month?"

"It sounds longer than it is."

"It sounds like countless missed shifts, surgeries, and patients that I won't have the chance to save. That's what it sounds like."

"Don't think of it like that. Think of this is an investment in *you*." He reached for a pen on his desk and scribbled something down, then slid the paper to Tabitha. "This is the website of the place we're suggesting you book with. Be sure to tell them you're affiliated with the hospital. Like I said, they have an entire program for professionals who need an opportunity to re-center and restart."

"Why does this feel like I'm being checked into rehab?"

The Chief's features softened for the briefest moment before he collected his expression. "Some of us are addicted to our jobs, Tabitha, especially when it comes to surgery. That high. That thrill and the rush of adrenaline. I'm not implying you're already there, but I'm also not saying you aren't on your way." He flipped his pen over and bounced the retractable end on his desk before dropping the writing implement. With two hands on the ledge of his desk, he pushed off to stand. "Do this, Tabitha. It will be a good thing. I promise."

CHAPTER FIVE

"*S*unrise sand yoga?" Camille took a sip of her coffee and returned the mug to the marble counter. She pushed back the laptop, shifting her weight on the barstool as she squinted at the small text on the screen. "Is there a way to make this any bigger?" She'd left her reading glasses at home again, not quite willing to admit they had become a necessity as of late.

"There's no need to read more." Tabitha reached over and pushed the laptop shut with her palm. "I won't be going."

"Seriously? You're going to turn down an all-expense paid Villa retreat? This place looks amazing, Tab, and it's not just the free Wi-Fi. Did you see they have seven different relaxation pools? That's one for every day of the week! I wouldn't even know what to do with that amount of potential relaxation!"

"I can't miss a month at the hospital."

"It sounds like the Chief thinks you can."

Tabitha's mouth flipped into a frown, reminiscent of the one she used to give their parents when they told her she couldn't do something she had set her mind to.

"I've been at Seascape Shores General five years longer than Chief Houston. He's never known the hospital without me. I don't think he really has any idea what he's getting himself into by proposing an absence of this length."

"You do know you're not irreplaceable, Tab, right?"

Tabitha's face paled. "Of course, I know that. It's just"—she paused and pulled in a breath that lifted her shoulders—"our unit is a well-oiled machine. Everyone has their own part to play."

"And you're a pretty big part."

"Shouldn't I be? I'm an attending trauma surgeon, Cam. I've worked my entire life to get to this point and now I'm just supposed to leave it?" Tabitha pursed her lips and blew across the top of her coffee mug. Steam rose in wispy tendrils around her face. "I'm not a quitter."

"You're not quitting. You're taking a break. You'll be back. Chief Houston assured you of that."

"And what if he decides he doesn't need me to come back?"

Camille wasn't used to seeing her sister's confidence waiver. Tabitha had never been one to request praise or have a need for any sort of flimsy affirmation. It was always a given that Tabitha was the best, and that was that. She knew it. They all knew it. It was an established fact that needed little further proof, like gravity. "He will want you to come back, Tabitha."

"I don't care if he *wants* me back. What I care about is that he'll *need* me to come back. There's a difference. I need to know that what I do is important. Necessary." She set her mug onto the counter with a bit too much force, and droplets of coffee splashed out and onto the pristine surface. "Because if it's not absolutely necessary, then what have I done, Cam?"

The sheen that came to her sister's eyes made Camille's stomach churn. This vulnerability was foreign. Startling, even. "What have you done with what?"

"My life." After a swallow that Camille could audibly hear, her sister muttered, "My marriage."

Tabitha never spoke of her failed union with Ben. It wasn't as though it was off-limits or taboo. Camille just assumed Tabitha didn't have any emotion tied to it. Tabitha was not an emotional woman—never had been, even as a young child when they'd lost their parents to a freak sailing accident.

Camille had been just twelve at the time and Tabitha was only ten. They'd ridden their bikes home from school that day, only to see their grandparents' gray station wagon parked in the driveway where the family sedan usually resided. That had been the first out-of-the-ordinary sign. The second was the plate of warm chocolate chip cookies Grandma Kay held over the threshold when the girls hurried up the walk, their backpacks slung over their shoulders and their expressions drawn in confusion.

"I told them they shouldn't take the boat out," was all Tabitha offered when Grandpa Carl sat them down at the dining table to break the tragic news. "The fog didn't lift until almost noon. They knew better than to go sailing in that."

Camille figured Tabitha would eventually break at some point in her life, but that never happened. Things broke around her, but she consistently remained tough as nails. Unshakeable. It was always a quality Camille admired in her younger sister, something she saw as a God-given strength. But Tabitha didn't seem strong now. And Camille didn't know what to do with that.

"What if I go with you?"

"Where?" Tabitha asked.

"On this retreat. What if I take a month off from the firm and we do this together? In fairness, it's so unbelievably slow at work right now that I honestly feel a little guilty about even taking a paycheck."

"You can't miss a month of work, Cam."

"Sure I can. I've got a good little nest egg in savings from the settlement with Mark. Plus, I've always wanted to have a sisters getaway. I just knew your schedule would never allow for it."

"Jeez, Cam. I'm sorry—"

"I didn't say that to guilt you, sis. I just think

maybe the stars are finally aligning and telling us it's time we do something for *us* for a change. Something so very out of the ordinary. I think it's a bit serendipitous, actually."

A smile that had been absent too long from Tabitha's face scrunched under her eyes and lifted her lips a fraction. "Only you would use a word like that."

"And only you would turn down an all-expense paid vacation at a five-star Villa. I'd say we both have our quirks."

Laughing, Tabitha said, "Truer words were never spoken."

CHAPTER SIX

*E*die pulled her phone from the nightstand and reread the text from Cal.

That's the last of them! Just sold your final piece. Pick that camera back up and help me fill my walls again! It's looking too empty in here.

She hadn't counted on selling a single piece, let alone the entire collection. Sure, she knew she was moderately talented, but it wasn't like her photographs would stand out in a crowd. If Cal hadn't been so generous in his offer to display her work, her bank account would still be low, along with her confidence as a professional photographer. She owed Cal a big thank-you. There was no question about that.

Punching her fingers across the screen, she typed a reply and an invitation and hit send before she second-guessed herself. She placed her phone back on the nightstand, determined not to glance at it until she finished getting ready for the day. Even with that resolve, her self-discipline proved weak. Minutes later, when her phone trilled with an incoming text, she flew across the room, her bare feet clapping on the hardwood floor as she snatched the phone from the bedside table.

I like that idea. That's right up my alley! I'll meet you there in an hour.

———

THE BRINY COASTAL air was heavy, the salt from the sea hanging as a blanket of humidity. Edie could feel it on her skin, balmy and damp as she pushed back the curly strands of hair that whipped around her face. She sucked in a full breath of ocean air, the sting reaching deep into her lungs.

Pushing up on her toes to look out across the shore, she propped herself up with her elbows pressed on the pier railing. Seagulls cawed from above, nose-diving low into the waters only to bob to the surface moments later with small fish between their beaks or gripped in their talons. Most people hated the birds for the messes and noises they made, but they'd never bothered Edie. If anything, she had them to thank for her introduction to Evan years earlier. If one particular seagull hadn't stolen her midterm notes and trekked halfway down the beach with them in tow, ultimately abandoning the papers in the sand next to

Evan's towel, the two would never have discovered they were in the same chemistry class at Seascape Shores University. They never would have become lab partners, and they certainly never would have fallen in love over beakers and petri dishes, study sessions and late night cramming.

As the saying went, the rest was history—a history Edie cherished with every fiber of her being.

"Penny for your thoughts?" Edie whirled around, coming face to face with Cal. His smirk was warm, making her stomach feel the same. "Sorry, Edie. I didn't mean to startle you. You looked so content. Mind me asking what made you look so peaceful?"

"Just a really nice memory." She pressed her palms to the thighs of her blue jeans and lifted her shoulders as she returned a smile. "Thanks for meeting me, Cal. I know it was a bit last minute."

"Not a problem at all." Slinging his leather messenger bag around, he pulled out two paint brushes and handed one to Edie. "I wasn't sure if you'd have one."

"That was thoughtful. Thank you." She took the proffered brush. "I think the only brushes I have are stowed away somewhere in our hall closet. And they're probably not even usable anymore, honestly. Back when she was a kid, Hannah used to love those paint-by-number activities. Our house was full of them."

"Another artist in the family?"

"Hannah? No. She's a math girl through and

through. She's actually getting her degree in Probability and Statistics. I think the only reason she liked paint-by-number was because of the structure of it all. Organized and methodical."

"What I like about painting is that there doesn't need to be any structure. There's so much freedom in a blank canvas. It's like a new beginning."

"That might be overwhelming to some. For me it would be, at least. I wouldn't even know where to start," Edie admitted.

"I can understand that. But I think you'd be surprised." Cal tilted his head as though searching Edie out. "So, where is this mural?"

"At the end of the pier. Follow me."

Recently, Edie had read an article in the Seascape Shores Tribune about a local seafood restaurant, Fin and Flounder, that had come under fire from the county. The building was long overdue for a good coat of paint, the salty air causing the old layers to peel and curl. Tony Backhaus, the owner, had suffered a stroke in the fall and while he had been able to keep the restaurant's doors open during his recovery with the help of friends and family, the upkeep to the exterior was an even larger task. One that went ignored longer than the timeframe city officials had given him to get things cleaned up.

Several painting companies offered their services, but all for a fee that Tony's medical bills and recent debt wouldn't allow. That's where the community came in with a call to action for local artists, citizens, and neighbors to come out with their paintbrushes and support. What started as a few simple coats of paint eventually became an ever-evolving mural. While Edie might have been intimidated to contribute to the painting on her own, she knew that with Cal's encouragement, she could come out of her creative shell. He'd been so successful in helping her with that so far.

Two hours later, Edie's hand cramped around the paintbrush. The long strokes were tiring and monotonous, but equally satisfying. She stepped back and surveyed their progress, rolling her neck as she shook out her arms.

"Cramp?" Cal dunked his brush into an old coffee can filled with murky water and then flicked it against his pant leg to blot the excess.

"I don't know how your hand hasn't fallen asleep yet. You're getting all those high places. Though I suppose that's part of the job requirement when you're that tall," Edie teased.

Cal tucked the brush handle into his back pocket and stepped closer. "Here." Reaching out, he took Edie's hand into his and flipped it over. Then, with his thumbs, he pressed deeply into her palm, his fingers massaging the cramped muscles with surprising dexterity.

It felt so good, Edie almost sighed. "Wow."

"Does that help?"

"Where did you learn to do that?"

"I was a masseuse for a brief period of time back in my early twenties."

Edie had a feeling Cal's twenties weren't the far-off memories hers had become. "Oh, so like yesterday is what you're saying?"

He flashed a toothy grin. "Just how old do you think I am? Or should I say, how young?"

Too young were the words that came to mind, but Edie left them unsaid. "I don't know. Mid-thirties?"

"Almost." Cal released her hand gently and then took up the other, working the same magic on the tired muscles. "Thirty-three."

She prayed he wouldn't reciprocate the question, and when he changed the subject without asking her age, he proved to be the gentleman she had always suspected him to be.

"I love this idea, by the way." He kept Edie's hand in his as he stepped back against the pier railing to take in the mural's entirety. "A constantly changing piece of community artwork. What a great concept. I, for one, really love our particular contribution."

"You *are* the one who came up with the humming-bird." Edie tried to relax her fingers, but she was suddenly aware of every nerve ending and that made it an impossible feat. She could feel her own pulse hammering in her wrist and prayed Cal couldn't sense its erratic rhythm, too.

"It was only fitting to include Hank. There was

already that beautiful flower just begging for its own little pollinator. Plus, I owe a lot to the guy. He brought you to me." The spark in Cal's eye was distinctive. Edie had never met a man who wore his thoughts so plainly on his face and spoke them so freely in his words. Like the artist he was, Cal's emotions were painted in his expression for all to see. "For that, I think the least we owe him is his rightful place on this mural."

"I suppose the art installation did bring a little bit of revenue to The Dock."

"Sure, it did. But I'm not referring to just your photography that I'm grateful for, Edie. I'm grateful for you."

Edie could feel the blush creep up her chest, hot on her neck. Without meaning to, she pulled her hand from Cal's. She couldn't tell if the whooshing in her ears was from the tumultuous waves at her back or from the words Cal had just spoken. It all swirled together as one indecipherable sound that felt a lot like drowning.

Running a hand through his hair, Cal swallowed before he dipped his head closer to Edie's and asked, "Do you think it would be okay if I take you out sometime?"

"Like a date?" The words blurted without permission.

"Yes, like a date."

"I'm not sure that's a good idea, Cal."

"I think I might've misread things. You're already seeing someone, aren't you?"

"No, that's not it. I'm not seeing anyone."

"But you don't want to see me…?"

"No. That's *definitely* not it." Edie didn't even know what she was trying to say, yet she managed to say all the wrong things. "I haven't been out with a man in a long time. Like a *really* long time."

"I'm pretty sure there's not an expiration date on those sorts of things."

"I feel like there has to be. I'm so out of practice, Cal."

He scooped up her hand again and began rubbing slow circles on her palm once more. "Then let's practice together. Tomorrow night? And we don't have to go out if that feels too official. My place. I'll cook."

Edie couldn't deny the pull of this man and her growing attraction toward him. But dating wasn't even on her radar, especially with someone a dozen years younger than she was. Even still, she found herself nodding her head and saying, "You know what? I'd like that."

"Me too, Edie," Cal said, his grip on her hand suddenly more firm. He stared into her eyes. "Me too."

CHAPTER SEVEN

"They should be in the top drawer of the nightstand."

"I've already looked there, Mark," Camille replied. "I don't see them."

"You'll need to look harder."

Camille fought to keep the irritation out of her voice, which was never an easy thing to do when it came to conversations with her ex-husband. "They're not in there."

"Did you get rid of them?"

"I don't know. Probably. I got rid of a lot of your things."

"But these were important."

So was our marriage, but you didn't have any problem getting rid of that, she thought as she yanked on the handle to the drawer once more, disappointed that she acquiesced to his demands. She didn't owe him anything, least of all favors pertaining to his attire.

"I need these for the gala, Cami."

"And you can't get another pair of cufflinks?" She squeezed the phone between her jaw and her shoulder as she rummaged through the drawer. "I'm sure Stephanie can run out and grab you a new pair."

"These were a gift from a big donor and he'll be there."

"You honestly think anyone will pay attention to your cufflinks?"

"Absolutely, I do."

The self-importance was nauseating. Camille knew this ego hadn't appeared overnight—that it was something developed over the course of several won elections and many successfully passed bills. As a young man, Mark had been ambitious, struggling up the corporate ladder with a reasonable sense of humility. But once he'd entered the political arena, things changed. He loved the attention of it all. He loved the wooing and the lobbying, and while she hated to admit it, his charm had grown exponentially over the last decade. The people loved him. He'd done great things on behalf of Seascape Shores up at the capitol. But he was a different man than the one she'd fallen in love with as a teenager. She knew she was a different woman, too. But she still had her integrity intact. The same couldn't be said for her ex-husband.

"Any luck?" Mark asked after a notable pause in their conversation. Of course, he had assumed she was looking for the missing cufflinks and not getting lost in painful memories.

"Nope. They're not here."

A groan of annoyance echoed through the phone. "Then I suppose I'll have to come over at lunch and look for myself."

"I won't be here."

"That's fine. Just leave the back slider open. I can let myself in."

"I'd like to be here if you plan to stop by, Mark."

"Are you worried I'm going to take something? I can assure you, I don't need any of your things, Cami. I got everything I had any interest in as part of the settlement."

That wasn't it. This rental was Camille's space, one Mark had never inhabited. They'd divvied up their possessions after the divorce. Mark had kept the house, which was fine with Camille. She'd needed to clear her head and her heart of that space—the space he'd brought other women into unbeknownst to her. But this townhome was hers, and she couldn't stomach the thought of Mark acting like he had any right to it.

"If lunch is the only time you can meet, then I'll make it work," she relented.

"Well, I'd appreciate that. And let me know if you happen to find them before then. It would be nice to avoid a trip out to your area of town if I can. As usual, I've got a busy day stacked with calls and appointments."

"I won't be looking for them. I have to leave for work now if I plan to make it in on time."

"You're still doing that receptionist thing?"

"Yes, still doing that receptionist thing." She slipped her arms into her pinstriped blazer and juggled the phone as she popped open the refrigerator door to pull out a chalky smoothie drink from inside. A breakfast of champions, she realized, but she really didn't have time for anything else. "For now, at least."

"I told you, I can put in a good word for you at Tommy Brighton's firm if you want. He owes me a favor that I should cash in sooner or later."

Though she knew favors were a big part of Mark's world, she didn't want to get wrapped up in any with him. "That won't be necessary. I'll meet you at my place at noon."

"Unless the cufflinks happen to magically appear before then. Let me know if they do."

"I won't be here to find out if they do." This man had an impossible time understanding the meaning of *no*. "See you then, Mark."

THE MORNING SLOGGED BY. Camille had lost count of the number of solitaire games she'd played on her phone to help pass the time. It wasn't that it was a bad job. For someone, it could be a dream job. Not much responsibility, but decent pay and the chance for advancement if one felt motivated. Camille had responded to the ad just a few months after Mark broke the news of his many affairs. She needed something to occupy her time, but she also knew her mental capacity wasn't where it should be. She could answer phones and paste on a cheery smile, but anything above that would require an effort she wouldn't be able to muster during that particularly painful phase of life.

Now that she'd landed back on her own two feet, she found herself easily bored with the repetition and simple monotony.

As Camille drove home at the start of her lunch break, she wondered if it had been a good idea to take the first job she'd applied for. Maybe she should've spent more time doing some soul searching before accepting the position. She hadn't been looking for a career, but she supposed any nine-to-five job inevitably became just that—a profession. She wasn't sure she could be satisfied much longer as a career receptionist in a firm she had absolutely no interest in.

Mark's sleek black SUV was already parked in her driveway when she pulled up to her townhome and shut off her wayward thoughts, along with the engine. She could hear a muffled exchange on his speakerphone and he turned off the vehicle once he saw Camille walk up to the side. Lifting a finger, he made eye contact through the window and wrapped up the call.

"Sorry about that." He stepped out of the SUV

and placed a quick kiss on Camille's cheek. "Conference call went long. Did the cufflinks turn up?"

"Not unless they grew legs. I told you, Mark, I've been at work and haven't had a chance to look for them."

"Right. Okay, well, I've got about fifteen minutes." He followed her up the cement walkway and stood close to her back as Camille fit her key into the lock and opened the front door. He peered in over her shoulder and asked, "Where do you suggest I look first?"

"You said they might be in your old nightstand, but I'm pretty sure you cleared it out before the movers brought it over here."

"I did, but I can look again if you think it's worth it."

"I really don't think they're in there."

Camille hated to admit it, but Mark looked handsome as ever in his slate gray suit and maroon tie. He carried himself with confidence in every scenario and dressed to fit the part. He was full of magnetism: his appearance, his smooth way with words, and his self-assurance.

"Another place we might want to check is my old jewelry box. It's in my back closet. I'll go grab it." Then, without meaning to, she said out of sheer habit and hospitality, "Make yourself at home."

Camille drew in a deep breath as she walked down the hall toward her room. She didn't have romantic feelings toward Mark—in truth, those had dwindled until they became altogether nonexistent years before their divorce was finalized—but their shared history was something so intricately entwined in the fabric of her life that she'd never be able to pull him completely out of it. She knew Mark in a way no one else ever would. Any amount of compassion she felt for him was born out of that place, which was why she—against all logic—had given up her lunch hour to help him look for a ridiculous pair of cufflinks.

With her wooden jewelry box in hand, she made her way back into the family room. The box was cumbersome and clunky, and when she saw Mark seated at her sofa with the leather-bound photo album spread across his lap, she had to keep from letting the box slip from her grasp. Mark's fingers held onto the corner of the page, but he didn't turn it. She knew exactly which photograph had caused this reflective pause. She didn't even need to look.

Mark didn't pull his eyes from the image as he said, "Just think how different our lives would be if we'd only been able to take him home."

"Mark." Camille lowered the jewelry box to the coffee table and then pressed a palm to her forehead, shutting her eyes briefly and inhaling sharply through her nose before saying, "I can't do this right now. I'm sorry. Can you please respect that?"

His gaze shot up, and he closed the album. "Of course. I'm sorry, Cami. I just think about him a lot."

"I do, too. Every day."

Mark leaned forward to place the album on the

table where it sat, often unopened but never ignored. The couch creaked beneath him as he shifted. He lifted the lid to the jewelry box, then cleared his throat. Camille had completely forgotten that she'd placed their newborn son's hospital bracelet in there for safekeeping when she'd organized her things for the move. When Mark pulled it from the box, letting it loop around his index finger, she had to steady her breathing so as not to fall apart right then and there. She couldn't do that in front of him.

"His birthday would've been next week," Mark said, like the date wasn't already permanently etched in Camille's heart and mind. There were some things that never needed reminding.

"Yes."

"Twenty-five. Hard to think we're even old enough to be the parents of a twenty-five-year-old."

"Well, we are."

Maybe the fact that Mark's new wife was just barely older than that made him feel as though he'd found some fountain of youth, but Camille felt each and every one of her forty-six years, down to the individual days, hours, and minutes.

Mark suddenly looked uncomfortable in a way Camille had only witnessed a time or two throughout their marriage. It wasn't the look of discomfort like those she'd seen him wear during a political debate or when under attack by a particularly ruthless journalist. It was a vulnerability, a shedding of his confident exterior that—though only briefly—hinted at the man she'd always hoped remained beneath the haughty exterior.

Hastily dropping the bracelet into the jewelry box and shutting the lid, Mark shot to his feet. "I think you're right. The cufflinks are a lost cause. I'll have to make do without them." He leaned in for a hug—the empty sort he seemed to have on reserve for Camille lately—and surprised her when he held on for a beat longer than necessary. "I'm sorry I wasted your lunch, Cami."

"It wasn't a waste, Mark. It's fine."

Glancing at the coffee table, Mark's voice cracked faintly but noticeably when he said, "You're right. I suppose it wasn't a complete waste."

CHAPTER EIGHT

*T*abitha didn't know what to do with herself. When she'd called Chief Houston the evening before to ultimately agree to the proposed sabbatical, she figured she'd have a few more shifts at the hospital before packing her bags for the beach. She hadn't expected the retreat center to have an opening for the following Saturday. And she certainly hadn't expected the Chief to be so persistent in encouraging her to reserve that particular booking.

So there she was, a Friday morning to herself, with no real plans or commitments. It should have felt like freedom, but Tabitha couldn't settle into it.

She had paced all morning, making sure things around the house were in order for her one-month departure. Was she supposed to place a hold on her mail? She knew Edie notified the post office last year when Hannah had been studying abroad in Spain and she took a three-week trip out to visit her. What about the water? Should she shut it off? Was it bad for the pipes to go that long without use? The tasks seemed insurmountable and tedious, which made leaving for the retreat feel like a burden and not the magical escape Chief Houston promised it to be.

By mid-morning, Tabitha had consumed four cups of coffee and texted her sister as many times with questions about her preparations. She had her phone in her hands to compose her fifth when it rang in her palm.

"I'm turning onto your street now," Camille's assuring voice greeted.

"Really? Thank you, Cam. Seriously." For the first time all day, Tabitha felt a wave of peace wash over her. Thank God for her sister. "I swear I'm not usually this incompetent."

"Incompetent is not a word I would ever use to describe you. This just isn't something that's in your wheelhouse and that's perfectly okay. I can help."

"Is planning a month-long hiatus from one's life really in anyone's wheelhouse?"

"Well, I had to plan a lifelong hiatus from my marriage, so I've got a bit of useful experience," Camille said in a voice wrought with sarcasm. "Open your door. I'm here."

"Camille, I'm not sure what I've gotten myself into," Tabitha said as she drew her sister into a long embrace upon letting her into the home. "I can't even seem to pack for this dang thing. The website says to bring clothes that allow your body 'freedom and openness.' Whatever that means. I'm assuming they're not referring to scrubs."

"No, most likely not." Camille pressed her mouth into a contemplative line. She always seemed to do this when a scheme was in the works. "You know what? I think a day of shopping is in order. I, for one, could use a little retail therapy after yesterday's run-in with Mark."

"Mark's in town?"

"Yes, for some fancy gala that apparently requires a particular set of cufflinks. He was certain I had them. So much so that he came by and insisted he look for himself after I told him they weren't there."

"Sounds about right."

"Doesn't it?" Camille rolled out her shoulders and shook her head as she set her keys onto the small table along the foyer wall. "Anyway, it rattled me more than I care to admit. He brought up Patrick."

Tabitha tried to suppress her surprise and keep her expression neutral. Camille rarely talked about her son. Mark spoke of him even less frequently. "Wow. That must've been hard."

"More unexpected than anything, really. I didn't realize he still cared."

"Of course, he still cares, Cam. Losing Patrick was awful for both of you. I remember vividly just how much it tore Mark up. He'd always wanted a son."

"I know he did. I just wasn't expecting to go there

with him yesterday, you know? He hasn't brought Patrick up in at least a decade."

"I get that."

"Anyway. I can't let my brain go there right now. Once the tailspin starts, I have an impossible time pulling myself out. But I'm totally up for playing hooky and not going back into work for the afternoon. I say we head over to the Promenade and get you wardrobe ready for your sabbatical."

"You sure you don't want to play hooky for more than an afternoon?" Tabitha really hoped she could twist her sister's arm. "Like maybe a month?"

***

TABITHA SLIPPED the strap of the shopping bag into the crook of her elbow to adjust its weight. She'd been pleasantly surprised. So far, the shopping trip had been a massive success.

A new store, Monarchs, was celebrating its grand opening, and the inventory was a perfect match. With the help of her sister and the eager young saleswoman who obviously worked on commission, Tabitha left with a pair of white linen pants, two loose V-neck shirts—one a pale yellow and the other the prettiest lilac—and a cable knit, gray cashmere cardigan that she could throw on if the coastal breezes picked up. She even found a pair of strappy leather sandals that were appropriate to wear both on a sandy beach, as well as out for a cocktail at happy hour. All in all, it was a win.

"Let's pop into this place really quick," Camille said, grabbing ahold of Tabitha's hand to steer her into a high end clothing boutique on the other side of the shopping center's courtyard. "I think we should get you at least one nice dress. You never know, there might be the occasion for something a little fancy."

Tabitha doubted that, but she'd been having such a nice afternoon with her sister that she didn't protest. She knew once she returned home, the anxiety she'd experienced over the impending retreat would creep back in. She'd stay out shopping until closing time if she could.

"That floral number in the window—that would be gorgeous on you, Tab. Really show off those great legs."

"I don't know. Feels a little formal."

The sisters walked into the store and were greeted by a saleswoman about their age who informed them that everything was twenty-five percent off for a current friends and family promotion. Tabitha perked up at that. She hated spending full price on an outfit she knew would be hanging on the clearance rack come the end of the season.

"Speaking of friends and family," Camille said, pulling Tabitha's gaze from an empire-waist black dress on a nearby mannequin.

"Oh my goodness, ladies!" Edie squealed as she rushed up to the women, shopping bags swinging at her sides. "I never thought I'd run into you two at the Promenade on a Friday afternoon!"

"I'm playing hooky and Tabitha's shopping for her beach getaway."

"That's not exactly what I'd call it," Tabitha amended under her breath as she pulled a leather jacket out from a rack and shoved it back after she looked at the price tag. Even with the discount, it was more than she felt comfortable paying for something she would only wear a handful of times.

"I wish I knew you'd both be here," Edie said. "I could've used your help finding something for tonight."

"What's going on tonight?" Camille held up a pair of dangling gold earrings and took in her reflection in the mirror on the display. Tabitha thought they looked great on her sister, but Camille must've felt otherwise because she returned them to the hook.

"Nothing, really." Edie shrugged. "Just going to a friend's house for dinner."

"You have friends other than us?" Camille clutched her chest, feigning offense. "I'm hurt."

"Well, it's technically a male friend."

"Good for you, Edie," Tabitha said, nodding. "That's really great."

"It's really something, I suppose. I don't know. I'm all in a tizzy over it. Actually, I could use your advice on a blouse." She held up a bag with the store's name printed across the side. "I've already purchased it, but I'm having second thoughts."

"Go try it on and we'll give it to you straight," Camille said, her hand on the hanger of a periwinkle blue shift dress. She shoved it into Tabitha's arms. "And you try this on. It's the perfect mix of carefree meets beach goddess."

Rolling her eyes, Tabitha took the dress and slipped into a fitting room next to the one Edie had just disappeared into. Bright, unforgiving iridescent lights framed the full-length mirror. Tabitha could hear a duo of chatty teenagers in the room next to hers and she tried not to eavesdrop as she stepped out of her jeans and pulled her white t-shirt over her head, but their bubbly voices carried too easily.

"I think you should go with the strapless. Who cares about your scar? Dylan definitely won't. All he'll be looking at are your boobs, anyway. They look huge in this dress, Stace."

"Dylan says he likes my scar. That it's a reminder that life's short and we're not all lucky enough to get second chances," one girl said.

"That's so sweet! I need to find myself a guy like Dylan."

"Tab?" Camille's voice filtered through the fabric dressing room curtain. "How does it fit? If you've got it on, let me see."

Pulling back the curtain, Tabitha stepped out from the fitting room. The dress fit well, hugging her curves in a flattering way, but at the same time loose enough that it didn't feel constricting.

"That's stunning!" Camille twirled her finger to encourage a spin. "Turn around."

Stepping from her own dressing room, Edie's eyes went wide when she caught sight of her friend. "Tabitha, that dress was made for you! You look gorgeous."

"You both are being very generous."

"I'm serious. You have to buy it." Camille pulled at the price tag and squinted as she read. "And with the sale, you can't afford not to. They're practically giving it away."

That wasn't entirely true, but Camille was right—the deal was too good to pass up. "Edie, that blouse is beautiful. What about it is giving you second thoughts?"

Edie tugged at the neckline of the hunter green silk top. The color complemented her fire red hair and pale, flawless skin beautifully. It was dressier than what she normally wore, but for a date, Tabitha thought it would fit the bill.

"I don't know. Don't you think it's a little low cut?"

"Not at all. It's plenty modest with just the right amount of sexy thrown in," Camille said, and Tabitha agreed.

"Oh dear. I'm not sure I'm going for sexy. It doesn't look like I'm trying too hard, does it? I feel like it's a bit young for my usual tastes."

"Do you feel good in it?" Tabitha asked.

"Yes, I think I do."

"Then I think it's a great fit."

Just then, the two high-school-aged girls tumbled out of their dressing room in a bundle of giggles, barreling headlong into Tabitha, who had to side-step to keep from being taken out completely.

"I'm so sorry," one blond girl blurted, and when her eyes locked with Tabitha's, she gasped. "Dr. Parker?"

Tabitha couldn't place the young woman. "Yes."

"It's me, Stacey Matheson. I'm not sure if you remember me, but you saved my life."

The memory came back at the mention of her name. It had been five years, but the surgery felt like yesterday; it had been one of Tabitha's most challenging to date. The girl's chances of survival were poor, the car accident narrowly claiming her life before she'd even arrived at the hospital. She'd been in the passenger seat when the driver had fallen asleep, and because she hadn't been wearing a seatbelt when the sedan collided with the big rig, she was ejected from the vehicle and left with little hope of even making it through the night.

"Yes, Stacey. I do remember you. It's so good to see you doing so well."

"Well is an understatement," Stacey's friend interjected. "Stacey's got a full ride to Stanford for rowing and is dating the best guy ever. Seriously, he's the sweetest. I'm totally jealous."

Waving off her friend, Stacey said, "I've always wanted to thank you, Dr. Parker, but wasn't sure how or if it was even appropriate. I read the articles that the newspapers published after the accident and I'm confident that if I wasn't in your care at the time, I wouldn't be standing here today. You're a big part of the reason I've actually decided to go pre-med."

Tabitha glanced at her sister and Edie, unsure how to respond to this unsolicited information. She was never good in these sorts of scenarios.

"My sister is certainly the best," Camille chimed in after a labored pause.

"Yes, she is," Stacey agreed. "Anyway, would it be weird if I gave you a hug?" she asked, turning back toward Tabitha. "Is that okay?"

"Oh. Sure." Tabitha tried to shake the uncertainty from her tone, and when she wrapped her arms around the young girl, she was surprised at the hearty squeeze Stacey returned.

"I owe you my life," Stacey said tearfully.

Tabitha pulled out of the embrace and replied, "I was just doing my job."

"Well, I hope it's a job you plan to do for a very long time."

CHAPTER NINE

"Wow." Cal flipped a checkered dishrag over his shoulder and leaned against the doorframe, his long legs crossing at the ankles. Edie couldn't help but detect the slight lift of his head and appreciative squint of his eyes as he said, "You look amazing."

After the hour and a half she'd spent in front of her bathroom mirror prepping for their dinner, she'd hoped for a compliment along the lines of nice or possibly even pretty. She hadn't prepared herself for amazing. Her *thank you* caught in her throat and came out as, "I brought a bottle of wine," instead. She held out the Syrah she'd purchased at the local market on the way over and nervously shoved it into his hands. "And you look amazing, too."

"I don't." Cal sidestepped out of the way to allow Edie into his home. "I'm covered in paint and spaghetti sauce. I look like a toddler after a messy day in preschool."

"You're always covered in paint." Edie smiled and quietly laughed. "But the spaghetti sauce is new."

She followed Cal through the house and into the kitchen. It wasn't a large home, but the white walls and cabinetry of the same stark hue, along with the marble countertop and ceramic subway tile back-splash, made the space appear open and airy. It matched in ambiance with his art studio, but rather than paintings and photographs bringing color to the otherwise bare space, his latest culinary adventure achieved that.

"I'm making lasagna," he said, tipping his chin toward the oven and then to the leftover ingredients that remained on the butcher block cutting board. "First time, actually, so we'll see how it turns out. I've got pizza delivery on backup, just in case." He extended a hand to gather Edie's purse and then helped slip the lightweight jacket from her shoulders. "I'll go put these in the spare room. Make yourself comfortable in the meantime. There's an antipasto plate in the refrigerator and I was just about to make up a cheeseboard with some cheeses I picked up at the farmers' market this afternoon. Feel free to grab them if you'd like something to snack on."

Once Cal had disappeared down the hallway, Edie tugged on the handle of the sleek, stainless steel fridge to retrieve the appetizers. She didn't mean to snoop, but she couldn't help but take inventory of the clear containers, all filled with leftovers ranging from chile verde enchiladas to fruit salad to what resembled a slice of a chicken pot pie. There were a few stacked takeout boxes from Edie's favorite Chinese food restaurant and she also saw a six-pack of wheat beer missing just one from the plastic rings. It looked like a bachelor's fridge, and Edie smiled at that.

"Sorry." Cal's voice at her back startled her, causing the door handle to slip from her hold. He pointed to the crisper drawer. "Everything's in here."

It wasn't a large platter, but it was just enough food for two, and they settled in on barstools around the island while they waited for the lasagna to finish. There were pickled onions and marinated artichoke hearts, along with huge garlic stuffed Kalamata olives and grilled red peppers. While Edie delighted in the variety, sampling each option, she couldn't help but notice Cal stick to the sliced focaccia bread and roasted almonds. Even though he didn't partake in the majority of the items he'd prepared for the platter, he seemed pleased with the fact that Edie was visibly enjoying it.

"Can I pour you a glass of wine?" he asked, pushing off from the bar to retrieve the bottle Edie had brought with her.

"Yes, please. I'd love one."

Edie's gaze followed Cal across the kitchen where he pulled a wine opener out of a nearby drawer. The cork squealed as it twisted before letting out a *pop* when Cal dislodged it from the neck of the bottle. He took two glasses from the counter and filled both with generous pours.

"Here you go." He handed one to Edie and then kept his fingers on the stem of his glass as he swirled it under his nose. "This smells delicious."

"The checker at the market said it's their top selling wine this month, so I thought I'd give it a try. It's from a local winery just a short drive over in Temecula Valley."

"Do you go wine tasting often?"

"No." Edie shook her head. "I went with the girls a few years back and I think I spent more time photographing the grapes than I did tasting the actual wine. I like a glass of wine with dinner every now and then, but I can't make an afternoon of drinking it. It all starts tasting the same to me. I think my taste buds get just as fuzzy as my head."

"When you say the girls, that's…"

"Tabitha and Camille. They're sisters, but they've each been like a sister to me since I don't have any of my own. We've been friends for the last twenty-five years."

Cal smiled, seeming genuinely interested. "Any brothers?"

"No. I'm an only child." Edie pulled in a long swallow of the red wine and instantly felt its warmth slide throughout her body. She'd been nervous all day in anticipation of their date, but now that it was finally here and with the help of the wine, she felt those nerves melting right away. "What about you? Any siblings?"

"I'm actually a twin. Identical, which is unfortunate because the world should only have to tolerate one of this ugly mug," Cal teased as his mouth curled into a playful grin.

Edie wondered if he truly knew just how handsome he was with his casual, yet confident carriage and easygoing attitude. His appeal was undeniable. To her it was, at least, but she figured she wasn't the only woman who appreciated Cal's charm.

"I've also got a sister who's a lot younger than Chris and me," he continued. "In fact, Angie's twenty-first birthday is next week. I might have to pick up a bottle of this wine as a gift for her since she'll finally be of legal drinking age."

Edie tried not to choke on the sip held in her mouth. She fought to swallow, the acidity burning her throat. "You have a twenty-one-year-old sister?"

"Yeah, as you can probably guess, she came as a bit of a surprise to my parents. They'd assumed they were done after my brother and me, but apparently the Big Man Upstairs had other plans."

Edie didn't think now was the time to divulge that her daughter was the exact age as Cal's baby sister. She lifted her glass to her mouth to dam up the words, but she choked on her next sip.

"You okay?" Cal shot forward as though he could come to her aid. But it wasn't the wine that Edie had choked on. It was the fact that she'd been pregnant at the same time as Cal's mother; that she seemed to have more in common with Cal's parents than with Cal. It was a tough reality to swallow.

"I'm fine. Sorry." She cleared her throat and softly tapped her chest with a fist. "Do you mind if I get a glass of water?"

"Of course not. Let me get it for you." Cal hopped to his feet to retrieve the requested glass just as the timer on the oven chimed. Edie sent up a silent prayer of thanks that she was quite literally saved by the bell. "Here you go." He passed off the cup before slipping his hands into oven mitts to pull the lasagna from the oven. Steam rose in thick billows as cheese simmered on the surface of the casserole dish.

"Cal, that looks picture perfect."

"You think?" His voice was chock-full of doubt as he surveyed the meal.

"It's better than any lasagna I've ever made, that's for sure."

"Hopefully it tastes as good as it looks. I'm pleasantly surprised that the entire thing didn't bubble right over. It seemed like it called for a mountain of grated cheese."

"You never can have too much cheese," Edie assured. "Did you follow a recipe? If so, I might have to steal a look at it. I'm always searching for new dishes to try out when Casey and Hannah come over."

"Hannah seems like a great kid," Cal noted in passing as he dished two heaping slices of lasagna into a shallow bowl. He handed it to Edie and then made one up for himself. "Would you like to eat here at the bar or in the dining room? And by dining room, I mean empty room with an unassembled table and matching chairs that are still in their boxes."

"The bar is just fine." Edie grinned at the way he presented the options. "I take it you haven't lived here long?"

"That's the embarrassing part. I've been here five years. I'm just not the entertaining type of guy, I guess. The only real reason I even have the table—albeit unassembled—is because I don't want to be the slacker uncle who never invites the family over for dinner. Chris has a wife and two kids—one boy and one girl—and by default, they always host for the holidays. But I'm determined to have Thanksgiving here this year."

"Well, you have six months to put that table together. I think you can pull it off."

"You give me more credit than I deserve." Cal leaned his head forward and lifted a brow. He held his fork to his mouth and said, "This really isn't half bad, is it?"

"It's delicious, Cal. As good as any Italian restaurant I've ever been to. Thank you for making it for me."

"Thanks for coming over. I wasn't exactly sure that you'd accept my invitation what with—" He paused, his gaze searching Edie out with an intensity that made her break into a sweat.

She gulped. "Me being so much older?"

She knew it was only a matter of time before they addressed the elephant in the room. She just hoped they could hold out a little longer. She was having such a lovely evening.

"That's not at all what I was going to say." Cal drew out his words and Edie felt each of them pang sharply in her stomach, her quick assumption making her want to crawl into a dark hole and never come out. "I was going to say with us being sort of like coworkers." Slowly, he settled his fork onto his dish and took up Edie's hands into his large ones, squeezing them with reassuring pressure like he had the other day on the pier. "Edie, I'm not bothered by our age gap and I hope you're not, either. I've dated older women before. I've also dated younger women. I like you and I'd really like to explore where things could go between us without either of us getting hung up on silly numbers."

She didn't want to admit that it was more like an age canyon and not just a gap, so she let that information be for the moment.

"I hope I'm not being too forward," he added.

"No," Edie replied, finally, shaking her head. "You're not, Cal. This dating thing—this is all just really new to me. If I'm being completely honest, I haven't dated since my husband passed and that was many, many years ago. I feel like I'm finally putting the pieces of myself back together and it's exciting and thrilling, but equally terrifying. I think I just got caught up in being a mom for so many years that I forgot how to be Edie, you know? But you've helped me discover her again through my photography, and I'm so thankful for that."

"Well, I hope you'll let me help to discover her in other ways, too," Cal said with a coy grin and before Edie could let his comment shake her senses completely off-kilter, he dipped the serving spoon into the casserole dish and asked, "More lasagna?"

CHAPTER TEN

*T*oeing the door open with her ballet flat, Camille squeezed through the doorway, careful not to let it clip her backside on her way out. With the confidence of a woman with a fabulous new haircut, she shook out her shoulders, angled her face skyward, and felt the early summer sun wash over her skin with invigorating warmth as she strode to her car, a large cardboard box in her grip.

It had all gone much easier than expected. Her boss took the news like he'd anticipated it, like it was an inevitable outcome finally coming to fruition. Camille wouldn't let herself feel the hurt that simmered in her spirit as a result of his unmoved—even if expected—reaction. It wasn't as though she'd envisioned some big, heartfelt plea to keep her on board. She knew there would be no going away party or even well-wishes. But deep down, she supposed she had hoped for a flicker of surprise, not the slow, steady nod from Theo, her boss, indicating he figured this was where things would eventually end up.

Still, it was good to end that chapter. So very good.

"I'm heading home to pack my bags," Camille said the moment Tabitha answered her call.

"You are not."

"I am. Just gave my notice."

"Don't you have to finish out your two weeks?"

"I don't know if I should celebrate the fact that I don't or if I should feel really, really replaceable," Camille admitted. "But no, I don't. I'm a free woman, Tab!"

"Well, my vote is to celebrate."

"That's just what I plan to do. An entire month's worth in retreat-style fashion. Are you prepared for this?"

Camille could hear Tabitha's laugh through the line. "I don't know how I could ever prepare for an entire month with my two best friends. No responsibilities. No plans. Just what on earth will we do with ourselves?"

"*Two* best friends?"

"Edie's coming!" Tabitha cheered. "She came over last night after her date and I convinced her to join us. Since she'll be working on building her ocean landscape portfolio, I figured this would be the perfect place for her to do just that. The ocean will literally be right outside our door. For the first time, I'm letting myself feel just a little excited about this whole sabbatical thing."

"I'm glad to hear it. I figured you'd come around in your own time." Camille dumped her box of office supplies into her trunk with a loud clatter and slammed the door shut. "And just how was her date? I'm dying to hear all about it in a very vicarious, *I-wish-I-could-snag-myself-a-hot-younger-man* sort of way."

"Oh, goodness. She'll have to fill you in on all the details, but they involve a shirtless man, a broken table, and a bottle of wine."

"Sounds scandalous! I can't wait."

"Is this the sort of story we should wait until tonight to share when we're in our jammies and have a big bowl of popcorn, or can you spill the beans now?" Camille caught Edie's gaze in the rear-view mirror as she flipped on the blinker on her sister's BMW to merge onto Highway 1. The road was already thick with traffic, especially for a Saturday morning. "And keep in mind, I'm an easily distracted driver, so if I get too excited, I just might crash this car."

"What on earth did you tell her?" Edie reached over the passenger seat and tapped Tabitha's shoulder.

"Not much," Camille answered for her sister as she pressed her foot to the brake pedal in anticipation of the slowing cars up ahead. "She just alluded to the fact that you and this Cal guy might've had a pretty exciting first date, if you know what I mean."

"I hate to ruin whatever bizarre idea you have about what happened, but I promise it's not as suggestive as it sounds."

"You're right. You *are* ruining it." Camille suddenly jerked the steering wheel, swerving the car into the next lane. "You turkey!" she shouted, flapping her hand at the driver, whose eyes were glued to his phone and not focused on the road, let alone Camille's emphatic display. "Get off your phone and drive!"

"Do you want me to drive, sis?" Tabitha asked, but Edie could tell it was more of a dig at Camille's less than stellar driving than it was a real offer.

"Oh, I'm fine. You promised I could drive your car, anyway. I just love this thing and heaven knows I'll never be able to afford one of my own," Camille said as she affectionately patted the dashboard. "I'm just getting out all of my aggression before we commit to this month of relaxation. Once we check in, it's all calm voices, loose muscles, and carefree spirits."

"Somehow, I doubt that." Tabitha rolled her eyes at her sister.

"You just wait. I'm prepared to go into full-on rest mode. Like a bear in hibernation. Anyway, tell me all about the date, Edie. I'm dying over here."

"It really wasn't a big deal." Edie smoothed her palms onto her thighs and looked out through the windshield from her position in the middle back seat.

Even without Camille's erratic driving, Edie was known to have a queasy stomach. The twisting highway that followed Southern California's curvy coastline was a surefire recipe for nausea. And the memories of the night before brought about a different sort of quivering in her stomach.

"Big deal or not, dish," Camille pushed.

"It was just a casual dinner. Cal made lasagna—"

"The man cooks? Wow, he really is too good to be true."

Edie loosened the seatbelt strapped across her chest, as it had locked into place when Camille hit the brakes. "We just ate and drank a little wine."

"At what point does his shirt come off? This is important. Don't leave out any details. I need to be able to visualize completely."

Gulping, Edie sighed. Her friend wasn't about to let up. "When I cut my hand on my wineglass."

"That's why she stopped by my place on the way home," Tabitha said, leaning toward Camille to fill her in. "To make sure she didn't need stitches."

"Wait, I thought it was a broken table?"

"Well, that broke, too." Edie rubbed at the bandage on her right hand, trying not to wince at the residual pain. "I was helping Cal assemble his dining room table. I'd set my glass on the edge, and of course, one of the legs that I thought I had screwed in correctly collapsed right out from under it. My instinct was to go for the glass of wine. I mean, you two should see his home. It's all bright, brilliant white.

I was not going to be remembered as the woman who spilled an entire glass of red wine all over that pristine carpet," she explained. "I reached for the glass and it shattered in my palm."

"You are leaving out the best part, Edie."

"Okay, okay." She schooled her expression and tried not to grimace at Camille's unrelenting inquisition. "It's not what you're thinking. Cal only took his shirt off to wrap it around my hand to stop the bleeding. That's all."

"What I'm thinking is that you are the only one in this car who has seen a half-naked man recently and you're keeping it all to yourself."

"I see a lot of half-naked men," Tabitha noted.

"Not the same." Camille angled a tight look at her sister. "Is he every bit as beautiful with his shirt off as he is with it on?"

Edie couldn't deny the very real attraction she felt toward Cal, and how that had only magnified in intensity when he'd tended to her injury the night before. Of course, Cal—without a shirt—was a major turn on, but the way he'd leapt to her aid, almost out of instinct, made the bundle of nerves wound within her unwrap and spread throughout every inch of her body. His close proximity and the way he'd cradled her injured hand, cautiously turning it over to examine it from every angle, turned her weak with desire. He had to be one of the most caring and attentive men she'd ever met.

"He's pretty easy on the eyes," she finally admitted

with the smallest giggle. She brought her hand to her mouth to trap it.

"Amen to that, sister!"

Even with the approval of her best friends, Edie couldn't squash the feeling that something was inherently wrong with the whole situation. Who was she to fall for a man so far out of her league? What on earth would they have in common past the initial attraction and shared interest in art and photography? Those commonalities couldn't sustain a relationship and she knew it.

Edie switched her gaze to the window on her right, fixing her eyes on the ocean waves and their repetitive assault on the shoreline. It felt as chaotic and tumultuously constant as the warring emotions within her, this back and forth of excitement and dread.

"When's date number two?" Camille asked.

"There's not one on the books. I don't know. Maybe next month, once I'm back home."

"Just to be clear, this sabbatical isn't a sabbatical from *everything*. I'm sure you can fit in an evening out, Edie."

"We'll see," was all she offered in response.

The three women sat in companionable silence as the vehicle wove its way toward the Villas. When her phone pinged within her purse, Edie worried it would be Cal. She wasn't sure she was ready for that. She'd left their evening in a flurry, tossing out the excuse that she needed Tabitha to take a look at her hand to make sure it didn't require further medical attention. The way Cal's features carved tightly onto his face, his brows drawn in apparent disappointment, let her know that he didn't buy her flimsy excuse. Even so, he was ever the gentleman as he walked her to her car and leaned over to leave a sweet, chaste kiss on her cheek.

Humility had forced Edie to shut the vehicle's door before she could throw her arms around Cal, pulling him to her in the embrace she so craved. She'd rolled down the window, keeping him outside along with the feelings she tried to push out of her head.

"Goodnight," he'd said, his hands hooked on the roof of the car as he dipped his head closer. "I really had a great time with you, Edie."

"Me too, Cal. I'm so sorry it had to end like this." She'd lifted her hand, still wrapped in his shirt, and shrugged.

"I hope I'm not being presumptuous when I say I hope this isn't an end at all." He'd tapped the top of the car as she'd started up the engine and flashed a knee-weakening grin. "I'd really love it if this is just the beginning."

Buzzing again, Edie's phone snapped her from musing over the previous night's events.

"Is that lover boy?"

"Please don't call him boy. It weirds me out." Edie glanced at her phone, relieved to see it was a spam coupon text from a local boutique. She shoved the phone back into her handbag.

"I'm just teasing you, Edie. He's all man."

"Since when have you gotten so insatiable, sis?" Tabitha tucked her chin back as she cast a leery look at her sister.

"Honestly, I really have no idea. I think I'm just feeling free without the binds of an unfulfilling job or a loveless marriage tying me down anymore. This is our time to shine, ladies!" Camille let out a loud *whoop* and punched a fist in the air in celebration. With the absence of her hands on the steering wheel, the vehicle veered across the divider before Camille over-corrected and sent them swaying the other direction.

"Let's save the celebrating for when we get to the Villas," Tabitha said, patting her sister on the shoulder. "I think the road needs all of your concentration right now."

"I've never been one to multitask. Good thing I won't have any tasks to multi for the next month."

"You are absolutely crazy, sis."

"And you love it. Seascape Shores Villas, you better be ready for us because here we come!"

Edie shook her head and laughed at their banter. At the very least, it promised to be an entertaining month.

CHAPTER ELEVEN

"Welcome, Dr. Parker. Camille. Edith. We've been expecting you. I'm Katherine and I'll be getting you all checked in this morning."

A young woman with an elegant blonde ponytail and equally sleek black shift dress stepped out from behind the front desk to greet the Seascape Shores Villas' newest guests. She extended a hand to Tabitha and gave it a shake. When she continued to speak, her voice came out in a soothing, hushed almost-whisper, like the low volume of a late night radio DJ. "I trust valet is currently parking your car?"

"Yes, they are."

"Great. The bellhop will get your bags delivered and situated at your Villa, so you don't have to worry about anything there. In the meantime, would you like a quick tour around the premises and a rundown of all the amenities available to you during your month long retreat here with us?"

"Absolutely," Tabitha said with a slight nod of her head.

Skirting the desk once more, Katherine gathered three brochures and passed them off to the women. "Our complete menu of services can be found in here. Everything listed is included with your Villa stay, we just ask that you make your reservations at least twenty-four hours before your desired service so we can be sure our staff is on-hand and prepared for you."

Tabitha's eyes went wide at the menu of spa options. She'd been to a day spa for Camille's bachelorette party over two decades before, but they'd only splurged for chair massages and painted toenails, and the salon itself was no larger than a postage stamp. Tabitha couldn't even pronounce some of the decadent services provided at the Seascape Shores Villas.

"Our most popular service is the mud bath. If you've never had one, I highly recommend it. We use only the finest montmorillonite mud imported directly from France to offer you an invigorating bath unlike anything you've ever experienced."

At her back, Tabitha could hear her sister choke back a snicker. How Katherine could make even mud sound lavish was a true gift.

"We have three saunas located on the property that you are welcome to utilize at your leisure. Our swimming pools are heated to ninety-two degrees and are open from seven AM to ten PM. There's one Olympic-sized lap pool located at the north entrance —you probably saw it when you drove in—and the other is right out here." She nodded her head toward the expanse of sliding glass doors that had to be at least twelve feet tall, reaching all the way to the beautiful arched ceiling and draped in thick, chocolate colored velvet that tumbled down and pooled onto the tile floor. "Let's step out here for a moment to take a closer look."

Tugging on the handle, Katherine slid the doors open wide. A rush of misty ocean air whooshed into the concierge area, lifting the woman's hair like she was in a shampoo commercial. "Right this way."

Tabitha, Edie, and Camille all exchanged a look, and Tabitha knew they were thinking the same thing. This place was phenomenal. Never in her life had she been to a resort, let alone one the likes of the Villas. The pool that Katherine had recommended they check out was straight out of a luxury magazine. Water in the deepest aqua hue slipped over the pool's infinity edge, making the separation between it and the ocean entirely non-existent. Gray and white striped umbrellas dotted the surroundings with plush, cushioned lounge chairs spaced underneath them. There were a few guests with dark sunglasses and expensive looking drinks in hand, already enjoying the beach air and the Villas' many amenities.

"Your Villa keys will gain you entry into both of our pool areas. Clean towels are provided, so no need to bring any down from your rooms. Robes can also be found in the changing areas, and there are lockers available should you need one. The cabanas that you see out on the sand,"—Katherine motioned her hand toward a row of white canvas covered tents located just at the water's edge—"those are available for you during your stay. We just ask that you reserve them ahead of time, as they are quite popular and fill up quickly, especially on the weekends. You'll find a full bar and restaurant menu located in a canvas pocket inside each of the cabanas, but everything is also listed online. That's another thing I should mention: room service is twenty-four seven, so if you have a craving for oysters or foie gras at midnight, just give us a ring. Our staff is here for you at any point throughout the duration of your stay. This retreat is all about meeting your needs and creating a space of healing where you can re-center and rejuvenate."

Splaying an arm out at her side, Katherine motioned for the women to follow her back indoors. "Watch your step," she said as she strode over the threshold. "The last thing worth noting," she continued while she walked toward the concierge podium, "are our additional therapies. Yes, we offer everything you could need to ensure the health and wellness of the body, but we also believe the health of the mind is equally important. We have several highly esteemed life coaches and therapists on staff should you wish to set up an appointment. We also offer daily services like yoga and meditation, which blend the soundness of both body and mind. It's truly an all-encompassing wellness retreat here at the Seascape Shores Villas and our hope is that this next month is just the beginning of a beautiful new you."

Even though it felt like a sales pitch, there was a sincerity in Katherine's tone that made Tabitha think people actually desired becoming something new. That was the entire problem here—she liked the "old" Tabitha and saw no need to create a new one. Hadn't she been living out her dreams already? Hadn't she achieved exponentially more in her lifetime than most people her age? It wasn't that she was arrogant, she just knew she had a gift and with that came an obligation to use it. Sure, she could get behind the idea of daily sunbathing and weekly massages, but life coaching? That's where she drew the line.

"Can I answer any questions for you? Or would you like me to show you to your Villa now?" Katherine asked, her hands folded in front of her on the counter.

"I'd love to see our Villa," Edie piped up.

"Me too," Camille agreed.

"Absolutely." Nodding, Katherine reached into a drawer and pulled three key cards from within it. She typed something on a computer in front of her and swiped each card, then passed them to each woman. "I have lanyards, too, if you'd like one. Some people don't love wearing their keys around their necks, but it does prevent you from losing it. You'll need your key to access each area of our property."

"I'll take one," the women all said in unison.

Katherine laughed. "Great. Three lanyards it is." She handed them off and waved her hand. "Follow me. Your Villa awaits."

"I just checked out the bedrooms. I've never seen a bed that big in my entire life!" Edie raced down the stairs, her bare feet clapping on the travertine tile floor. "I did snow angels on it and still didn't reach the edge."

"Forget the size of the beds. I've never rested my head on a pillow that felt like an actual cloud," Camille said. "A *cloud*. Seriously, even if we never leave this Villa for the next thirty days, it will be well worth it."

Tabitha couldn't disagree. When Katherine had shown them around their place, Tabitha had been impressed at every turn. Lavish, rich fabrics covered throw pillows and the two couches in the living room were the softest, supplest leather she had ever laid her hands on. The granite countertops in the kitchen shone like they had been freshly waxed and the fixtures throughout the Villa were the most beautiful brushed silver. Everything became even more stunning when they were told housekeeping would come by daily for a light cleaning. That she got to enjoy this decadent space without needing to clean it tipped the scales for Tabitha. She was sincerely beginning to look forward to this month away from the responsibilities of the hospital.

"What should we do first?" Edie snagged the pamphlet from the coffee table and plopped onto the couch. It hissed beneath her as the full cushions practically enveloped her entire body. "Oh my goodness," she said with a giggle. "I might need one of you to pull me out of here when I want to get up. This is the fluffiest couch I've ever sat on! I've nearly been swallowed alive!"

Tabitha grinned, sinking lower into the loveseat. "Seriously, right?"

"I think I'm going to set up an appointment with a life coach." In the kitchen, Camille popped one of the complimentary chocolate covered strawberries into her mouth and chomped down loudly.

Tabitha tried not to bristle at her sister's words. "Really?"

"Um, absolutely. I kind of feel like I'm in the perfect place to talk with someone about my life goals. As of yesterday at noon, I had exactly zero."

"That's not true at all, Cam." Edie shook her head at her friend. "I think the fact that you quit your job means that you actually *do* have goals. Goals like not wasting your time on a dead-end job that was literally sucking the joy out of your life."

"When you put it that way, I guess you could be right."

"I know I'm right. And I fully support you digging deeper in an effort to identify those goals. I think a life coach can certainly help you do that."

Tabitha was glad for her sister's epiphany, but she didn't hold out hope of experiencing any of her own. She was willing to acquiesce when it came to a little pampering, but opening up to a complete stranger about her goals and aspirations? That wasn't going to happen.

"I'm kind of interested in the mud baths," Edie said, flipping the brochure over and squinting her eyes as she read the text.

"I'm going to be honest," Camille started. "It was all I could do not to totally lose it when she was talking about their imported, fancy mud. Seriously, no one can make mud sound appealing, not even that super sophisticated woman."

"I don't know. Aren't you just the slightest bit intrigued?" Edie gave Camille a sidelong glance.

"Don't get me wrong, I'm absolutely going to sign up for it. But I still think it's just going to be a bunch of glorified dirt. I'm down to get covered in it though. What about you, sis? You in?"

Tabitha groaned. "Are we all doing it?"

"Yes," Edie said as she tossed the brochure back onto the low table and leaned her head further into the couch cushion. "We are all doing it."

"And I suppose you'll pressure me into it if I say no, right?"

"I believe you're the one who pressured us into

joining you on this retreat, actually, so it's really only fair that we do the same."

"You're not wrong." Tabitha laughed. "And I'm beginning to wish I hadn't been so insistent on you coming."

"Oh, please. You are *so* glad we are here right now, encouraging you to join us in a tub of pig slop." Camille came around the loveseat and flopped down next to Tabitha. She nudged her shoulder into her side and looked up with pleading eyes.

"It's not pig slop, sis. It's imported from *France*," Tabitha teased in a fabulously terrible French accent.

"Okay, so French pigs rolled around in it first." Camille shrugged. "You'll join us?"

"I'll join you."

"Yay!" Edie waved two hands in the air in celebration. "Let's get our mud-fest on!"

CHAPTER TWELVE

*T*hey spent the first night in, opting for a Lifetime movie and room service. Camille had ordered seared ahi over a bed of mixed greens, tossed with a citrus vinaigrette that reminded her of the one she used to make for the salads Mark took to the office for lunch. Tabitha and Edie had shared a wood-fired margherita pizza. They couldn't pass up the warm chocolate chip cookie and vanilla ice cream combo featured on the dessert page, the mouthwatering picture doing its job to lure them in. It was heavenly in every way and the fact that they didn't have to cook made everything taste even more delicious.

It was Sunday, and they decided to hold off one day before scheduling any spa treatments. Camille loved that idea. The infinity pool had been calling her name and she couldn't wait to grab her book and her pink sunhat to cozy up under one of the huge umbrellas. The temperature was mild and by mid-afternoon, the sun was high in a cloudless sky.

In fact, to her surprise, it was nearly noon when Camille finally rolled out of bed. She couldn't remember the last time she'd overslept at that length. Rarely a day went by when her alarm clock wasn't her blaring wake up call. Today, she felt like a teenager and reveled in the fact that she could do this every single morning for the next month if she so pleased. No rules. No plans. It was almost too good to be true.

When she'd finally moseyed her way downstairs, there was a note on the granite island, her name scribbled across the top in familiar cursive. Edie had headed out with her camera to get a jump start on her newest portfolio and Tabitha had just left for a run.

Camille remembered back to when they were teenagers, when her younger sister had convinced her to join the high school cross-country team. If only to appease her, Camille had agreed, but her joints and her muscles protested every inch of every mile. Tabitha had a runner's body with her lithe frame and sinewy build. She was made for running. Yet, despite their shared genetics, Camille most certainly was not, her feet too flat and her ankles too prone to twisting. She hated running just about as much as she hated Brussels sprouts or enduring a root canal. Even so, she couldn't help but smile at the fact that Tabitha was out on the beach at that moment, her legs stretching and feet meeting the sandy coastline with every marked stride.

"I need to go clear my head," Tabitha used to say, crouched down while she laced up her sneakers by the front door of their childhood home. *"I'll be back when I've cleared out all the cobwebs."*

Camille pictured the wind whipping at her sister's long hair and prayed that it would invigorate her spirit, enabling her to let go of whatever demons she had pent up inside.

Camille knew they were there. Tabitha's brief comment about her failed marriage with Ben was just a hint into her sister's trove of regrets. Of course, Camille had wanted to dive deeper into that startling admission and peel back the layers—sweep out the cobwebs spun over the many years—but she knew it wasn't her place. Tabitha had scoffed at the idea of talking to a professional, but Camille believed it would be the best thing for her sister.

One step at a time, she reminded herself. That Tabitha had even checked into the Villas was a small miracle in and of itself. Who knew what an entire month could accomplish?

Camille thought about these things as she made quick work of getting ready for her day at the pool. She slipped into her black one-piece swimsuit with the flattering, scalloped neckline and pulled a floral print cover up over the top, finishing her sunbathing attire with the cutest wedge sandals that she'd picked up on clearance the week before at the mall. After spreading a generous helping of sunscreen across her face, shoulders, and neck, she tossed the bottle into her wicker handbag, along with a thermos of ice cold water and her latest romance paperback from the library.

All set.

She flipped the note on the counter over and wrote that she'd be at the pool if anyone needed her.

The pool was no more than twenty yards from their Villa, which proved to be the perfect distance: not too far, but not so close that they could hear splashing or conversations that grew louder in volume with each poolside drink.

On her short walk over, Camille nodded at the other guests that passed, tipping the brim of her wide, floppy hat and offering a genuine smile. Everyone was so friendly here, so seemingly at peace and carefree. Camille could already feel the stresses she'd bound up in her shoulders start to melt away rapidly, like she'd shrugged off a too-tight jacket and could finally shake her limbs loose.

While falling asleep the night before, she'd promised herself that she wouldn't dwell on her job any longer. She would not look at quitting as the failure some might be inclined to label it. Edie was right. It was the only thing to do. Camille had to leave that particular workplace in order to find success elsewhere. She just wished she had never taken the silly job in the first place.

"Why do you always settle, Camille?" she murmured aloud as she waved her key across the keypad on the entrance gate to the pool area.

"Maybe because you don't know your true value."

The husky voice at her back had her shooting sky high, clutching her handbag the way she instinctively did when in an unlit parking lot or crowded airport. Camille spun around, about to give this stranger a real piece of her mind. What kind of person went around joining rhetorical conversations uninvited?

"Excuse me?" The assertion died in her throat when her eyes met those of the man in question. His head was cocked coolly to the side, and he rubbed at the salt and pepper stubble on his jawline in the most nonchalant manner. Camille fought the urge to stare. He was the picture perfect definition of a silver fox and she had to calculatedly time her blinks just to make sure she didn't gawk at the man.

"You asked a question. I gave you an answer," he said, leaning his upper body forward, directly into her bubble of personal space.

"Yes," Camille began, but she needed to train her voice to keep it from shaking. "I was talking to myself."

"But you weren't really, were you?"

"Um, yes, I really was." Flipping back around, she scanned her key against the pad once more, but the gate failed to open. It appeared she was trapped in this dreadfully awkward conversation.

"Need some help?" The man gestured toward the gate. Camille stepped aside, albeit reluctantly. With one wave of his key, the latch clicked and unlocked. "After you."

"Do you make a habit of offering unsolicited advice to strangers?"

"Only those in fuchsia sunhats."

"It's more of a magenta, really."

Lifting his hand to his chest, the man produced an exaggerated, guilty expression. "My apologies. I really need to study up on my color wheel."

"It's an honest mistake." Camille played along, if only as a small olive branch for being so rude initially. "But thank you for opening the gate. I'm not sure why my key isn't working."

"These things are really easy to deactivate. I'm on my third already and I've only been here as many days." He tugged at the lanyard looped around his tanned neck and smiled before adding, "Name's Foster."

"Camille." She reciprocated the greeting. "But you already know that from my little pep talk back there." She dropped her things onto the nearest empty chaise and pulled her sunglasses from her eyes, tucking them into the pocket of her cover up. "And I do value myself, just so you know. It's the whole reason I recently quit my job. I deserve better and I'm going to make sure I never settle again. Not with work. Not with relationships. Things are going to change."

"Good for you, Camille," Foster congratulated. "That's really great."

"It is, actually. I'm living my best life."

"I think it's fair to say we're all living our best lives

here at the Villas. I mean, have you ever been to a place that offers complimentary sunset s'mores?"

"It is pretty surreal, isn't it?"

Foster motioned toward the lounge chair next to the one Camille had staked her claim on. "Do you mind if I join you?"

"Not at all." She nodded. His company—though unexpected—would be nice. "So what brings you here, Foster?"

"A wedding planning retreat. My oldest daughter's."

"They have entire retreats for planning weddings? I had no idea."

"Right? Back in my day, I just rented a tux and showed up at the church. Now they have vision boards and vow writing sessions and these elaborate ways of asking their friends to join the bridal party. Honestly, I'm just signing the checks. Whatever Becca and her fiancé want is fine by me. The less I have to be involved in making the decisions, the better. They don't really need this old geezer's input, anyway."

Without meaning to, Camille's gaze landed on Foster's empty fourth finger. Something foreign surged within her at the absence of a wedding ring and she tried to tamp the feeling down, knowing she had no right to it. They'd only just met, for goodness' sake. "Are they getting married here?"

"Here, as in Seascape Shores, yes. But not at the Villas. My construction job doesn't allow for that sort of hefty price tag. Her fiancé's parents are covering this retreat bill. It's the only way I'd ever be able to set foot on this property." He blew out an inflated breath. "Whew! I feel better letting that little secret out. I feel like I have *sham* written all over my face. Is it obvious?"

"Not at all. You fit in just fine here," Camille assured. "And to make you feel better, I'm in the same boat. My sister is paying for my stay. The only reason I don't feel guilty about that is because her employer is paying for hers, so it's kind of a pay it forward sort of thing in my book. And let's be real; I'm happy to mooch off of her if it means I get to live in the lap of luxury for a month."

"Spoken like a sibling."

"I take it you have a few of your own?" Camille leaned back onto the chair and blocked the sun from her eyes with the palm of her hand.

"Here, let me get that." Reaching over, Foster swiveled the large umbrella until Camille was completely shaded by its covering. Even though the temperatures were moderate, she knew she'd burn if she didn't take precautions to keep out of direct sunlight. "Is that any better?"

"That's great. Thank you."

He leaned deeper into his lounge chair and reclined, kicking off his flip-flops before crossing his legs at the ankles and propping his hands behind his head. "And yes," he continued, rotating his face to angle it her direction. "I'm the youngest of three brothers. Plus, I've got five kids of my own. You could say I've been surrounded by siblings my whole life. A bit of a sibling expert, if you will," he joked.

"Five kids."

"I know, right?" He laughed, a hearty sound that originated deep in his belly. Camille liked the warm, full tone of it, how it felt familiar even though it was her first time hearing it. "I can't tell you how many times my wife and I got the whole *'Man, your hands are full!'* or *'You do know how babies are made, don't you?'* We'd always just nod and smile. I think my wife wanted to cry sometimes, but she just bit her tongue. Raising five kids under eight was not easy back in those early years with all the teething and diapers and tantrums. They're all grown now, but it was a real struggle for some time there. Total survival mode."

"I bet you and your wife are loving it now that they're out of the house," Camille said, trying to squash the unmerited disappointment she felt over the revelation that he was married. "Several of my friends say being empty nesters is a bit like having a second honeymoon, but one that lasts forever."

"Well, Darla's already had her second honeymoon with her second husband, so there goes that."

A golf-ball sized lump formed in Camille's throat. Or maybe that was her foot. She felt like an idiot. "I'm so sorry, Foster. I didn't realize—"

"Don't be sorry. She left when the twins were twelve, so we've been on our own for a while. We've managed just fine." He picked up a menu from the poolside table between them and squinted his eyes as he surveyed the lunch items. "Shoot. I left my reading glasses back at the Villa. I have such a hard time seeing anything nowadays without those dang things. Anyway. What about you? Any kids?"

"No kids," she lied, unable to be as frank and unabashedly open with Foster as he had been. "And my ex-husband recently had his second honeymoon, too, so I understand what that feels like. But I know I deserve better than anything he could ever offer me, so I've wished him well and moved on."

"Sounds like I was wrong then," Foster said.

"Wrong about what?"

"When I said you didn't know your true value." He grinned, his cheeks producing two deep-set dimples beneath the fine layer of stubble.

"I'm getting there," Camille agreed. "So. Anything look good on the menu?"

"I was thinking of ordering the carne asada nacho plate, but it sounds enormous. Any chance you want to share?"

"I'm never one to turn down Mexican food. Well, any food, really."

"A woman after my own heart."

The smile hooked on after his words would've made Camille's knees unbuckle had she not been reclining already. Foster was strikingly handsome. She figured he was several years older than herself, the crow's feet at the corners of his friendly eyes a bit more pronounced than the ones that spread out from her own. His thick, ash gray hair swooped right above strong brows, which framed in eyes that rivaled the ocean with their piercing blue. And there was a rugged masculinity about Foster that couldn't be denied. Camille was particularly surprised by her attraction to that specific trait. Mark had been anything but rugged, his demeanor sophisticated and highly refined.

"One order of nachos, coming right up." Foster pulled up the app on his phone to submit their order. "Anything to drink?"

"I'd love a lemonade."

"Two lemonades," he said as he punched his fingers across the screen. "I'm just figuring out how to use this new operating system on my phone, so bear with me. My son had to give me an entire tutorial yesterday and I still don't understand any of it. Apparently, there are a bunch of new features that are supposed to make things easier. But to me, they just make it more complicated. Can't we just go back to flip phones and landlines?"

"I'm so glad I'm not the only one who's intimidated by technology."

"Intimidated?" Foster guffawed. "I'm downright terrified!" His phone made a trill sound and a proud grin pulled at his lips as he read the incoming alert. "Hey, looks like I figured it out. Our order has been submitted! Danny will be so proud."

"Danny's your son?"

"Yes, Becca—the one who's getting married—he's her twin. If you stick around here long enough, I'm sure you'll meet them. They were all planning to come down to the pool later this afternoon after their massages."

Camille couldn't explain it, but the idea of meeting the children of a man she'd known less than ten minutes didn't scare her off the way it rightfully should.

"You didn't want to get a massage, too?" she asked.

Foster grimaced. "No ma'am. Not my kind of thing."

"Have you ever had one? It's really one of those things you shouldn't knock until you've tried it."

"I don't need to try sushi to know that I won't enjoy it. I've been myself enough years now to know what I will and won't like. I figure a massage is the same."

"You've never had sushi?" Camille gaped. "You really are missing out."

"I like my fish baked, fried, or grilled. Even smoked. But not straight out of the ocean."

"Foster, we have to remedy this."

"Is that so?" he asked, his right eyebrow cocked in curiosity. "Let's just say I was up for remedying this— how would you suggest we go about doing that?"

"The good, old-fashioned way. We flip a coin. If I win, you have to let me take you out to sushi. There's a great little place not too far from here. It's won all kinds of awards and has a fantastic Yelp rating."

"And if you lose?" She could see Foster was

intrigued by the proposition by the way his mouth tightened and his eyes slanted her direction.

"That's for you to decide."

"You're on." He reached his hand into his pocket and pulled out a quarter, then balanced it on the knuckle of his thumb. "I pick tails."

CHAPTER THIRTEEN

*T*he ocean had been cooperative for Edie that morning, showing off with grand waves that crested like pipelines and dazzling with sands that left behind new grainy patterns with each receding tide. It was the largest subject she'd ever attempted to capture through her lens, so very different from the close-up photography she'd grown comfortable—if not complacent—with over the years.

Edie typically preferred to focus on the minute intricacies of things. And here, at the ocean's edge, there were millions upon millions of sandy details at her disposal. As much as she wanted to pull it out of her bag and slip it onto her camera, she kept her macro lens tucked away for another time. The wide-angle lens she'd rented for the month was spectacu-larly heavy, requiring the use of both hands to hold it steady while she struggled to compose the shot. At the very least, she'd get a great workout from lugging around the beast and maybe she'd even tone her biceps a little by the end of her project.

There was so much to marvel at, she scarcely knew where to start. A short walk down the coastline had her head dizzied by the potential. Mother Nature had gifted Edie with the very best, and she hoped she'd be able to do it justice.

Just offshore, craggily rocks jutted out of deep blue waters and the spray of waves that struck them left froth and foam along the seam where the sea met the massive stones. Birds with scoop-like beaks bobbed, undulating on the surface. Now and then, a fish would thrust itself skyward with unexpected ease, as though taunting its loitering predator. There were tiny holes along the shore, little sand burrows for creatures to escape the midday heat. There was sunlight and reflection like thousands of mirrors swathing the ocean in mosaic form. It was already a masterpiece. It didn't need Edie's help.

To see a world in a grain of sand, Edie recited silently from the first line of one of her favorite William Blake poems. That was her very issue, after all. She *did* see a world in just that single grain of sand. The ocean itself? That was an infinite universe. How could she ever tell its story within one frame?

By noon, she could sense the sun beginning to burn her fair skin and felt the frazzling of her nerves, so she packed up her gear to retreat to the Villa for a quick shower and to change out the bandage on her hand. Honestly, it hardly hurt anymore and was healing well, but Edie still thought it best to keep the cut covered for the next few days to avoid re-injury or the possible infection Tabitha had warned against.

When she'd left at sunrise, Camille had still been asleep and Tabitha had followed her out, running shoes on her feet. They had their individual plans for the day and agreed they'd circle back up for dinner. Edie was grateful for the freedom to do her own thing. Sure, they had been friends for over twenty years, but a month in close quarters could put a strain on even the most rock-solid of relationships. Especially since each woman was accustomed to living on her own.

Over a gooey cookie and melting ice cream, they'd made a pact to come out on the other side of this month even closer. Unbreakable. Allowing each woman her own breathing space within those days was the only way they could achieve that desired outcome.

By the time she'd gotten back to the Villa and had her shower, Edie's stomach let her know she'd neglected it for too long. She'd skipped breakfast, her only priority that morning to add images to her nonexistent portfolio. Even if she photographed the ocean every day, she doubted she'd have enough useable images to cover the walls of The Dock for her next installment. She wanted Cal's opinion on the pictures she'd taken so far, but she knew it was too early to ask for it. When she scrolled through the photographs on the back of her camera, all she experienced was overwhelm, not the confident rush of excitement she often got when she knew she'd nailed the perfect shot. This was like learning an entirely new skill, one she didn't feel very adept at.

As she was towel drying her hair, replaying a slide in her mind's eye of the pictures she'd captured earlier in the day, she heard her phone buzz across the bathroom counter. Snatching it up, she read the incoming text.

I miss you already. Any chance you're free for lunch? I'm out in your neck of the woods delivering a painting and could pick you up in 10. I'd really love to see you.

It had been their first communication since the date. Edie hadn't intended to hold out on texting, but every time she thought to, nagging doubt stopped her fingers in their tracks. She'd made a fool of herself in more ways than she cared to count, and she wanted to regroup both her feelings and composure before she saw Cal again. She'd pass up this particular offer. She just wasn't ready.

Thanks, but I already ate, she began to type, but the lie wasn't natural and her finger wouldn't let her press *send*.

Backspacing, she sucked in a breath that lifted her shoulders to her ears. Her desire to see Cal proved so much stronger than her ability to keep him at bay. What a hold he had on her.

That would be great. I'm in Villa number 6. See you soon.

His thumbs up emoji reply made her think he was

likely driving, and the ten-minute window he'd given her was barely long enough to cover her mouth with some raspberry-tinted lip gloss and sweep her hair into a low ponytail. She smoothed her hands down the front of her sundress and took in her reflection in the full-length mirror. Just as she'd suspected, the sun had kissed her complexion, turning her skin a soft pink. For now, it made her look bright and refreshed, but too much more and she'd be peeling, thanks to her fair Irish complexion passed down on her mother's side.

Moments later, when Cal knocked on the door, Edie had talked her nerves down, then back up, and then finally down again, so the kiss he placed on her cheek when she swung the door wide didn't send her into a complete tailspin. In fact, it felt nice. Appropriate, even.

"You look really beautiful, Edie," he said, producing a single white daisy from behind his back. "I picked this on the walk up from the car. I'm sure there are all kinds of security cameras around and I'm fully expecting to be chased off the property by a groundskeeper, but I couldn't help myself. Something about it reminded me of you. Cheery. Bright."

"It's lovely, Cal," Edie said, taking the flower from his hands and sliding it just above her ear. She pulled the bobby pin she'd used to tuck her long bangs back and secured it to the stem. "Thank you."

"Do you have everything you need? There's a seafood restaurant just a couple of blocks away that

I've been wanting to try out if that's alright. Does that sound good?"

"That sounds fantastic," Edie said as she placed her keycard into her woven clutch and closed the Villa door behind them.

Cal's hand at the small of her back as they meandered along the pathway to his parked car made her insides flutter like she was a schoolgirl on her first date, and it was almost more noticeable than the growl that rumbled her stomach.

"Sorry," she blurted, totally embarrassed. "I'm really hungry. I spent all morning out on the beach and have yet to eat anything."

"I would've been happy to come over for breakfast," Cal said, grinning mischievously in a way that had become so him. "All you have to do is call. My place is only twenty minutes from here. Not far at all." Stepping in front of her, Cal reached to open the door to his 4-Runner before Edie had the chance to grasp the handle. He waited until she was fully situated and buckled before he rounded the front of the vehicle to hop into the driver's seat. He had his keys in the ignition, but before he turned over the engine, he paused, catching Edie's eye. "Is it just me, or did we leave things sort of weird the other night?"

Cal broke the ice and Edie felt as though she'd fallen right through it, about to drown in a puddle of her own insecurities.

"Cal, I don't know what got into me or why I left

in such a hurry. I acted so strange. I'm not normally that flighty, I promise."

"You were hurt, Edie. I get it. Tabitha definitely needed to take a look at that hand to make sure you didn't need stitches. By the way, how is it feeling today?"

She glanced down at the small bandage on her palm covering the injury. "It's fine. I'll be good as new in a few days."

"That's really great news. So, everything's alright between us?" There was a touch of doubt in his voice and a lingering glint of unease in his eye.

"Everything's alright, Cal."

"Great." Satisfied with that, he started up the vehicle and pulled away from the curb. Even before they'd reached the first stop sign, Cal had Edie's hand in his, taking possession like it was the natural thing to do. "Is this okay?" He lifted their joined hands and glanced across the cab in her direction.

"This is okay," Edie assured as she gave his firm grasp a squeeze. "More than okay."

The seafood restaurant was actually a sushi place, which was fine with Edie, even though she didn't care for raw fish. Camille had hauled her to so many sushi restaurants over the years that Edie knew she'd be able to find something edible on the menu. Usually, she opted for chicken teriyaki or miso soup. She was sure she could do the same here.

The young hostess at the podium near the entrance of the swanky restaurant showed them to the long sushi bar and gave them each a pair of chop-sticks, along with a leather-bound menu.

"Your sushi chef will take your order, but I can get any drinks started, if you'd like."

"What would you like to drink, Edie?" Cal asked as he held out her chair for her to take a seat. "A glass of wine?"

"Oh, no, thank you. I'm fine with water," she said to both the hostess and Cal. She pressed closer over the table and admitted, "I don't think I'll be having any wine for quite a while. Evidently, it makes me do stupid things."

"Knocking that glass over had nothing to do with how much wine you had, Edie. It was an accident. That's all it was."

"Still, I think water will do me good. I didn't realize how hot I'd gotten out on the beach this morning. I need to be better about staying hydrated."

"Were you able to get some good photographs?" Cal peered over the menu while he spoke.

"I'm not sure. I think this is going to be a real test for me. I'm struggling to feel comfortable with such a large subject. I don't know how to compose any of my frames. It all just feels random and messy. Landscapes are quite difficult for me."

"As an artist, it's good to push yourself outside of your comfort zone every now and again."

She didn't need reminding. In truth, Edie couldn't think of any area of her life where she felt exactly *in* her comfort zone. Certainly, dating a man a dozen years younger didn't fit into that category.

Looking around her, Cal suddenly straightened his back, perking up like a dog asked if he'd like to take a walk. "Wait a second, isn't that your friend over there?" he asked. "That man she's with—I think I know him."

Edie spun around in her chair so quickly that she almost tipped right out of it. "Camille's here? With a man?"

Lo and behold, Cal was right. There, in the middle of that very restaurant, was her dear friend, seated across from a striking older man Edie had never seen before.

Cal rubbed his chin, as though searching his brain. "How do I know him?"

"What on earth is she doing here?" Edie mused under her breath.

"Let's go find out. Looks like they've got two extra seats at their table. I'm sure they wouldn't mind a little company." Cal scooped up their menus and stood to his feet before the protest could fall from Edie's lips.

She had wanted to spend more one-on-one time with Cal, but the unfolding mystery surrounding Camille and her lunch date took precedence. She rushed to catch up, nearly knocking over an empty chair on her way.

"Mr. Spaulding?" Cal said as they got closer to the table. "I sure thought that was you!"

The man rose to his feet, a smile bursting onto his

lips. "Cal, son. How the heck are you?" He grabbed onto Cal's hand and shook firmly, then tugged him closer and slapped a friendly palm on his shoulder the way men half hug one another.

"I'm great, sir. Just grabbing some lunch here with my girlfriend, Edie." Camille and Edie, who had yet to say anything up to that point, locked saucer-wide eyes. Cal continued on, like he hadn't just dropped a huge bombshell of a relationship declaration. "I saw Danny the other day at the Farmers' Market. He said Becca's wedding is this month. Congratulations, Pops. You're finally getting some of those kids of yours married off!"

"Only took thirty-two years! I'm hoping the others will soon follow suit." Foster elbowed Cal in the side. "It's really great to see you, Cal. You know what? Why don't you two join us?"

"Oh, we wouldn't want to impose," Edie interjected, trying with desperation to read Camille's vapid expression. She couldn't tell if their company was wanted on her end. Her friend gave her nothing to work with.

"It's no imposition. We literally just ordered." Foster motioned to the empty seats and then returned to his. "And don't tell the waiter, but I've got a takeout box of carne asada nachos here as backup in case Camille lets me down with this whole sushi adventure." He nodded toward the out-of-place container settled in the middle of the table like a Styrofoam centerpiece. "I lost a coin flip, so here we are." He looked apologetic for a passing moment as he said, "I'm sorry. Where are my manners? Edie, Cal, this is Camille."

"We all actually know each other already," Camille said tightly. "Edie's one of my closest friends."

"Get out!" Foster's deep voice was rich with the surprise that matched his expression. "That's a riot. So you gals know each other, seems like you both know Cal, and I also know Cal? This is the weirdest seven degrees of separation I've ever been a part of."

"Oh, this is weird, alright," Camille agreed.

"So Foster, how do you know Camille?" Curiosity pushed all of Edie's tact right out the window. How long had Camille been keeping this man a secret? She suddenly felt silly, blathering on and on about Cal, when Camille evidently had a man of her own waiting in the wings. How hadn't Edie known? Wasn't this the sort of thing best friends shared with one another?

"We don't know each other, really," Foster explained, much to her relief. "We just met at the pool this afternoon. Got to talking, placing bets and all, and I lost—to the tune of three sushi rolls."

"Foster's oldest son, Danny, and I graduated high school together," Cal chimed in as he took a water glass from the server who had located them at their new table. "Thank you," he acknowledged, then returned to the conversation. "I can't tell you how many times I crashed at the Spaulding home back in the day. I think I was there every weekend of my senior year. Yours was always the go-to house when anyone got kicked out of their own."

"I figured I already had five kids. What were a few more?" Foster shrugged. "It's really good to see you, Cal. Has life been treating you well?"

"It absolutely has. I've got my own art studio—it's how Edie and I met, actually—and I just sold my one-hundredth painting this morning to a client down the road from here. So I guess you could say I can't really complain."

"You always were such a phenomenal painter. Remember that mural the high school commissioned you to paint on the back side of the gym when you were only a junior? Now that was a real work of art. It's still there, I believe. They've painted over all the others from that year, but yours still remains. And rightfully so. None could compare."

"Thank you, sir." Edie could tell Cal felt uncomfortable accepting the compliment. He was always so modest when it came to his talent.

Just then, Camille slid her chair back from the table and announced, "I'm going to use the lady's room real quick before our food gets here."

"I'll join you," Edie blurted.

"I think we should probably order—" Cal started to say, but Edie waved him off with a flapping hand.

"Get me anything. I'll be right back."

The two walked briskly toward the back of the restaurant like they were in some power walking race, neither speaking until they were finally within the confines of the women's restroom with the door shut securely behind them.

"What is happening out there?" Edie whisper-shouted.

"Honestly, I have no idea. Looks like your boyfriend and Foster are old friends." Camille looked stunned for an instant before she let out a hoot of laughter. "Boyfriend!"

"You heard him say that, too?"

"I did. Is it the first time he's called you that? His girlfriend?"

"Yes. And I'm not sure how I even feel about it."

"I think you should feel great about it, Edie. Cal is a real catch."

"So is Foster," Edie pointed out, her eyebrows raised clear to her hairline. "Did you two really just meet at the pool?"

"There's nothing there, Edie. We're just friends. And barely that. I don't even know the guy." She paused. "But is it just me, or is he not drop-dead gorgeous?"

The startling whoosh of a toilet flushing had Edie and Camille both buttoning their lips. They stood in silence as a waitress emerged from the closest stall and washed her hands at the sink, then grabbed and unwound a roll of paper towels to dry them. The moment she left, the women erupted in a fit of laughter.

"What are we doing, Cam? I mean, I'm here with

my apparent boyfriend, and you're lunching with a man pulled straight out of a magazine."

"More like an AARP ad."

"Oh, come on." She slugged Camille on the shoulder. "He's not that old. He's just mature."

"Evidently, he's old enough to be Cal's dad. You heard Cal say he graduated with his son, right? That means *my* lunch date could be the father of *your* lunch date."

Edie bit the side of her cheek. "I think that says more about me than it does you. Cal's too young for me and this just proves it. I've always known that."

"Or," Camille began, her finger held up in the air like a pause button, "this just means we've reached some magical age where we can go older *or* younger. I knew there had to be perks to our forties. Hot flashes and mood swings deserve some sort of tradeoff. I think we might've just discovered it!"

Edie wasn't sure she subscribed to Camille's theory, but she laughed all the same. "So, what do we do now? Do we just go back out there and act totally normal?"

"Have you ever known me to act totally normal?"

"You know what I mean. How do we handle this? I haven't been on a double date since Evan was alive and you were still married to Mark. Remember that awful diner on 6th that you made us try out, even though the reviews were terrible? I've never been that sick in my life."

"Our first clue should've been that the power was

out. Hard to keep food fresh without any sort of refrigeration," Camille recalled. "But this isn't a double date, Edie. I'm serious. I don't even know Foster."

"But wouldn't you like to?"

"I don't know. I mean, he seems decent enough. And adventurous. He didn't even bat an eye at some of the rolls I chose. I picked some pretty weird ones."

"Speaking of, Cal's out there ordering for me right now. I probably should've let him know my aversion to sushi before I rushed back here."

"What's the fun in that?" Camille bumped Edie with her shoulder as she grabbed onto the door handle. "Come on girl, our men await."

CHAPTER FOURTEEN

Sweat slipped over Tabitha's forehead in a sticky trail. She reached up to wipe it clean with the back of her hand and flipped her wrist over to glance down at her smart watch. Eight miles; twice what she thought she'd run.

Doubling over at the waist, she pulled in a measured breath, closing her eyes as she hissed it back out through her mouth. A gust of sand-filled wind caught her hair, swirling the long brunette strands around her face like a blindfold. She reached down to toe off one shoe, then the other, and collected them in one hand as she whisked her hair from her face.

She tiptoed to the water's edge.

The Pacific Ocean was notoriously cold and the sharp temperature made her gasp even though she'd readied for the shock of it.

Water lapped at her ankles as it spread over her

bare feet like a pair of icy socks. She couldn't fathom how the surfers she'd watched in the early morning hours did it. Sure, they had full wetsuits on, but it must've been freezing when a swell would take them under, soaking their unprotected face and hair. But there was a rush there, both in the excitement of the shouts that carried over the water's surface and in the vigorous way they swam to chase each promising wave.

Maybe one morning she'd join them. Better yet, maybe she could convince the girls to go with her. She laughed out loud at the thought, the ridiculous visual all too easy to conjure up.

Spinning around, Tabitha peered back up the shoreline. Palm trees strung along the coast and sea lavender burst like fireworks in the sand with their brilliant clusters of purple blooms. The prime beach-front properties alternated back and forth between restaurants and hotels, like a game of real estate leap frog. There was no denying the very real splendor of the Southern California coastline, and though she'd lived near it all her life, Tabitha appreciated its unmatched beauty.

She appreciated it, but she wasn't quite willing to retrace those eight miles back up it.

She dusted the sand from her feet and shoved her toes back into her shoes, knowing the sneakers would need a good shaking out before bringing them back into the Villa. Even though they weren't required to clean the place, she could at least do her best to keep it relatively tidy for the housekeepers. Those sorts of things were just common courtesies.

Plunking down onto a large piece of driftwood, Tabitha pulled up the Ride Reserve app on her phone to request a ride to the Villas. The nearest driver was five minutes out. What had she done before this particular technology? It had proven itself to be a godsend, especially after late nights at the hospital when she'd leave her car parked in the garage, opting instead for someone else to navigate her home. Half of the time, she'd fallen asleep on those rides. She'd seen the repercussions of a tired driver behind the wheel one too many times and knew better than to take her chances.

Camille had always been leery of the driving apps and the drivers that worked for them, a worry Tabitha felt was unwarranted. There were background checks for those sorts of things, she figured. And if not, sometimes you just had to choose the better of two evils and today, her screaming muscles won out.

Moments later, Tabitha's pinging phone alerted her that her driver was pulling up in a white Toyota Camry, and when she looked toward the parking lot behind her, she saw the vehicle angling into an empty spot. Jogging up the pathway of sand that gradually transitioned to gravel and then to blacktop, Tabitha hurried over, her legs like jelly underneath her, threatening to give way. It was all she could do not to collapse into the backseat of the car upon opening the door.

"Hi there," she huffed out. The seatbelt was wedged in a deep groove in the cushions, and she fought to free it while she slammed the door. "I'm just headed a few miles north. Not too far."

"Tabitha?"

Heart stuttering, the smile dropped from her face. "Ben? What are you doing here?"

"I'm working," her ex-husband said, just as Tabitha finally had a chance to catch her breath. Once she rallied and pulled in another, she breathed in a thousand memories all at once, both the scent of his car and his cologne tugging her into the past like a thrown lasso.

"You're working as a Ride Reserve driver?" Her words caught on the lump in her throat.

"Here and there, when I don't have a house to show."

Casey once told her that Ben had quit his job as the editor-in-chief at the Seascape Shores Tribune and that he was working toward getting his real estate license. The conversation had been an uninteresting one, and Tabitha wasn't sure if it was the botched appendectomy that she'd replayed in her mind that forced that piece of information into a space where she'd later forget it, or if she just hadn't cared to begin with. By the time Ben had served her with divorce papers, Tabitha had become indifferent toward nearly every facet of both their marriage as a whole and her husband as an individual. It wasn't an ugly ending, but it was an expected one.

That indifference no longer existed when she saw him seated in the driver's seat of what once had been their family vehicle. She couldn't explain the knotting of her stomach that wouldn't go away, even when she wrapped her arms around her middle to ease the discomfort.

"I'm surprised you're not at the hospital," Ben said as he backed the car from the parking space, his eyes never leaving hers through their connection in the rearview mirror.

"I'm on a sabbatical." She tried not to notice the way Ben's eyebrows jumped up on his forehead in unchecked surprise.

"Good for you, Tabitha."

"It wasn't my decision." She gnawed at her bottom lip.

He offered her the silence her statement demanded before finally speaking as he turned onto the highway. "I'm dropping you off at the Seascape Shores Villas?" Ben glanced down at the app on his phone.

"Yes."

"Beautiful place."

"It is."

Tabitha looked at her lap, at her fingers clenched together there. The stain where Casey had once spilled a glass of grape juice as a child could still be made out on the floor mat, the color faded, but the memory vibrant. Tabitha winced. She'd gotten so frustrated with Ben over that stupid spill. How on earth could he let a five-year-old drink a glass of bright purple juice without a lid? And in their brand new car, no less! Ben had remained calm, his composure always kept. That only aggravated Tabitha more.

"It's just a car," he had said while she tried to scrub the blemish from the carpet with furious might. *"No one got hurt."*

That was his mantra. *No one got hurt.* Like getting physically hurt was the worst-case scenario. What an irony, given Tabitha's line of work.

The day their marriage ended on the courthouse steps under a colorless sky of gray, he'd given her one last hug and she'd given him a weak smile, the only thing she had left to offer the man she'd once promised her life to.

"It's okay, Tabs," he'd said, squeezing her tightly before letting her go. *"No one got hurt."*

Tabitha's teeth found the inside of her cheek and bit down.

When was the last time she'd even seen Ben? It had to have been well over a year. At first, she'd figured they'd still get together for the holidays. For their son's sake, of course. But she hadn't protested when she'd been scheduled to work on Thanksgiving the year their marriage ended. And when Christmas rolled around that December, she was the first to volunteer to cover one of her colleague's shifts.

Gradual avoidance turned into permanent evasion, and here they were, four years later, Tabitha riding in the backseat of the very car she used to pilot. Fate was such a strange thing with the most obscure sense of timing. All promises of relaxation, rejuvenation, and whatever else the Villas had to offer flew right out that sedan's window. This encounter rattled her, made her head spin with thoughts she usually kept suppressed under the weight of work. But there was no emergency here, nothing that demanded her immediate attention above everything else.

Questions she never wanted to ask suddenly took forefront in her mind.

How was Ben doing? Did he enjoy driving complete strangers around for a living? Was he okay financially? How was his mom? She hadn't been well during their last Easter together. What about their old dog, Boots? Was he still around?

Tabitha knew many divorced parents often put their children in the middle, placing them in the awkward position of relaying information back and forth like a go-between. Ben and Tabitha had never done that, and other than knowing of his job change, Ben's life now existed one-hundred percent outside of Tabitha's.

Well, except for the fact that she was currently in the backseat of his car.

Though the drive was a matter of minutes, Tabitha felt the silence in each individual second.

In the mirror, she saw Ben's mouth drop open as though he were about to speak when his phone suddenly dinged. He snapped his jaw shut and glanced down at the phone balanced on the center console.

Tabitha couldn't help but read the name that flashed across the screen—Dawn, she thought it said —and she couldn't mistake his nervous glance as her eyes connected with his in the rear-view mirror again. Tabitha quickly switched her gaze out the back window, knowing full well it was none of her business.

Still, when Ben finally positioned the vehicle against the curb in front of the Villas, she noted how quickly he snatched up his cell phone, like he'd been anxiously waiting to reply to the text the entire drive. His fingers flew over the screen and the smile that lifted the corners of his mouth as he read the incoming message made Tabitha's forehead crease with tension.

Had he ever been that excited to hear from her? In truth, they didn't text much during their marriage. Tabitha used to call on her way home from the hospital after her shifts, but Ben was usually out at one of Casey's basketball games or up late editing his latest piece for the newspaper. Over time, she found it best just to circle up with him in person back at the house. They were never big talkers. Well, Tabitha never was, at least. Ben would always carry the conversations at parent-teacher conferences or holiday parties, even at her work gatherings for the hospital. She'd never minded. She was grateful for it, in fact. Ben was good at connecting with people in a way Tabitha knew she never would be.

Even with their son, Ben was the go-to parent. She knew Casey would never be a "mama's boy" and she had been fine with that. Motherhood didn't come easily for Tabitha.

When she'd first met Edie at a local toddler playgroup, she'd been amazed at how nurturing she was. Edie would smooth Hannah's hair absentmindedly while talking with the other moms. She'd give her daughter a look of adoration even while disciplining her. Tabitha would just stand there, gaping in awe at the easy way she projected her love.

Of course, Tabitha loved her son. She'd die for him. But it didn't pour naturally out of her the way it dripped from every word, look, or touch Edie gave to Hannah.

And maybe that was Tabitha's ultimate problem as a wife, too. She couldn't even recall the last time she'd told Ben she loved him, and here he had a text from a woman whose name he stored in his phone with big heart emojis placed on either side.

Tabitha coughed to clear her throat as she exited the vehicle.

"Thank you—" she began to say, startled when the driver's side door popped open and Ben jumped out.

He tossed his cell phone onto the vacated seat and shut the door. "I'll walk you up."

"You don't have to, Ben."

"I'd like to."

Nodding, Tabitha conceded. "Alright."

He looked different. Slimmer, that extra padding around his middle gone and the sculpt of his jaw tighter. His near-black hair had more flecks of gray, mostly concentrated in his sideburns, and he was clean shaven, which surprised Tabitha because Ben had always sported a five o'clock shadow. She must've been staring because he leaned toward her and said, "You won't believe this, Tabs, but I've been training for a half marathon." He smiled, pride pulling his lips into a wide grin as he shoved his hands deep into his pants pockets. "I bet you never thought you'd hear those words come out of my mouth."

"You're right about that. You always hated to run."

"That was because I got drunk that one night and bought that stupid treadmill from the infomercial. It did not live up to its promises of a 'thinner, fitter, firmer new you'." He placed air quotes around the words. "The dang thing broke after a month. Running on the beach in the sand is a whole different experience. I love it."

"I know it is. That's exactly what I did this morning. In fact, I brought half of the beach home with me in my shoes. A few more runs and I should have enough sand collected to build my own castle."

Ben laughed. "That's funny, Tabs," he said, like he was surprised by her attempt at humor. She was a little surprised by it, honestly. "We should go running together sometime."

"What?" She shrugged her chin back into her neck, eyes bugging.

"We should run together. I think you'd be impressed that I can actually keep up with you now. Next time you head out for one, you should give me a call. Seriously. You have my new number."

"I do?"

"Yeah, it's in the Ride Reserve app. Just text me and I'll meet you out at the pier. I live right by it now. Renting, but only until I decide where I want to land permanently."

"Oh, okay," was all she could form as an answer.

"Anyway, I've got to go pick up another customer." He started shuffling backward, but still faced her as he spoke. "It was good to see you, Tabs. And I'm serious about that run. Let's do it."

Before she could offer any sort of reply, he had spun around on his heels, jogging back toward the old car. Her heart skipped at the memory it conjured up of a young Ben, jogging down their driveway, Tabitha's hand in his, a shiny white sedan wrapped in the largest red bow she'd ever seen parked along the curb.

It was both a lifetime ago and yesterday all at once.

CHAPTER FIFTEEN

"*I*s there a way to calculate how many pounds we'll gain if we do this every night for the next month?" Camille scraped her spoon against the side of the dish to get the last bit of vanilla ice cream pooling there. It was too good to even waste a drop.

"You didn't hear? Calories don't count here," Edie said, a full scoop already melting in her mouth. "It was stated in their promotional material on the website. It's the only reason I agreed to come."

The two women laughed, but Camille noticed her sister didn't join in. Tabitha had been in one of her *off in another world* moods, the kind where she'd stare blankly, smile robotically, and just go through the motions of interaction.

Camille had noticed it the very moment she and Edie came back from sushi. They'd tumbled through the doorway in a mess of giggles as they replayed their lunchtime antics. In any other scenario, she would've been eager to tell her sister all about Foster and the bet and their unexpected run-in with Edie and Cal, but she knew better than to divulge all of that right then. The glass of zinfandel, along with the uncorked bottle next to it on reserve, indicated Tabitha was going through something. Processing. Camille would wait until her sister was ready to talk.

Apparently, that time came after Tabitha had consumed two glasses of wine and three under-baked chocolate chip cookies.

"I saw Ben today."

Edie froze, her dessert spoon suspended inches from her mouth. "Wow, Tab. I had no idea."

"It wasn't anything big."

Camille gave Edie a sidelong glance that didn't go undetected by her younger sister.

"I'm serious," Tabitha said firmly, her eyes narrowing. "It wasn't a thing."

"How is he?" Camille placed a hand on Tabitha's forearm. It was quickly shaken off.

"He's fine. Good, I think, actually. He's taken up running now, if you can believe that."

"No, I can't believe that."

Ben hated to run, but more than that, he'd hated that Tabitha spent what little free time she had doing it. One Thanksgiving, when he'd poured more of the cooking wine into his glass than into the cranberry sauce, he'd divulged to Camille that he didn't entirely love his wife's hobby.

"It's just one more thing for me to compete with," he'd murmured after Tabitha had announced that she would be going on a post-meal run around the block before the tryptophan kicked in.

He'd said it in passing and never mentioned anything of the sort again, but Camille knew there was more to his admission. That he would take up the sport on his own was just about as believable as Ben picking up a scalpel and joining Tabitha in the operating room.

"He's training for a half marathon," Tabitha continued. She spun the stem of her wineglass between her fingers. The liquid coated the sides, leaving a purple film on the glass where it swirled. "And he has a girlfriend named Dawn. At least, I think it's Dawn. I couldn't really read it clearly on his phone, but there were a lot of hearts around her name. I know there was a D and an N. Maybe it was Dayna, now that I think about it. I'm not sure. His phone was too far away to get a good look."

"Tabitha, this is a lot." Edie's voice was full of compassion for her friend when she asked, "Are you okay?"

"Of course, I'm okay." Tabitha reached for the bottle of wine and refreshed her glass, then threw back a considerably large guzzle. "I'm totally fine."

"Where did you see him?"

"It's funny, really." Tabitha snort-laughed the way she often did when she'd had a few too many. "He drove me home after my run this morning. My legs were too dang tired to retrace my way back up the beach. I wasn't planning to run eight miles when I set out. Running in sand is a whole lot harder than on pavement. I'd forgotten that."

"But why did you call Ben for a ride? Edie or I could've used your car to come get you." Reaching across the dining table, Camille slyly retrieved the cork and placed it back into the wine bottle, then took the bottle to the fridge to store it. They'd all had enough for the evening.

"I didn't call him. Well, I mean, I guess I sort of did, but I didn't know it was him."

"This isn't making any sense, Tab." Edie's mouth thinned into a line. "How did you call him without knowing you were calling him?"

"He's a driver for Ride Reserve. It was random, really. He was only assigned to me because he was the closest one, I think. I'm not really sure how it works," Tabitha rambled. "But get this, he's using our old Camry. That thing must have close to two-hundred-thousand miles on it already. Anyway, I didn't even know it was him until I had gotten in and buckled up. Man, that car still has the same smell. Remember those pine tree-shaped air fresheners he always bought at the gas station by our place? The vanilla ones? I didn't see one hanging in there, but it sure still smelled like it."

She looked beyond her sister and squinted out at the dark ocean framed in by huge picture windows that stretched wall to wall.

"The car smelled like his cologne, too. The same one he's worn for years. I only bought that particular brand for him because the saleswoman said it was masculine and woodsy. Ben had dressed up as a lumberjack for Halloween that year, remember? I thought maybe he was trying out a new style or something." She lifted her glass to her mouth, then cleared her throat softly. "I didn't particularly like that cologne then and I don't really like it now."

Camille wrestled to find the right thing to say, unable to land on anything that would be of comfort. Instead, she covered her sister's hand with her own and this time Tabitha didn't shake her off.

"Are you glad that he seems to be doing well?" she asked. "Or was it hard for you to see him doing well?"

"It wasn't one or the other, I suppose. It just was." Tabitha let out a breathy huff that almost sounded like a laugh. "And I guess that right there sums up our entire marriage: *it just was.*" Tilting her head back, she drained the contents of her wineglass in one lengthy swallow. "It just was, until it wasn't." She looked at her glass for a prolonged moment, almost surprised to see it was now empty. "This is super boring, guys. I'm sorry. Let's talk about something else."

"We're not bored. We're concerned."

"I shouldn't have even said anything. It really wasn't a big deal. There's no reason to be concerned. It was just a ride."

"I understand that, but it still must've been hard to see Ben so out of the blue like that. I mean, I get

that the divorce was amicable—we all know it was
—but you must've experienced some emotion over
seeing him for the first time in what? A couple of
years?" Camille knew if she pressed too hard, her
sister would shut down altogether, so she tiptoed
gingerly around the real questions she wanted
to ask.

"The truth of the matter is, I don't know what I
felt. When I saw that woman's name on his phone
and the way Ben's face lit up when he read her texts—
I don't know. Maybe it was jealousy, but it didn't feel
like it was. If I felt anything at all, it was guilt. Guilt
because I don't think I was ever able to make him
that happy."

"You made him happy, Tab," Edie assured, a
forced smile tacked on after her words.

"Maybe at one point in time I did, but I couldn't
keep him happy."

Camille felt that comment in the depth of her gut
like a sucker punch. It had been the same with Mark.
Even though she knew one person wasn't responsible
for ensuring another's happiness, Mark had thrown
that accusation around heavily throughout their
divorce proceedings.

*"I'm just not happy anymore, Cami. This life—with you
—it doesn't make me happy like it used to."*

Tabitha whipped her head suddenly, like she was
shaking off the present conversation. "Enough about
that. What did you gals do all day?"

"Well, Edie has a boyfriend."

"Oh my goodness, Cam!" Edie smacked Camille's shoulder. "He's not my boyfriend."

"Yes, he is. That's exactly how he introduced himself to Foster. Well, he said you were his girlfriend, but same difference."

"Who is Foster?" Tabitha looked back and forth between the women like she was watching a fast-paced tennis match.

"Your sister's new friend," Edie said.

"We've been over this—we're not even in the friend zone yet. He's just another guest staying here. I met him at the pool and we ended up spending the afternoon together. Nice guy."

"I feel like you're leaving out a lot of details here, sis."

"Yes," Edie agreed. "The main one being that he is crazy attractive. Silver fox status."

"He's pretty easy on the eyes, I'll give you that," Camille conceded. "But he's just here for a wedding planning retreat for his daughter, so it's not like anything will go anywhere."

"The man tried sushi for you, Camille."

"Because he lost a coin flip. If I had lost, I would've had to be his date for his daughter's wedding this summer."

Edie and Tabitha's mouths gaped simultaneously.

"What?" Camille shrugged.

"That's a pretty forward request," Tabitha pointed out. "Especially from someone you just met."

"Really? It didn't feel forward. He'd mentioned

something about his date moving to Nepal to photograph the wild water buffalo there. How he didn't have a plus one any longer and that his daughter said it would mess up the seating arrangements since the guest count was now off. Yada yada yada."

"Okay, so he was definitely coming on to you," Tabitha said. "I see."

"Oh, he was not."

"That's not true, Camille. He flirted with you throughout our entire lunch. Cal noticed, too. He even commented on it on the ride back—how it was interesting to see Foster with someone since he was always known as the single dad back in the day. Apparently, he didn't date much then since he was so busy raising five kids all on his own."

"Well, he's not dating anyone now, least of all me." Camille glanced at the clock on the wall, surprised to see the hour hand creeping up on ten o'clock. "Listen ladies. We've got pedicures early in the AM, so I suggest we all hit the sack. Today has been a long, eventful day, and even saying that feels like an understatement. I think a few hours of shuteye would do us all good."

"A few hours?" Edie laughed. "I think you slept for a dozen or more last night. We're going to have to wake you or you'll sleep past noon again. I swear, Camille, you're like a teenager. Or a puppy. Or maybe a sleep-deprived sloth."

"I'll set an alarm," Camille assured. She gathered the dishes left from their dessert and took them to the sink, resisting the temptation to wash them. "There's no way my feet are missing out on some much deserved pampering. I'll be up bright and early with bells on. You'll see."

CAMILLE SHOOK her head and crumpled the note on the kitchen island before tossing it into the trash bin.

"You should've just woken me up, girls," she muttered under her breath. She pulled out her phone from the pocket of her robe and dialed concierge. After two rings, a recording picked up, listing a menu of options to select from. Camille punched option number three onto the keypad on her cell and waited for the connection.

"Seascape Shores Villas Salon. How may I help you?"

"Um, yes, hi. This is Camille Todd—"

"Oh, Camille. I'm so glad you called. We've been trying to get ahold of you all morning regarding your scheduled pedicure appointment."

"Yes, well, it seems I've overslept and completely missed my appointment altogether. I believe Tabitha and Edie are there right now. We had nine-thirty pedicures."

"Tabitha and Edie? Yes, it looks like they are just finishing up their services as we speak. Unfortunately, we couldn't hold your appointment, but we would be happy to reschedule it. Would you be able to come in this afternoon, say, around one o'clock?"

"I sure can. And don't worry—I promise I won't fall asleep again and miss this one, too."

The woman laughed through the phone line, a quiet, polite laugh that felt rehearsed. "It's really not a problem. At Seascape Shores Villas, we pride ourselves on creating an environment of relaxation and leisure. Napping is definitely part of that. Don't apologize for taking care of yourself, Camille. We look forward to pampering you at one o'clock."

Well, if this wasn't the most enabling place on the planet.

Camille fixed herself a quesadilla with sour cream dip for an early lunch since she'd missed breakfast altogether. She reveled in the quiet of the Villa while she had it all to herself and meandered throughout the house as she munched on her snack. Her particular bedroom was spacious, filled with a massive king-sized canopy bed and heavy wooden furniture. There was a beach motif that flowed throughout the space, splashed with turquoise and peach hues that felt so very coastal. There was even a large conch resting on the nightstand and when she held it up to her ear, Camille heard the faint echoes of ocean waves mimicked in its hollow shell.

Her parents had had a similar one that they kept on their sailboat back when Camille was just a little girl. Her dad would blow into the spiraled end, producing a loud, horn-like blast that he'd use to communicate with other sailors out on the waters. Camille had often tried to "play" the shell like an instrument the way her father had, but she always failed miserably, sounding more like a dying goose than any kind of horn. Even after playing the trumpet for a semester in the middle school band, she still had little luck producing that same distinct sound. Oh, what she wouldn't give to hear her father and his conch now.

They'd been gone for almost thirty-five years, but the ache her parents' absence created in her life still panged occasionally, especially when Camille would see something that pulled at a specific memory. Picking up the conch, she moved it out of her room and settled it onto the hallway table, where it would be a less noticeable fixture.

When she'd finished getting ready for her day, opting to add loose curls to her shoulder-length blonde hair and a light face of makeup, it was almost time for her appointment. Edie and Tabitha had just texted her a picture of their polished toes. Tabitha chose a nude color, while Edie's nails were painted a sparkly pink. They were headed to the pool for the afternoon and told Camille to join them when she was ready.

At five to one, she made her way across the property and stepped into the salon located on the north side of the Villa's grand entrance. A glass wall of water separated the front desk from the rest of the salon and thousands of tiny bubbles pushed upward from jets at the bottom of the fixture. It was like a floor-to-ceiling aquarium—minus the fish—and Camille could make out rows of leather pedicure chairs lined up on the other side, slightly obscured by the water feature.

"Camille?" The young woman at a podium greeted Camille as the salon door shut behind her.

"Yep, that's me!"

"Right this way," the woman instructed in a deliberately soft voice, indicating Camille should follow suit. "I'm Trina."

Camille wasn't sure she was cut out for this sort of refined lifestyle, one that required hushed tones and impeccable manners. Even so, she figured she could pull it off for a month—it would be a bit like playing house or make believe, but she could manage and play the part.

"This is Amy. She'll be giving you your pedicure today. Please go ahead and have a seat and make yourself comfortable." Trina motioned toward an open chair with a girl who looked a lot like Edie's daughter, Hannah, seated on a low stool. She waited until Camille was fully situated before she stepped closer, then picked up a remote attached to the arm and pressed a button. Instantly, Camille felt two roller balls jab deeply between her shoulders. She couldn't help but squeal. A group of women midway through their own pedicures shot sidelong glances in her direction, holding their furrowed gazes long enough to indicate their displeasure in her sudden outburst.

"Sorry." Camille made a face. "I wasn't expecting that."

"You can adjust the pressure and duration of your massage using these buttons."

"Okay." Camille took the remote and set it on her lap. "I'll do that. Thank you."

"How is the temperature of the water?" Trina asked. "Not too hot, I hope?"

Slipping off her sandals and sinking her feet into the small tub, Camille let out a sigh. "No, this is just perfect."

"Great. I'll be back with a glass of ice water, unless I can interest you in some wine or champagne?"

"Ice water will be just fine." She'd already been sleepy enough and figured any alcohol consumption would only exacerbate that. "Thank you."

The young girl at her feet handed her a color wheel of polish choices as Trina strode off to fetch her drink.

"Oh, wow. There's a lot to choose from." Overwhelmed, Camille waved off the pallet. "I'm okay with anything. You pick."

When Trina came back with Camille's promised glass of water, Camille was already deep in relaxation, Amy's hands working at her tired calf muscles with firm, almost painful strokes. It was embarrassing how long Camille had neglected her poor feet. She knew Amy would have quite a job ahead of her, and she almost felt bad about that. *Almost.*

"If you want to recline your massage chair a touch more so you can lean back, I have a couple of cucumber slices that you can place on your eyes during your treatment. Would you like that?"

"I'd love it!" Camille tempered her excitement to avoid another look of judgment from the salon's patrons, mainly from the women who had already made known their disapproval of her unbridled excitement. "Thank you." She took the cucumbers and situated them onto her eyelids. They were cool and crisp and she had to resist the temptation to ask for a side of ranch so she could pop them into her mouth.

As Amy continued massaging her legs, the lazy, instrumental music playing over the salon speakers and the bubbling of the footbath joined to slow Camille's thoughts. She'd originally been upset that she missed out on this experience with her two friends earlier that morning, but it turned out the quiet and lack of conversation was exactly what she needed to fully unwind.

The women a few chairs over, though—they didn't get that memo.

"Ladies, let me tell you—this entire wedding is turning into my worst nightmare. Not only do I have to pay for everyone's week-long stay here, but evidently now I have to hire a wedding photographer since the bride's father failed to do so."

Camille lifted one cucumber from her eye and peered over at the group to her right. There were four or five women, all around Camille's age, who had smooth foreheads, plump lips, and wrinkle-free faces, like they each had their plastic surgeon on speed dial. When the woman who had been speaking glanced her way, locking onto her gaze, Camille dropped the cucumber back down and squeezed both eyes shut.

"Honestly,"—the woman lowered her voice just a touch—"it's as though he's unaware of the age-old tradition that the bride's family pays for the big day. Or at the very least, offers to. It's a good thing we have money or poor Jeremy would probably be getting married in a run-down Vegas chapel with Elvis officiating." The woman snickered and when her friends joined in, it only encouraged her. "I'm not even sure what Jeremy sees in her. She's so very plain. All the girls in the family are. You know their story, right? The mom ran off with their father's brother when the youngest was barely out of diapers. Talk about your dysfunctional family. I ask Jeremy each and every day if he's sure about bringing these people into our lives, *permanently*." She seemed to pause to take a sip of something before adding, "I just pray he'll come to his senses one of these days. And the sooner, the better. He's a smart boy."

Another woman giggled, her laughter dripping with pretension. "At this point, you may need to do more than pray, Monica. Sounds like you might need to take some action."

"Oh, believe me. I have my ideas. Starting with that father of hers."

"Just what do you have up your sleeve?" Another voice chimed in.

As Camille strained to hear the conversation, Amy scraped at the arch of her foot with a pumice stone, sending the sharpest shiver racing down her spine. She yanked her foot back, her entire body recoiling. The cucumbers tumbled from her face.

"Sorry," Camille whispered loudly as she shoved the veggies back onto her eyes and settled in. She had turned off the massage feature on her chair so she could eavesdrop without the humming sound of the motor as competition.

"You know me. I have my resources. Plus, I've been digging around," the woman continued. "There are more skeletons in that man's closet than in a graveyard."

Camille wished she hadn't zeroed in on this particular salon conversation and as much as she tried to convince herself it was a different bride and a different family that filled the woman's lips with idle gossip, her next statement disallowed for any question about that.

"Foster Spaulding may be one heck of a looker, but he's a dangerous man with a criminal's past. I plan to do everything within my power to bring his sins into the light. It'll be a cold day in hell before I ever call that man family."

CHAPTER SIXTEEN

"*I*'ve shot a couple of weddings in my day. None in the last few years, but I'd be happy to pull up some albums of my most recent work if you'd like to see them." Edie shaded her eyes as she squinted up at Foster, who stood above her on the pool decking, an orange slushy drink with a paper umbrella in his large hand.

"That would be really great, Edie. Yesterday, when Cal mentioned you were a photographer, it didn't dawn on me that we still needed one. Honestly, this whole wedding planning thing is pretty far outside my wheelhouse. I'm just doing whatever Becca asks at this point."

"I think that's our role as parents when it comes to our kids' weddings," Edie said. Though Hannah wasn't even engaged, Edie knew when the day finally came, her only real job would be to support her daughter by helping her create the wedding of her dreams. It was something she greatly looked forward to.

"I just want my girl to be happy," Foster agreed.

"Spoken like a proud father," Edie said. "I've already got plans this evening, but would you like to come by our Villa tomorrow night? I can pull up the photographs on my laptop and you can see if my work fits with Becca's style. And if she and her fiancé are able to join you, that would be even better. I'd love to get her opinion and chat with her a little about my process and what to expect on the day of the wedding if she chooses to go with me."

"Wow, I really appreciate all of this, Edie. You're a total lifesaver. I'm beginning to think it's kismet—me meeting Camille yesterday. It looks like it might lead to some really great things. If it works for you, I'll swing by around six."

"That's perfect. See you then."

Tabitha waited until Foster was out of sight, following his movement behind sunglass covered eyes. She lowered them and peered above their tortoiseshell rim. "*That's* Foster?"

"Right? I told you he was handsome."

"You did, but I wasn't expecting *that*."

"Do you think Camille will care that I invited him over? I probably should've asked her before I offered."

"Um, if I know my sister, I think she'll be absolutely okay spending more time with that man."

"I just wanted to make sure I'm not overstepping at all," Edie said. "You know, the thought of photographing a wedding again is kind of exciting. I've only shot a handful, just to make a little money on the side, but they were really fun and I'd love to try my hand at another. Plus, anything will be less of a struggle than photographing this stupid ocean." Edie nudged her head past the infinity pool toward the waters that roared up ahead. The coastline was crowded with throngs of beachgoers taking an afternoon dip in its salty shores.

"Stupid ocean? Really?" Tabitha chuckled.

"Okay, maybe it's not stupid. But seriously, I am having the worst time, Tab. Cal's been asking to see what I've photographed up to this point and I feel like a kid who forgot to study for a final exam. I've got nothing."

"I'm sure you have something."

"Yeah, I guess I have *something*, but nothing that's any good. Have you ever felt like you were just so far out of your depth that you didn't know what to do?"

"Oh, absolutely. Every hour of every day of my residency. Yes, I was technically a doctor at that point, but I had only begun my training as a trauma surgeon." Tabitha twirled her straw in her diet soda and ice clinked against the glass. "There's a learning curve to things, Edie. You're a photographer—a great one at that—but you're gaining a new skill. It'll take time before you're any good at landscape photography, and even longer before you're an expert. But you'll get there. You just have to be willing to put in the hours and the hard work that goes along with that journey."

Knowing Tabitha once struggled with self doubt was comforting. If Southern California's top trauma surgeon could have insecurities, then Edie was certainly entitled to her own.

"Thank you, Tabitha. I needed to hear that." Pulling at the strap of her swimsuit, Edie could see a faint line forming on her shoulder next to the freckles that appeared a few summers ago and decided to never leave. "You about ready to head in? I think I'm currently my preferred shade of pink, but any longer in the sun and I'll turn lobster red. There is no in between."

"I'm going to wait out here for Camille, but you go on ahead. She just texted and she's almost done with her pedicure. It shouldn't be long. She said there was something she wanted to talk about. Something about a conversation she overheard at the salon. Who knows?" Tabitha said. "You're headed to The Dock for the evening, yeah?"

"I am."

Edie had confessed her insecurities to Cal over a text the night before and he'd suggested she swing by his studio. He had an idea that just might help her out. She'd been intrigued. Plus, she wanted to follow up on their recently declared relationship status. Not surprisingly, it had kept her up tossing and turning the entire night.

Tabitha smirked and asked, "Should I wait up?"

"Oh goodness. It's not like that."

"You're allowed to have a little fun, Edie."

"That's just it. I'm having *lots* of fun. But once the newness that goes with that phase wears off, where does that leave us? Look at Becca, Foster's daughter. She's the same age as Cal and she's getting married. Next, she'll be starting a family. I'm so far removed from that stage of life, Tab. I'm not going to be able to give Cal any of that."

"What makes you think that's what he wants?" Tabitha reached into her large beach bag and pulled out a tube of SPF 50 sunscreen. "Have you asked him?"

"No."

"And why is that?" She squirted a dollop of the lotion in her palm and then held the bottle out for Edie.

Edie lifted a hand. "I haven't asked him because I don't want to know the answer, I guess. And I also don't want to answer the questions that *my* questions will lead to. Like how old I am."

"Jeez, Edie, you're not old. You're only a year older than me and I definitely don't consider myself old. I'm totally in my prime."

"Right, but I'm twelve years older than Cal. That's a lot. He was born when I was in junior high school."

"Sure, but you're not in junior high now. You're a grown woman who can date whomever she pleases. Plus, Cal's a grown man. One who seems very interested in you, regardless of the age discrepancy. I think you should just be honest with him about all of this. It can only help."

"Or everything could blow up in my face."

"I honestly don't think that's going to happen."

Edie sighed. "You know what the strangest part of all of this is? He's actually the oldest man I've ever dated. Evan was twenty-eight when he died. Cal's thirty-three."

Even though she couldn't see her eyes through the dark lenses, the fallen expression on Tabitha's face conveyed all the empathy in the world. "I really like Cal, Edie. I think he's good for you and I think you're good for him. Don't let fear stop you from exploring something that could turn out to be really beautiful for both of you."

"Is Tabitha Parker now in the business of offering relationship advice?" Edie feigned shock. "I never thought I'd live to see the day."

"Right? Given my history, I suppose you should take it with as much salt as the Pacific Ocean can hold," she said, laughing. "But still, I do believe there's some truth to it all."

"I do, too," Edie said. She reached over to give her best friend's hand a tight squeeze. "And I think that's what scares me the most."

TABITHA'S CAR WAS LUXURIOUS. The leather seats were so supple that they almost felt like velvet to the touch and the scissor doors that opened upward like wings looked like they belonged on a stunt car in a blockbuster movie. Edie had only driven the BMW once before, the same night Tabitha pulled it off the dealership lot. She'd been so nervous about wrecking her friend's new car back then that she hardly paid any attention to the way it hugged the road's curves or how it accelerated from zero to sixty in four seconds flat. Edie had been overly cautious that first time behind the wheel, like she was sixteen years old, applying for her driver's license.

Not tonight. She drove the car like she owned it. Something about that made her feel undeniably sexy. The black cocktail dress that stopped mid-thigh only bolstered that newfound confidence. When she slowed up to the red light at the intersection of Coral and Beachwood Avenues, pulling alongside a dark-colored sedan with lightly-tinted windows, Edie could feel the eyes of the other driver land heavily upon the vehicle without even turning her head to confirm. The smirk that drew up the corners of her lips turned into a full-fledged grin when she lowered her foot to the gas pedal and launched down the roadway like an arrow released from a bow.

She rode that high all the way to The Dock.

When she stepped out of the car, heels meeting the blacktop one at a time, Cal openly gaped, his jaw slack and expression stunned.

"I know. I know. This car is pretty gorgeous," Edie said, stepping up onto the curb to meet him. "You should've seen all the stares it got on the ride over. Men sure do like their cars."

"I'm not looking at the car." Cal whisked her into his arms, binding her tightly there against his chest, the rhythm of his heart thrumming strongly against hers despite the fabric between them. "Edie, you are the most beautiful woman I have ever seen."

In any other scenario, she would've called it out for the lie it was, but there was a vulnerable lilt to Cal's voice that made Edie's breath catch and her heart lodge in her throat.

"Do you have any idea what you do to me?" he half-growled near her ear.

A blush crept up her neck, hot and tingly. "I forgot the camera in the car," she said, pulling back. Reluctantly, Cal let her slide out of his grasp, but not without an audible grumble. "Give me just one second," Edie assured.

His appreciative stare while she stooped down to gather her camera from the passenger seat was enough to make her fan herself. Cal had told Edie she was beautiful on more than one occasion and he always made her feel pretty, but there was something in the air tonight—an unmet desire that crackled between them like a current of electricity.

"I'm embarrassed to even show these to you." She held up the camera and shrugged. "But I really do need your advice, so I'm willing to risk potential humiliation."

"You have no reason to be embarrassed by your art, Edie." He took the camera from her and slung the strap over his shoulder. "But let's wait on that. I have something I want to show you first. Come with me?"

Taking her hand possessively into his, he led her up the sidewalk to The Dock. It was after hours, the studio long closed up for the night, so she shouldn't have felt the pang of excitement shoot through her when he locked the door behind them. It would make sense to secure the building in case any late night patrons decided to stop by. Still, her heart raced in her chest. There was a change in Cal's demeanor this evening, and it allured her to no end.

The front room was dark, save for a small pendant light that shone just above the street facing window. All of the sconces used for illuminating the paintings and photographs on display had already been turned off. It was dark, and something about that made Edie feel like she was a teenager sneaking around after curfew, trying not to get caught while hiding in the shadows.

Edie followed Cal down the narrow corridor to his studio at the back of The Dock where the lights were still on. No question, this was her favorite part of the building. While the front space reminded her of Cal's home—sterile and pristine—his studio was a beautiful riot of color. Paint spattered the walls, the floor, the ceiling. She figured there was a remnant from every one of Cal's pieces, a mark of each creation left behind. Cal wasn't tidy about his art. He painted with flying strokes and passionate movement.

"Wait right here."

He left her standing in the middle of the room before he disappeared into the broom closet just a few paces away.

Edie looked around. There were three canvases— all as tall as she—at various stages of completion, propped up on large easels. Tilting her head, she tried to make out the scenes in each, but she couldn't decipher anything concrete, only the mood they evoked within her.

One was a blur of crimson, black, and gray, crashing together in tight swirls of paint that looped across the canvas. Another was composed of cool blues spread together like soft waves. The last was an ombré blend of orange and yellow and white, alternating in threes across the stretched frame.

Cal was one of Southern California's most renowned abstract expressionists, his works selling for top dollar at both Los Angeles' and San Diego's prestigious art auctions. Even in their small town of Seascape Shores, the longest he'd ever held onto a completed painting was a few days. There were waiting lists of local clients eager to buy his pieces. His talent was raw, the kind that couldn't be taught. It was part of the reason Edie felt so uncertain about her own skills. She'd wanted to be able to effortlessly create the way he did. She'd hoped to shift from macro to landscape photography like the flip of a switch. She just couldn't do that.

"Here." Cal emerged from the closet with an old newspaper clipping in his hands. He held it out for her to take. "I wanted you to see this."

The article was dated ten years back, and the headline read *Local Artist Lacks Vision and Leaves Viewers as Empty as His Bank Account.* Underneath was a picture of a smiling young Cal. He stood next to a painting that surely belonged to someone else. Nothing about the precise lines and intricate detailing hinted at his hand. It was a painting of a seashore, congested with beach chairs, blankets, and umbrellas. White-capped waves rippled in the distance. While it was a nice painting—pleasant even—it looked like something that belonged on a greeting card and not on display at The Dock. Certainly not up for bidding at any auction.

"Is that yours?" Edie looked up and locked eyes with Cal.

"Yes." He snickered. "It's terrible, right?"

"It's not terrible," Edie said. "But the things this critic says about you—that's what's terrible. His comments are incredibly hurtful, Cal."

Cal leaned forward and scanned the article over Edie's shoulder. He pointed to the second paragraph and tapped it with his finger. "The bit where he says the only thing my paintings are good for is fire kindling was my favorite part."

"That's so insensitive." Edie's heart squeezed for him, even though the words had been written a decade earlier.

"Maybe, but he was right. They burn incredibly well. You should've seen the bonfire my friends and I had on the beach. That one in particular lit up like a Christmas tree. The flames rose higher than our heads."

"You burned your painting just because some art critic didn't like it?"

"No, I burned my painting because *I* didn't like it."

Edie folded up the piece of newspaper and handed it back to Cal, unable to read more of the journalist's harsh criticism. Cal tossed it next to a stack of paint palettes and jumped up to sit on the butcher-block table's ledge, legs dangling beneath him like he was on a swing.

"I'd been commissioned to paint Seascape Shore for a Memorial Day event—you know, the one where they auction off original pieces from artists to raise money for our local VA? At the time, I had been dubbed the up-and-coming artist of the year and Craig Cantrelle—that was the journalist—he wanted to do a piece on me and my work for the paper. As you just read, he wasn't a big fan."

"But that's just one opinion."

"Right, and only one opinion matters."

He wasn't giving himself enough credit. "Cal—"

"The only opinion that mattered was *my own*." He lifted Edie's camera from its place on the table and handed it to her.

Taking the heavy camera into her hands, Edie brought up the images on the back screen. As she advanced one by one, she felt nothing. It wasn't until the image of the starfish popped up that a spark lit up her spirit. The starfish had washed up by her feet while she was attempting to fill her frame with the rising tide. The texture of the sea creature had intrigued her, demanding a closer look. Water glistened off its grainy surface, beading on the five points that spread out on the wet sand. She loved the juxtaposition of the glassy water droplet resting like a crystal ball on the coarse, orange exterior. She'd zoomed in as far as she could, steadying her hand to get the shot. And boy, it was a good one.

"I love that," Cal whispered at her back.

"Me too," Edie agreed. "The others, not so much."

"So delete them."

She bristled. "But you wanted ocean shots for my next installment."

"Right. And that starfish is phenomenal. I doubt it will last a day hanging on these walls. It's going to fly out of here."

"But it's not a landscape photograph."

"Edie, I wanted you to photograph the ocean, but I didn't say it had to be a landscape. That's what your daughter suggested. I just wanted your take on the ocean. I wanted to see it through your eyes. You've done that here. In fact, this starfish might be my favorite photograph of yours to date. The colors, the textures. It jumps right off the screen. I can almost feel it."

"You really think I should just delete all the others?" She swallowed thickly. She wasn't sure she could bring herself to do that, to erase all the long hours of work with the click of a single button.

"It's up to you, but as an artist, burning that painting was the turning point in my career. I finally gave myself the freedom to paint the way I wanted to paint, not the way I thought others expected me to. It took me a few more years before I refined that passion and found my home with abstract expressionism. But you're the opposite. You've already discovered your sweet spot. I say you stick with what makes you happy and continue doing that. Life's too short to do anything else."

At that moment in time, Edie knew exactly what made her happy, both in her art and in life. She discarded the camera onto the table and slid into the space between Cal's legs, lifting to wrap her arms around his broad shoulders. With uncharacteristic boldness, she curled a hand around his neck and drew him close, her chest flush with his as she rose up on tiptoe. Cal's eyes flashed with wild expectation.

"You make me happy, Cal," she murmured, her

lips so close to his mouth she could feel his erratic breaths on her skin.

"You make me happy, too, Edie." He worked on a swallow.

Cautioning herself not to overthink it, Edie pushed her lips onto Cal's in the kiss she'd craved for so long it had become a constant ache within her. To her relief, Cal met her mouth with equal enthusiasm, his lips hungry and his breathing ragged, like her own.

"Edie," he groaned against her parted mouth. "You seriously have no idea what you do to me."

She couldn't fathom how a man as attractive and successful, and yet as kind and compassionate, as Cal could have any interest in her. But whatever doubt taking root in her gut was obliterated when he hopped down and spun her around, pinning her against the ledge of the table, his hands bracketed possessively on either side of her as he searched out her gaze with alluring intensity.

Cal lifted a finger and grazed her cheek, running a trail down to Edie's trembling lips, all the while never breaking their stare. Then both hands surrounded her face, cupping it not as a way to pull her close, but to hold her steady in preparation for what he was about to do. His thumbs brushed gently against her mouth, and with painstakingly slow movements, he brought his lips just over hers.

"I want you so badly."

Edie's hands fell to her sides, her head heavy, her limbs like leaden weights.

It had been decades since she'd been kissed and she feared she'd forgotten just what to do. She was unsure how to kiss him and worried she'd ruined it already.

So he showed her.

This is how, his mouth indicated as it pushed into hers again, meeting it so gently, almost as a whisper.

And like this, as his tongue slipped out and slowly teased her lips apart. It swiped into her mouth and tangled with her own, swirling around, softly but rhythmically. They chased one another like this, warm and wet caresses.

Edie couldn't breathe.

Cal was tender yet firm, greedy but still giving. He took the lead, moving his mouth expertly against hers in an increasingly frenzied pace that had her head spinning and her heart thundering within her ribcage. It was almost too much.

"You are really good at this," she said, giggling against his lips when they'd parted for air. She stared deeply into Cal's eyes, beckoning him toward her again by tugging at the collar of his shirt.

"It's been awhile," he admitted and then he kissed her with eagerness, not even attempting to mask his desperate want in the low sound that rumbled in his throat. He stopped only to say, "But I've been thinking about this moment for the entire month we've known each other. I knew it would be good, but I had no idea it would be this good."

Edie looked up at Cal under half-lidded eyes. The table's surface was rigid against her backside, but his large body pressed against hers in the most wonderful, exhilarating way and she didn't want to move. She melted into a puddle of emotion when he brought his face near and said, "I'm totally falling for you, Edie. I'm a complete goner."

That admission pulled all the air from Edie's lungs.

"Cal, I'm forty-four."

"Okay." Reaching down, he gathered her hand into his and lifted it to his mouth. With his full lips, he pressed a feather-light kiss against her skin. He peppered kisses all along her hand, her wrist, her arm.

"That's twelve years older than you."

"Yep." His mouth trailed up her bare arm, hovering on her shoulder before nuzzling against her neck. "So?"

"Doesn't that bother you?"

"No." He leaned in and placed a kiss just under her ear. A shiver shot through her body as his warm breath tickled her tender skin there. "Does it bother you?"

"Honestly? A little bit. It does."

Cal slumped back. "Okay. What about it bothers you?"

"You called me your girlfriend yesterday. I'm not

even sure that's what I am, but do you really want a girlfriend who's a dozen years older than you?"

A long sigh slipped from his lips. "I'd wondered if I misspoke then. Honestly, it just came out. As a kid, I'd always looked up to Foster. Kind of like a father-figure, you know? Yesterday, I was just so proud to show you off, I guess. And even more proud to call you mine. But I apologize if I overstepped. I shouldn't have called you my girlfriend without asking you if that was okay first." He kissed the tip of her nose and drew back. "So let me ask now. Is it okay to call you my girlfriend?"

It wasn't where she expected the conversation to go. Edie's head was still stuck on the age gap that had only briefly been addressed and then skimmed right over.

"Yes," she said, surprised that, in fact, it was okay with her. More than okay. "I do want to be your girl-friend, Cal. You make me feel…I don't know, I don't want to say young again, but you make me feel something I haven't felt in a long time. You make me feel like *me* again. I've felt so lost for so long. But discovering myself again, and discovering this—with you—this is exactly what I want."

"Good, because it's what I want too, Edie. Sounds like we're on the same page."

"But I'm still a lot older."

"Age is just a number that I'm not particularly all that worried about right now," he said in a throaty voice that reverberated against her collarbone. His mouth found a spot against her neck that nearly made her toes curl. Man, he was an expert at this. "All I'm currently concerned with is making sure my girlfriend gets kissed absolutely senseless. Sound good?"

After the next kiss that left Edie seeing stars, she discovered that was all she was really concerned about, too.

CHAPTER SEVENTEEN

*T*abitha hadn't intentionally selected the restaurant based on its proximity to the hospital. But each doctor, nurse, or hospital worker who entered its doors in their periwinkle scrubs pulled her attention from the Chinese chicken salad in front of her and out of the conversation with her son seated across from her. She'd become so easily distracted by their presence. She wondered what sorts of procedures they'd performed or what cases they were currently handling. Had they been up for twenty-four hours yet? Were they just finishing their shift? Just beginning it?

She used to do a similar thing with Ben. Whenever they'd go out to eat, they would pick a random couple in the restaurant and make up a story about how they met. What they'd gone through that day. The things they fought about. They'd construct these elaborate narratives in such vivid detail, Tabitha swore they had to be true. She knew she'd be disappointed to learn the reality of the couple's situation because there was no way it would ever live up to what they'd conjured up over lunch.

"Mom?" Casey swiped his lower lip with his cloth napkin and then folded it back onto his lap. "Did you hear me?"

Tabitha pulled her gaze away from the doorway. "What's that, sweetie?"

"I asked how things were going at the retreat center."

"Oh." She stabbed at a piece of cabbage with her fork and brought it to her lips, holding it there. "Things are going okay." She popped the bite into her mouth.

"Hannah said her mom is loving it. That they wait on you hand and foot."

"Yes." Tabitha nodded. "They do."

"Sounds amazing." Casey's eyes followed the path that Tabitha's took when the restaurant's door swung open again and a group of scrub-clad patrons stepped inside. He rotated back to face his mother. "You missing work?"

The question made her bristle. "I know I'm not supposed to, but yes. I do. Very much."

"I don't think it's that you're not supposed to miss it, Mom. I think it's just that you're supposed to have a healthy break from it. That's all."

"I'm not entirely sure what a healthy break even

means. What other professions require 'healthy breaks'?"

"Lots of them." Casey offered a half smile. He sure looked like his father when he did that. "All the important ones, at least."

She knew her son was just trying to be kind, but the words felt hollow and fell flat. "I'll just be glad when this month is over and I can get back to my real life. Don't get me wrong. I love spending time with Edie and Camille, but it's closer quarters than I'm used to."

"You always did like to be alone."

Casey surely didn't mean it the way she felt it, but it stung all the same. "I've always enjoyed *your* company," she offered with a contrived grin, feeling the need to prove herself. Not that she was a loner, but her drive from the hospital to home didn't give her much time to decompress. And some days, that decompression time was absolutely vital. She'd seen things others would never see, made decisions others would never be forced to make. She'd had to shake that off and out of her head before she could fall back into her role as mother and wife. She'd had to be alone to do that.

Casey offered an empathetic smile. "I know you enjoy my company, Mom." Pointing the tines of his fork at her salad, he asked, "Is that any good? Hannah always orders it when we come here."

"It's really good. A little too much dressing this

time, so the noodles aren't very crunchy, but it's my favorite thing on the menu. Want a bite?"

"No. I'm good with my French dip. Thanks, though."

Tabitha nodded. "How are things with you and Hannah?"

"Things are fine. She's taking this really hard biostatistics class right now, so I don't see her much. She's always either studying or doing homework. But we're good. We make it work."

Tabitha didn't like the surrendered tone of Casey's voice. Like his smile from earlier, it also reminded her of Ben. "Maybe you two could study together? Find a way to spend more time with one another while also doing your schoolwork?"

"Yeah, we do that. I don't know." He shrugged and took a large bite of his sandwich. She could see his thoughts brewing as he chewed before saying, "I think maybe our relationship has run its course. We'll see."

That wasn't the news she'd hoped to hear. "Oh, Casey. I'm so sorry. I had no idea."

"It's fine. I mean, I really like her. I might even love her. But I don't think we're in the same place right now. Her number one focus is graduating on the Dean's Honor List, which is an amazing goal. But I've got more than just school going on, you know? I just booked a gig at Curly Joe's for this Saturday night."

"You did? No way! That's really great, Case."

"Thanks. I'm excited about it. I've already written

up the set list. Actually,"—he hesitated—"do you want to see it?"

"Are you kidding? I would love to see it!"

Casey pulled his phone from his back pocket and swiped at the screen, then passed it off to his mother. He'd been a musician since he could crawl his way into the pantry to pull out pots and pans to bang on. In recent years, he'd focused on singing with acoustic guitar accompaniment. Like any proud mother, Tabitha recognized her son's God-given talent. However, he'd recently gained attention outside of his immediate circle, and there was a deep validation in that. Securing a gig at Curly Joe's—the largest coffeehouse in Seascape Shores—was just the confirming proof of his talent that Casey needed. Tabitha was elated for her son.

"You'll be singing On Bird's Wings? That's my favorite."

"I know. That's why I stuck it in there. I'm hoping you'll be able to make it." Casey took the phone back and placed it on the table, face down.

"I wouldn't miss it."

He beamed, a full, broad smile this time. "See? There are some perks to this sabbatical. You usually have to work on Saturdays."

He was right. She couldn't deny that. Her schedule didn't fall into the nine-to-five, Monday through Friday routine. If she could be thankful for this time off, this opportunity to watch her son sing provided a valid reason.

"Dad's coming, too."

"Oh, is he? That's great. He's always been so supportive of your music."

"Did you know that he just sold a house to Brooks Falcon?"

"No. I hadn't heard that." Brooks Falcon was a bit of a local celebrity, well on his rise to stardom with his rock band, Falcon's Flight. That Ben had a client of that caliber was quite impressive.

"I got to tour his old house before he put it on the market. He had an entire wall of Fenders. It was like a museum. He'd also converted the basement into a studio so he could record all of his music right there at home." Just then, their waitress came by with the check, and when Tabitha went to reach for it, her son shooed her away. "That's my goal. To own a home with my very own studio. I realize I'm about a million gigs and a non-existent record deal away from that, but I've told Dad to keep his eye out for anything that pops up."

"Sounds like your father's doing pretty well with work these days."

"Honestly, Mom, this is the best I've ever seen him. Happiest, too. He's lost a bunch of weight training for a half-marathon. And he even signed up as a driver for one of those apps to save a little extra cash for our upcoming trip out to Nashville."

Tabitha tried not to react visibly to that information. "You're going to Nashville?"

Taking his credit card out of his billfold, Casey

slipped it into the leather check holder and leaned back in his chair. "Yeah, this summer. Neither of us have ever been, so we just decided to plan it. That's another reason Hannah's not all too thrilled with me right now. She had told me once that she wanted to visit Nashville. I think she's a little upset that I'm not taking her, but I told her this is just a father-son trip."

"It's important for you to have those." Tabitha was happy that Casey was making a relationship with his father a priority, and even more glad to hear that Ben was reciprocating. "You two will have a lot of fun. I've heard Nashville is the music capital of the world. I think they call it Music City or something along those lines. Honkytonk bars and aspiring musicians on every corner. It's supposed to be a really exciting place."

"It'll be a nonstop party. You know me and Dad. Party animals," Casey said around a laugh. "I've got a couple of city and museum tours lined up and there's a 10K Dad wants to do while we're there."

"So he really has taken up running, huh?"

"It's pretty unbelievable, Mom. Considering how resentful he was each time you'd head out for one."

Tabitha stiffened.

"I didn't mean it like that."

"No, Casey. I get it. I'm just glad he's found something he enjoys. And I'm really happy to hear about your trip. You'll have to tell me all about it when you get back. I've always wanted to travel."

"You could come?" Even though the invitation

was extended out of obligation, it was still undeniably sweet.

"Casey. This is for you and your father. You just said that. A father-son trip."

"I know. Sometimes, I just get this crazy idea that we can do stuff together like a family again. I know I'm an adult now and shouldn't crave that anymore, but sometimes I just do."

Tabitha's shoulders fell, along with her heart. Even though Casey had been eighteen when the divorce happened, Tabitha knew it still affected him. "We will always be family, Casey. That won't ever change."

"Sure." He didn't add to it, and that word suspended between them like an ellipsis.

"Thank you so much for lunch. It was delicious." She tried to cut through the tension that had formed, but didn't feel all that successful. There was still an unmet yearning in her son's eye, and she knew she was to blame. Well, she and Ben, at least.

"Anytime, Mom." Casey gave her a closed-lip smile. "I'll see you on Saturday?"

"You can count on it."

CASEY HAD SENT over a few of his recent recordings and while their tempo didn't match her usual running playlist, Tabitha found they fit the pace she was able to run that particular afternoon. She'd pushed herself too hard the day before and her legs were still angry. But Casey's classical guitar strumming, paired with his soothing tenor, kept her moving forward at a comfortable speed, one that stretched her muscles without fully punishing them.

She only had an hour until Foster was supposed to arrive to meet with Edie about the wedding. Edie had asked that Tabitha be there, if only to help her sell herself and her talent. Tabitha had assured her that there was no need for that—that Edie's work spoke for itself—but she agreed all the same. It was an exciting opportunity for her friend and she'd do whatever she could to make it happen for her.

Checking her watch, Tabitha gauged just how far down the coastline she had time to run before she needed to double back toward the Villa. The shores were less crowded today, and she'd only passed a few other joggers, one with a massive dog who pulled at his owner's leash with oxen-like strength, dragging his person down the sandy beach. It made Tabitha smile. That dog would be really useful right about now. She'd been a runner long enough to know what her body could handle, so she couldn't understand why she'd overdone it the day before. It was going to take her a couple days to rally from that, and maybe as many soaks in her bathroom's Jacuzzi tub, too.

When she got to the point in the sand that lined up with a huge craggy ocean rock—the locals called it Pirate's Peak—she used that as her marker and pivoted on her heel to turn toward home. The sun was still high in the sky, only just beginning its gradual descent into the horizon, and it reflected off the ocean's surface in metallic waves. Shards of blinding light forced her to squint her eyes. Looking around, Tabitha made sure there weren't any other joggers or beachgoers in her path. The coast was clear.

She shut her eyes completely.

With Casey's songs on repeat, she jogged, eyes closed. *This* was her therapy. She knew Camille wanted her to talk with someone. About what, Tabitha wasn't quite sure. But this right here, the waves crashing in a steady rhythm in the distance, her son's beautiful voice in her ear, and her feet landing softly against the sandy shores, this was all the therapy she needed. She reveled in it, and let the cold ocean air fill her lungs and clear her mind.

She'd gotten so lost in her meditation that she certainly didn't feel the presence of the jogger just up ahead. She couldn't see that every step brought them closer. In her mind, she was alone, the entire beach all to herself. So when she crashed into another runner, shoulders clipping in a jarring and unexpected collision, it sent her flying backward with the force of a football tackle. Sand flew up around her like confetti when her backside met the ground.

"Oooof!" she cried, the wind knocking out of her. She yanked her earbuds out and shook her head.

"Tabs?" Ben's voice startled her even more than the collision. He pushed his headphones off of his ears and shoved his phone into the pocket of his running shorts.

"Ben? What are you—?" Tabitha shaded her brow as her ex-husband's silhouette came into view.

"I'm so sorry." He shot out a hand to help her up. "I was looking at my phone and had my music up too loud. I wasn't paying attention. Didn't even see you there."

Tabitha dusted off her backside and rolled her shoulders, flexing her neck to work out the kinks.

"Are you hurt?" Ben asked, his voice fraught with worry.

"No, no. I'm fine."

"I'm really so sorry, Tabitha. I was totally distracted by my phone."

Tabitha wondered if it was a text from a certain someone that had Ben off in his own little world, but she wouldn't let her mind latch onto that thought.

"I was distracted, too. I had my eyes closed."

A laugh burst out of Ben's mouth. "You run with your eyes closed?" He tried, but failed, to keep from snickering openly. The fist lifted to his mouth did little to conceal his laughter. "Yesterday, I asked you to text me if you wanted to go for a run, but now I think I should insist on it. You clearly need someone to be your eyes and ears out here on the beach if you're going to run with your eyes totally shut."

"I don't usually run with my eyes closed. Just today. And only for the last few minutes, really. You managed to catch me right in the middle of it."

A look of concern fell over Ben's features as he sized Tabitha up. "And you're sure you're not hurt?"

"I'm sure. But I do have to say, you're a bit of a brick wall, Ben."

"I don't know if that's a compliment. I seem to remember you calling me that once before. That sometimes speaking to me was like '*speaking to a wall*.'" He smiled, even though the memory gave Tabitha nothing to smile about.

She'd said it their first year as new parents, when Ben seemed to have no opinion on whether or not Tabitha should apply for the night shift that had recently opened up at the hospital. She'd figured it would allow her to be home with their baby during the day, but it wasn't a decision she felt comfortable making on her own. Ben had been totally indifferent, saying she could do whatever she wanted. But what she'd wanted at the time was his direction and input. She could make life-altering decisions for others in an instant, but this decision—one that affected the rhythm of their new family—seemed impossible.

"I'm glad you're okay," Ben redirected, almost as if he could bury his last comment in the sand beneath them. "Are you finishing up your run? Or just getting started?"

"I'm heading back. Probably only a half mile left."

"Can I run it with you?"

"Oh. Yeah. Sure."

"I should be heading back in that direction, too,"

he said. "I'm showing a house this evening and I need to make sure I've got all my ducks in a row before my client shows up. This one's new on the market, so I haven't had a chance to scope it out yet. I was actually looking at the listing when I ran into you."

Together, they picked up the pace, jogging side by side. Tabitha tucked her earbuds into her pocket and turned off her playlist. "I had lunch with Casey today. He said you're really killing it as a realtor."

"Killing it isn't a term I would use, but I've had some lucky breaks recently, which has helped. I enjoy that I can make my own hours, too. I think that's my favorite part. Each day is different."

"You never did like to have a schedule."

"No, and I still don't. Casey and I are taking a trip out to Nashville this summer. He's planning our whole itinerary since he knows I'm awful at it." Ben's words were choppy, like he struggled a little to run, breathe, and talk all at the same time.

"He mentioned that. He's really looking forward to it."

"So am I."

They continued their run in comfortable silence. Every once in a while, Tabitha would look over out of the corner of her eye, just to see if Ben was maintaining their pace or if she should slow a little to meet his stride. To her surprise, he kept up without issue. It was clear he'd been training for some time. She wanted to ask what prompted this sudden interest in running, but it wasn't any of her business. Ben was free to take on whatever hobbies he liked.

"I was surprised to see you yesterday," he said after several moments of prolonged quiet between them. "You don't have a picture uploaded in your Ride Reserve profile, so I had no idea it was you. And as far as I know, your given name isn't Wanda Morales."

"Is that really the name that comes up?" Tabitha scowled. "I have a feeling that's Camille's doing. She never likes it when I use my real name for things. And she's really not a fan of those driving apps. She seems to think all the drivers are serial killers."

"There's screening for that."

"Exactly what I told her."

"But there's not a whole lot of screening for passengers, you know?" Ben pointed out. "I've had some pretty sketchy clients in my car. Luckily, nothing I couldn't handle. But you do have to be alert and maybe even a little on the cautious side if you're going to share your car with complete strangers."

"Do you enjoy it? Driving around people you don't know?"

"I do. You know I've always liked meeting new people. And it's good money for not a lot of effort. Originally, I just started doing it to earn some extra spending cash for things like the upcoming trip to Nashville. But I've got plenty saved up for that now and I'm still doing it," he explained. "Plus, I have the app to thank for my girlfriend. She was my very first customer."

"I didn't know you were dating." It wasn't quite a lie, but not entirely the truth.

"Four months now, so I suppose we're still in the honeymoon phase. Her name's Donna. She's a vet tech. It's a funny story, really. When I say she was my first customer, I should clarify that she and an alpaca were technically my first customers."

"You had an alpaca in that car?"

"They're super bendy animals. You'd be amazed at how easily it just folded itself up in there. Like an accordion," Ben said, like it wasn't absurd to have a farm animal in a Camry. "The little guy had somehow escaped from his farm and Donna found him on the side of the road when she was out for a morning run. He was really dehydrated and in need of medical attention. So she pulled up the Ride Reserve app. The first guy who accepted her request had a truck, but when he got there, he wasn't willing to take them. Not even in the bed of the truck. So when I showed up and she told me the story—and that sad look in the poor alpaca's eye—well, I just couldn't leave them on the side of the road, you know?"

Tabitha's thoughts hung back to the part of the conversation where Ben said his girlfriend had been out for a run. It all made sense now. She felt foolish for ever thinking any of it had been related to her in any way. Ben took up running to impress his new girl-friend. Of course.

Without intending to, Tabitha's legs spurred into another gear, her arms pumping quickly at her sides.

"Oh, wow," Ben said, almost panicked, as he noticed her uptick in speed. "So you want to sprint the last bit, huh?"

"Yep," Tabitha gritted through her teeth. It was so much more relaxing to run with music playing and closed eyes than it was to race next to a chatty ex-husband.

"This is really fast," Ben panted.

"Yep."

Like there was a ribbon at the finish line—some prize to be won—Tabitha ran as fast as her legs could carry her. Ben matched her stride for stride. When she'd pull forward a few feet, he'd kick it into high gear to take the lead. Then Tabitha would summon whatever strength she had on reserve to accelerate even more, leaving Ben lagging several paces behind.

This back and forth continued all the way up the beach. When the Seascape Shores Villas came into view, Tabitha put on the brakes, nearly skidding to a stop. She doubled over, her hands on her knees as she recovered her breath.

Ben slowed up to a jog. She could hear him cough loudly at her back, wheezing and sputtering like an old jalopy.

Spinning around, they locked eyes. Tabitha's were

watering from the salty sting of the ocean air. Ben's were squinted in confusion. They paused a moment, then, simultaneously, the two erupted in a roar of laughter.

"What was that?" Ben asked after coughing to clear his throat once more.

"I honestly don't know. But for someone who's only recently become a runner, I'm really impressed you were able to keep up. That was fast."

"I've been running for three years now, Tabs," Ben said as he rolled his shoulders and swiveled his head back and forth to stretch his muscles in a cool down. "Not quite like *that*, though. You've got some crazy speed."

Oh, she had some crazy, alright. What had gotten into her? Why had she been so bothered by the information about Donna? Why did she care? This wasn't like her.

"I'm sorry I pushed us like that. It had just dawned on me that I was going to be late for meeting Edie back at the Villa if I didn't quicken the pace a little. She's got a guy coming over who might be interested in hiring her to photograph his daughter's wedding. She asked that I be there."

"It's no big deal. In fact, it was kinda fun. I haven't raced like that since I was a kid and mom would call me into the house for dinner on pizza night."

"It *was* kinda fun, right?" Tabitha had her hands on her hips, stretching her legs from side to side when her phone buzzed against her thigh. She withdrew it from her pocket. When she pulled up the incoming text, she almost dropped the phone to the sand.

"What is it?" Ben looked over at her. "Everything okay?"

"It's a text from Camille." Eyes wide, Tabitha gulped. She flipped the phone around and, with trembling words, she said, "It's a mug shot of the man we're supposed to meet."

CHAPTER EIGHTEEN

*C*amille had paced back and forth so much, she feared she wore a track on the travertine floor beneath her. The cell phone gripped in her sweaty palm remained quiet. Why hadn't anyone texted her back yet? Were Tabitha and Edie not even the least bit concerned they were about to welcome a convicted felon into their Villa? Or that Edie was contemplating doing business with him?

Camille had to admit, when she'd overheard the salon conversation involving Foster's potential criminal activity, she'd assumed the story was as fake as the ample cleavage on the woman making the far-fetched claims. And much to Camille's relief, a quick internet search proved that to be the case. Foster was a foreman at Horizon Heights Construction, a mid-sized construction firm based out of Seascape Shores. Camille had heard of it and recognized the logo instantly, having seen their signage on plenty of building projects throughout town. He'd been with the company for twenty-three years and made a modest salary with no jobsite violations or customer complaints.

Foster Spaulding didn't have much of an internet trail.

Stephen Foster Spaulding Jr., however—well, that was an entirely different story.

"Thank God! There you are!" Camille shouted when the front door to the Villa opened just before six o'clock and Edie walked through its frame. "Did you hear that Foster—?"

"Is right behind me?" Edie cut her off, her rounded eyes hinting that Camille should promptly zip her lip. "We ran into each other at Seascape Shores S'mores, so we thought we'd come back here a little early to get a head start on looking at my portfolio. Becca and Jeremy will be here in just a few."

"I wish I'd known you'd be here, Camille." Foster grinned as he sauntered in behind Edie. He had an untucked white linen shirt on, with khaki shorts and leather flip-flops, yet all Camille could envision was an orange jumpsuit in her mind's eye. "I would've brought you a perfectly toasted marshmallow. Would you believe they had a marshmallow roasting contest and my marshmallows won three times over? Beautiful golden brown. Who knew I had such an obscure and completely useless talent?"

Oh, there are a lot of things we don't know about you, Foster. Or should I say, Stephen? Camille tried to hush her thoughts, but they played loudly in her head, just as distracting as Foster's booking photo that was also permanently ingrained there.

"I'm going to go grab my laptop from upstairs," Edie said. She turned to their guest. "Foster, you can make yourself comfortable at the dining table. I figure we'll set up there since there's lots of space to spread out."

"Will do," Foster said, his hands shoved casually into his pockets. He gave Camille a telling look, one that conveyed his appreciation for the chance to be alone. Up until two hours ago, she would've appreciated the opportunity, too. Right now, though, she felt like they needed supervised visits.

"I'll go with you!" Camille whirled around and raced to catch up with Edie, who was already halfway up the staircase.

"Don't be ridiculous. I'll only be a minute. I'm just fetching my computer, Cam," Edie flashed a goofy smile and lowered her voice in an insistent way. "Go hang out with Foster."

Clearly, Edie had yet to read her texts.

Camille's stomach roiled. With reluctant strides, she made her way back down the stairs.

"So, what did you do all day, Camille?" Foster glanced around the Villa as he spoke, rotating on his heel in a complete three-sixty. "Take advantage of any spa services?"

"No. I actually had some things to take care of back at home."

She'd spent the morning going through Patrick's photo album and when her tears had run dry, she decided to be a real glutton for punishment and visit the cemetery where his tiny body had been laid to rest. A yellow rose was propped against his gravestone and Camille noted Mark had also stopped by to visit their son on what would have been Patrick's birthday. Though she and Mark had their differences, they shared this connection—however tragic—and always would.

Sometimes, it still felt surreal that they'd celebrated twenty-five birthdays without him, their son never having the opportunity to experience one of his own while here on earth.

"Doing something fun, I hope?" Foster raised an eyebrow.

"Just celebrating a birthday of a loved one," she answered tightly. It felt like more information than she needed to give.

"That's great, Camille. Birthdays are always a cause for celebration."

Their small talk was stilted, so very different from the easy flow of their conversation at the pool and at sushi. Camille knew she was to blame for it, but this new information about Foster hindered her ability to interact with him the way she once had. It changed everything.

Right then, the front door flew open with such force it would be a miracle if the doorknob didn't leave a dent on the wall it careened into.

Tabitha burst into the Villa, panting and covered in a sheen of sweat. "I came back as soon as I got—"

"A leg cramp? I told you that you really need to eat more bananas, Tabitha." Camille clenched her teeth and jerked her chin toward Foster at her back. She swooped over and took Tabitha by her shoulders. "You need more potassium in your diet so you can avoid getting those pesky Charlie horses. I keep telling you that. You're so prone to them. Always have been."

Unlike Edie, Tabitha quickly caught on, the many years of sisterly scheming working to their advantage. "Yes. More bananas. Absolutely."

But then, what really struck Camille as bananas was that Ben stepped out from behind her sister, also clothed in running gear and coated in just as much sweat. What in the world was going on?

"Leg cramp," Ben said, shrugging impishly as he looked at Foster. "Terrible way to cut a good run short." He extended a hand. "Hi there. I'm Ben."

"Foster. Glad to meet you."

"Let's get you that banana."

Camille grasped onto her sister's elbow and swiftly directed her into the kitchen just off to their left. She cornered her near the stainless steel refrigerator. Camille opened the fridge, then motioned to Tabitha to join her behind the large doors, out of sight.

"You got my text?" she asked, hoping they were out of earshot.

The men discussed the importance of a healthy diet in the other room, which was certainly an odd topic, but nothing about this evening proved normal, so it was par for the course.

"He's a convicted felon?" Tabitha's eyes bugged out of her skull. "You can't be serious."

"As a heart attack. Aggravated assault. He served two years in the county jail and paid a hefty fine." Camille's voice was barely a whisper. She pretended to fiddle around in the produce drawer, taking out a head of iceberg lettuce and rotating it in her hand like she contemplated fixing a salad. "Apparently, he got out early for good behavior."

Tabitha's brows rose. "Well, that's good to hear, right?"

"Tabitha. We have a convicted felon in our living room at this very moment. I'm not sure any part of this is good."

"Does Edie know?"

"I texted her, but based on our interaction when she came home, I don't think she's received them yet. If she has, she definitely hasn't read them. This is awful, sis. What on earth do we do?"

"I'm honestly not even sure," Tabitha said. "But I'm getting really cold in this fridge. Plus, we're supposed to be getting bananas. Those are on the counter."

"Good point." Camille dropped the lettuce back into the crisper drawer and shut the refrigerator door. She walked a few steps over to the fruit basket placed next to the toaster and grabbed the bunch of bananas stored there. She tore one off, then handed it to her sister. "I feel like we're trapped in an episode of Dateline."

"Well, it's not a dark and stormy night, so at least there's that." Peeling the banana, Tabitha took a bite. "Yuck. I hate it when they taste green. This still needs to ripen for a few more days."

"Focus, Tab. I really need your problem-solving skills here. You don't actually have to eat the banana."

"Sorry." She put the partially nibbled fruit down and slumped against the counter. She wove her arms across her chest. "You don't think he's actually dangerous, do you?"

"I honestly don't even know the guy. And I couldn't find a whole lot pertaining to his case or the exact charges. It was a bit of a rabbit hole that ended with his mug shot. That's when I panicked and texted you both."

"It's so unlike you to panic," Tabitha deadpanned.

"This is not the time to make a mockery of my paranoia. In this instance, it's completely warranted."

"I don't know, sis. I mean, it's not like he escaped from jail and we're harboring him or anything. From what you've said, it sounds like he's served his time and was even released early. Maybe we should give him the benefit of the doubt. There might be an explanation for all of this."

"You do realize that aggravated assault means there was likely some sort of threat involved, right? I mean, even *I* have watched enough Law and Order to know that."

Tabitha's gaze shifted toward her ex-husband and Foster, who were still conversing in the other room. "I really have a hard time believing that man right there threatened or assaulted anyone."

"Why? Because he's so handsome? That should be the first indicator, Tab. It's always the impossibly good-looking ones that turn out to be serial killers."

"I thought it was the Ride Reserve drivers that were the killers."

"It's all of them!"

"Okay." Tabitha placed two steadying hands on her sister's shoulders. "Let's just take a breather for a moment here. Foster has a checkered past—"

"More liked a striped past, what with the prison uniform and all." Camille groaned.

Tabitha rolled her eyes. "I say we just ask him about it."

"You're suggesting we ask him about his jail time? And just how does one weave that into a normal conversation? Hey Foster, any favorite meals from your time in the slammer?"

"I don't know." Tabitha bit her lip. "I need to think on it for a bit, but I'll come up with something."

"I don't think we have the luxury of time." Camille's gaze moved toward the door where a woman who bore a striking resemblance to Foster had just walked in. She had the same piercing blue eyes and contagious smile, and she wore her auburn hair in curls that skated just above her shoulders. A slender man with a flash of white-blond hair followed behind, and there was no question that he was the son of the woman from the salon. The genetic traits were undeniably strong.

"Hey kiddo, you made it!" Foster rushed to the foyer and wrapped his daughter in a big bear hug. Camille's heart squeezed at the sight. His fatherly love was evident, and the hard criminal exterior she already had a difficult time envisioning now seemed like pure fiction. "How was cake testing?"

"Filling!" Jeremy, Becca's fiancé, answered with a rub of his belly like he was Santa Claus himself. "I think I sampled twice my weight in cake."

"Did you two settle on a flavor?"

"Vanilla cake with buttercream and fresh strawberries," Becca answered.

"You've always been a strawberry-loving girl. I remember when we went strawberry picking at that little farm down the road when you were just five-years-old. Heritage Acres Farm, I think it was called. You stained your fingers bright red from eating the strawberries as fast as I could pick them. I think it's a great choice for your cake." Foster left a kiss on the crown of his daughter's hair before he pulled away from their sweet embrace. "Edie's just grabbing her laptop. Let's take a seat at the table so we're ready to go when she gets down here."

Camille's eyes tracked Foster, watching his every move.

Out of nowhere, Edie's voice bellowed from upstairs. "Hey, Camille?" Her tone wavered like she'd seen a ghost. "Any chance you can come up here and help me find my charger?"

Camille flew up the stairs, grabbing onto the railing to steady herself as she bounded two at a time.

"Foster's got a prison record?" Edie was sitting in the middle of her bed, her phone in her hand, her mouth ajar. "What in the world?"

"I know. It's crazy, right? For *aggravated assault*." Camille said it like she actually knew what that meant.

"So what do we do? Do you think I should retract my offer to photograph the wedding? This feels all kinds of uncomfortable now."

Camille pursed her lips. "I don't necessarily think Becca should be punished for her father's transgressions. But the whole thing is truly bizarre. I'll give you that. Did you really need help finding your laptop charger, or was that just a ploy to get me up here?"

"No. It's right here. I've just been sitting here stalling as I waited for Cal to text me back. I asked him if he knew anything about all of this since he has a history with Foster. Unfortunately, he's not responding. He's at an art show with one of his buddies from college, so I don't think he'll check his phone anytime soon."

"Well, I don't think we can stall much longer. Becca and Jeremy are here, and they're all set up and waiting for you in the dining room. Things are going to look suspicious if we put them off."

Edie frowned. "What if I download some really hideous wedding photographs from the internet and pass them off as mine? Then there's no chance they'll want to book with me and we can cut them all loose and never think about Foster again."

Though it sounded like a plausible plan, Camille wondered if—when it came down to it—she'd actually be able to forget about Foster. Something about the man intrigued her to no end. She would also be lying if she didn't admit that the mystery surrounding his unknown past was intriguing in and of itself. Not that she was ever one to fall for a bad boy. Mark had been as straight-laced as they came, up until the point where his morals slowly unraveled, right along with their marriage.

But Foster? There was something about him that made it hard for Camille to completely write him off. And she was bound and determined to figure out just what that was.

"Let's go downstairs. Treat Becca and Jeremy like you would any potential client and let me handle the situation with Foster. I think I might have an idea."

"I'M IMPRESSED you were able to round these up so quickly." Foster skewered a fat marshmallow and leaned forward, elbows propped on his knees, as he held the stick over the fire pit. Flames licked up toward the marshmallow in a bright white and orange blaze, bubbling the sugar and charring the underbelly. Foster jerked it back and blew out a powerful breath.

"They really aren't kidding when they say their main goal is to ensure all of their guests' needs are met around here, marshmallow emergencies included. Plus, after you came in bragging about your roasting skills, I had to see if it was all talk," Camille said. "Based on the looks of that particular marshmallow, I'd say it was."

Camille discreetly peered over her shoulder at Edie, Becca, and Jeremy, who sat just on the other side of the glass sliding doors, huddled around Edie's laptop as they scrolled through her pictures. Tabitha and Ben pretended to watch the evening news, but Camille caught them glancing her direction every few minutes, just to keep tabs and make sure everything was alright. Apparently, that was the reason Ben came back to the Villa. Why Tabitha was with him in the first place was a question Camille would have to ask her sister later that night, but for now, she was grateful for Ben's presence.

"I'm not all talk, Camille." Foster sucked gooey marshmallow residue off of his thumb. He lifted just the corner of his mouth into a smile. "You just make me nervous."

"*I* make you nervous!" Camille snorted. "Well, that's something."

"You do. You're beautiful and fascinating and—"

"I'm going to stop you right there, Foster." Camille lifted a halting hand like a stop sign. "You need to know that I know."

"You know what?"

"I *know*," she emphasized the word like it would clearly convey her meaning.

"You gotta give me a little more than that to work with here. You already know that I think you're beautiful?"

"No. *That* I didn't know." She shook her head and took another marshmallow from the bag as she tried to let that admission pass without blushing. "I know about you."

"This is very cryptic, Camille. What do you know about me?"

She couldn't believe she was going there, but she was going there. "I know about your time in jail."

Like he'd been socked in the gut, Foster slumped back in his Adirondack chair. He lowered the marshmallow into the fire and watched as flames engulfed it, his eyes glazed over and face expressionless. "I see."

"It wasn't like I was conducting some sort of background check on you or anything. I was just at the salon getting a pedicure and I overheard your future in-law mention something about your criminal history."

"Criminal history," Foster repeated. His shoulders lifted and dropped in a surrendered blow. "Wow."

Suddenly, exposing Foster didn't feel like the most important thing anymore. The dejection—maybe it was even a little shame—that cloaked his face as he processed her words was enough to make Camille's stomach flip. She swallowed hard against the bile threatening to rise up her throat.

"I hadn't realized I was the hot topic of salon gossip these days."

"It wasn't like that," she lied, because it was exactly like that. "She just mentioned that you…" Camille had no idea where to go with the statement, so she let her words trail off.

Foster dropped the skewer to the ground and rubbed his hands, one over the other. The evening breeze caught his hair, ruffling it, and he lifted two frustrated hands to rake it back. Taking a breath that expanded his lungs so fully his shirt pulled taut against the effort, he closed his eyes and when he opened them, Camille nearly lost her own breath. The look of vulnerability was disarming, and she surrendered all resolve to expose him right then and there.

Foster's throat forced a swallow, one that strained the muscles in his neck and clamped his jaw.

"Have you ever loved someone so much that you would die for them?" he asked, his unblinking gaze holding hers with such intensity she felt it down to her toes.

"Absolutely." Though Camille had only known her son for three impossibly short weeks, she would've gone to the ends of the earth for him, would've given her very last breath just so he could take one more. Every day, she wished that had been an option.

"Then you would surely understand going to jail to protect them," he said. "That's what I did. And given the chance, I'd do it all over again."

CHAPTER NINETEEN

*I*t had been a sleepless night for the women of Villa #6.

The meeting with Becca and Jeremy went well, and by the time Edie had snapped her laptop shut, she was already holding a deposit check for her wedding photography services. For the largest package she offered, no less. In any other scenario, Becca and Jeremy would've been Edie's ideal match. The young couple was easy-going, and all of their preferences were right in line with exactly what Edie knew she could provide for their big day. They understood her vision and how she planned to bring it to fruition at their early June beach wedding.

Edie wanted to let the excitement of a successful pitch swell within her, maybe even celebrate it a little, but she kept it quiet, unsure if it was right to feel any pleasure in it at all.

Camille was still visibly rattled about the whole

thing with Foster, and that hadn't changed with the sunrise.

"Coffee?" she asked Camille when she staggered into the family room, sleep still heavy in her eyes.

Edie was on her second cup. She'd gotten up at seven, but remained in the bathrobe and fluffy slippers provided by the Villa, curling up on the sofa that rivaled the comfort of her bed. She'd tried to read the morning paper, but nothing held her interest. Ultimately, she found herself just staring out the Villa windows, the ocean framed perfectly within it like a picture. Like the very picture she had such difficulty taking.

"I'd love some coffee. Thank you." Rubbing her eyelids with a balled up fist, Camille yawned. "I sure tossed and turned all night. I feel like a zombie."

Edie retrieved a mug from the cupboard and filled it nearly full, leaving room for the milk she knew Camille would want added to it. "I didn't sleep well, either." Edie opened the fridge and took out the carton, then poured enough milk into it so the deep black liquid turned a sweet caramel color. "Let me know if it's not hot enough. I can pop it in the microwave for you if you want."

"This is perfect. Thank you, Edie."

"The whole bit with Foster really got to you, huh?" Edie tugged the sash on her robe tighter as she sat to join her friend at the table.

Camille blew across the top of her mug with a large sigh. "It did, but my reaction to it all is what bothered me the most. I was acting like a crazy woman, Edie. I mean, seriously. It's not really any of my business what kind of past Foster has. Why I felt the need to interrogate him is totally beyond me."

"It sort of is your business if you're interested in the guy, right?"

Camille cut Edie a look. "I'm not interested in Foster."

"Okay." Edie humored her with a nod.

"I'm really not."

"Right."

"Why do I get the feeling you don't believe me?" Camille set her mug down and pushed it toward the middle of the table with an outstretched arm. She sat deeply in her chair.

"Your words say one thing, but when you're around him, your body language says something completely different. I've known you enough years to know when you're interested in a guy."

"Well, even if I were, I don't have time to be interested in anyone. I'm on the brink of a major life change. I'm going to need to find a new job as soon as I leave the Villa. I can't be bothered by a man. Especially a man as complex as Foster."

Edie figured that's all she would get out of Camille, so she had to be satisfied with it for now. "Did you at least find out what he did time for?"

"No, and ultimately, I don't think I even want to know. It felt like a Band-Aid on a deep, deep wound that I didn't have any right to peel back."

"We all have those, in one form or another, I suppose."

"Exactly. Plus, it's not like I'll have any real reason to see him again. The information isn't mine to know."

"Unless you *wanted* to see him again." Edie attempted to interpret the emotion behind Camille's blank expression. "That would be okay, Camille."

"I don't want to see him again. I mean, he's gorgeous and he seems to really like me, but that's neither here nor there."

"He likes you, huh?" Edie hid her growing smile behind her mug. "Did he tell you that?"

"He said something along the lines of me being beautiful and fascinating. You know, your typical gibberish."

"That's not gibberish, Cam. It's the truth."

Camille rolled her eyes with such exaggeration, Edie worried they would get stuck. "You're my best friend. You're obligated to say that."

"I'm not obligated to say anything. Just like Foster wasn't obligated to share his feelings with you. I think it's a good sign that he opens up so easily with you. A lot of men can't do that." Edie was thankful that Cal was the sort of man who could.

"Maybe, but I'm not ready for any of it. I'm not ready to reciprocate. And let's be real. It wasn't like he came clean completely. He just gave me enough information to satisfy my inquiring mind. A little tidbit to tide me over. There's still a reason he was convicted.

If twelve people saw his obvious guilt, why should I be the one person to turn a blind eye to it?"

"Because sometimes all we need is one person who's willing to overlook our shortcomings."

"Well, if his shortcoming was that he picked his nose or left the toilet seat up—and I'm betting those are real contenders, too—that would be one thing. This is another thing altogether."

"Fair point."

Edie was just about to get up to pour herself a third cup of coffee when there was a light knock at the door that redirected her path.

"You expecting anyone?" she asked, brow drawn, as she padded across the room to answer it. The knock got louder with a second, more insistent rasp.

"Nope." Camille yawned again. She stretched her arms skyward and let out a satisfied grunt. "Other than you and Tabitha, no one really knows I'm here."

Opening the door, Edie was met with a shock of bright red, a bouquet of roses suddenly shoved over the threshold and into her hands. She stumbled backward a few steps, unprepared for the handoff.

"Edie Lancaster?" the small man behind the massive bouquet asked in such a nasally voice that it sounded like he had a clothespin pinching the bridge of his nose.

"Yes, that's me." Edie shifted the vase from one hand to the other.

"Okay, great. These are for you from a Cal Burton. Have a nice day."

"Ooooh. Looks like lover boy is quite the romantic, huh?" Camille came up behind Edie and before she could be stopped, she'd snatched the note from within the sprigs of greenery. "*I think twelve is my new favorite number,*" she read aloud as Edie propped the enormous vase on her hip and shut the door. "*Love— your boyfriend—Cal.* Oh my gosh, Edie. Don't tell me there are a dozen roses in there. This is just too good!"

Edie did the quick math, totaling up the flowers arranged in the crystal. "Yep. There are twelve."

"So I'm guessing you finally told him your age?"

"I did." Edie pressed her nose into one of the blooms and inhaled its scent. It reminded her of her grandmother's garden, the sweet aroma transporting her to one of her most cherished childhood memories and places.

"And here you were, all worried that it would bother him. The man literally sent you one rose for every year that separates your ages. His affection— and creativity—truly knows no bounds, Edie. What do you think is next? Any chance he'll spring for a dozen donuts. A dozen eggs? I could really use some breakfast right about now."

"I'd be happy to cook something up."

The male voice at their backs had the women reeling around like pirouetting ballerinas.

"Ben?" Edie fumbled the vase, but Camille grabbed onto it before it had the chance to shatter onto the floor. "I didn't realize you were still here. Is Tabitha…?" Her eyes shifted toward the stairs, to the bedrooms that were just off the hallway. The vision of Ben standing in the living room in only a borrowed robe had her blinking her eyes so rapidly she became dizzied.

"Tabitha went out on a run. I slept late, so she went without me."

Edie couldn't bring herself to ask out loud what she was really wondering.

To her relief, Ben cut her off before she could form the awkward question. "Before either of you gets the wrong idea about any of this, I'd fallen asleep on the couch last night while we were watching TV. I guess it was after you all had turned in for the night. Tabitha decided to just leave me be rather than wake me up and send me home."

"But you were…" Edie flicked an index finger toward the ceiling. She lowered her voice. "You were just upstairs, Ben."

"I was showering, that's all. Before Tabitha left, she told me I could get cleaned up in her bathroom if I wanted to. I was still in my running clothes from yesterday. They're in the wash now." He waved a hand over his body. "Hence the robe."

"So nothing happened?" Camille slowly lowered the vase onto the center of the kitchen island and stepped back. Her arms woven across her chest likely weren't meant to mimic the act of intimidation, but it couldn't be helped. Even Edie felt the threat in her posture.

"Nothing happened, Cam. It wasn't like that. We're not like that."

"I know. I'm just surprised to see you here today. Truth be told, I was surprised to see you here yesterday, too." Camille sized up her once brother-in-law in a scrutinizing, drawn out look. "We really haven't seen you in years, Ben. And now—right when Tabitha's supposed to be figuring things out in her life—she sees you two days in a row? Something about this doesn't add up."

"I can assure you, I didn't plan any of this, Camille. And I *definitely* didn't plan to skip out on showing a new listing to one of my most promising clients yesterday. But when you texted Tabitha that mug shot, well, I guess I just realized some things take priority over work," Ben said. "I might not be married to Tabitha anymore, but I'll always care about her. And her safety—all of your safety—is important to me."

The sincerity in his words was enough to appease Edie, but Camille didn't look so easily persuaded.

"Alright. I'll buy it. For now," she conceded. "But I'm going to ask you the question I know my sister won't: what's with the running, Ben? You always hated it. Like truly despised it. It seems so odd that you've suddenly taken it on as a hobby after all of those years of having such an aversion to it."

Ben nodded, like the question was one he ultimately expected to hear. "Tabitha is not an easy woman to understand. I'm sure I don't have to tell either of you that." He glanced between the women. "But I've always wanted to get her, you know? I wanted to see the world how she sees it. I'll never fully understand her line of work or how it's almost as though she craves being in the operating room as much as she craves oxygen. But running…that was something I could at least try. Our marriage was complicated. Our divorce was simple. But those questions I had about who Tabitha was at the core didn't go away when I signed the papers. If anything, it only led me to more questions."

"So she is the reason, then," Camille verified. "I suspected so."

"She's been the reason for almost every decision in my life."

Edie hadn't realized she'd been standing there clutching her chest as she listened to Ben's heartfelt explanation. She understood every bit of what he'd said, having had her own questions about her dear friend. That Ben had given up on their marriage, but not entirely on Tabitha, made something inside Edie's chest squeeze. There was a compassion there that couldn't be dismissed.

Like he could tell Camille wasn't convinced, Ben continued. "I blamed Tabitha for so much of what went wrong in our marriage. I hated the long hours and how she'd have this glassy-eyed look when she'd finally come home. The days when she'd go for a run before even acknowledging Casey or me were the worst," Ben recalled. "We'd been divorced a year before I bought my first pair of running shoes. The first time I laced them up, I only ended up running a quarter-mile. It was pure torture. But I did a lot of thinking. Praying mostly. Praying that I didn't kill myself out on that stupid run. Over time, though, I noticed that after a good run, I felt like my thoughts were untangled. Like I could think through things more easily while my feet hit the pavement. I figured that must've been the case for Tabitha, too. And something about that common- ality helped me understand her, if only a small portion of her."

Ben scrubbed a hand down his face.

"I focused so much on what Tabitha wasn't giving to our family that I never once thought about what I could give to her. She needed that headspace—that time apart from both work life and family life—and I forced myself into it when I didn't have any right to be there."

Camille slumped a hip against the kitchen island and let her arms fall to her sides. "Wow, Ben. Not the answer I was expecting."

"No?" He chuckled. "You seemed pretty convinced it did have something to do with Tabitha."

"I mean, sure, of course I thought it was related to her one way or another. But I hadn't realized you'd processed so much over these last few years. I only wish Mark had been as insightful when it came to our relationship."

"What makes you think he's not?" Balling up a

fist, Ben pretended to knock on the side of his head. "Not all of us are completely empty up here."

"That's up for negotiation," Camille teased.

"Have you ever thought about telling Tabitha any of this?" Edie spoke up. She decided Ben could use a cup of strong coffee after that admission. She took down another mug and poured the last of the coffee from the carafe, then walked it over to him.

"Thank you," he said as he took the cup. "No, I haven't. It's taken me a lot of hours of running—and as many hours in therapy—to be able to put any of those thoughts and feelings into real words. In fact, this is the first time I've said all of it aloud in any sort of way that makes sense." He pulled in a sip of coffee and held it in his mouth a few seconds before swallowing. "It doesn't change our past, but it does help me see it in a different light. I've been able to let go of some of the resentment I'd been harboring toward her all these years. That's been huge."

"I think, in your own time, you should open up with Tabitha and tell her the progress you've made. It could go a long way," Edie offered.

"Not sure what the end goal in that would be."

"I don't believe Tabitha is in the same good head-space that you are in right now, Ben," Camille divulged. "This sabbatical, it wasn't really her choice. Things have been slipping at work and she just hasn't been herself. Her confidence has obviously been shaken, and that's a first for her. I don't think she necessarily sees that change in herself, but we all do."

Understanding filled Ben's eyes. "She has every reason to be confident. She's always been the best."

"I think she might be at the point where being the best isn't even good enough," Camille said, shrugging. "Or at least the knowledge that she's the best doesn't fulfill her the way it used to. Unfortunately, if that's the case, I'm not sure that she'll ever find anything that does."

EDIE THOUGHT about Ben's confession the whole way to The Dock. She'd gotten a ride through Ride Reserve and while she usually made pleasant small talk with the driver, the replaying conversation in her head didn't allow for her to have one in real life, too.

It didn't seem right that Tabitha wasn't privy to Ben's true thoughts, but they certainly weren't Edie's to disclose. Plus, she didn't know if it would go over well had Tabitha found out her friends had shared such a vulnerable conversation with her ex-husband. Meddling in someone's marriage was never a proper thing to do. And meddling in someone's divorce was even less acceptable.

When the car pulled up to the curb, Edie thanked the driver and hurried up the walkway into Cal's studio. She could hear reggae music filtering out from the back and through the wash of afternoon light that flooded down the long corridor, she glimpsed Cal swaying back and forth to the lazy beat, paintbrush in hand. She stopped in the doorway and leaned a shoulder against the jamb.

Cal was lost in the music and his art. There was a half-painted canvas before him, and he dragged the bristles across it in a diagonal line—top corner to bottom corner—leaving textured layers of brilliant yellow in the paintbrush's wake. When he turned toward the table to dip his brush into a different color, his eyes caught Edie's.

A slow smile spread onto his full lips.

"Sorry," Edie said. "I didn't want to disturb you."

"How long have you been standing there?" Cal set the brush onto the butcher block and grabbed a nearby rag, then wiped his hands with it.

"Not long. Promise." She pushed off the doorframe and walked over.

"Good, because I was seriously belting out that last song. The one on now, this one I don't really know." He stepped toward Edie and gathered her into his arms.

"I'm sorry I missed it, then."

"You shouldn't be. If it's any indication of how well, or poorly, I sing, I was cut from my school's fourth grade talent show. And they were required to accept everyone who tried out."

Edie laughed. "That bad, huh?"

"You've heard the phrase *'you can't carry a tune in a bucket'*? Well, I can't carry a tune in a dump truck. Or maybe that's just it—my singing is trash and that's where it belongs."

"Well, you can't be good at everything," Edie said, surprised by the easy flirt in her tone.

Tugging her closer, Cal's mouth met Edie's in an ardent kiss, one that showed he felt too much time had lapsed since their last one. She pressed up onto her toes and curled her hand around his neck, letting her fingers tangle in his disheveled hair.

"This is one thing you are really, really good at," she spoke against his mouth.

"Yeah?" He placed a quick kiss on her lips. "You think so?" Another kiss. "I think I could use a bit more practice."

"I'm happy to give you that opportunity," she spoke through a smile.

They kissed like they were teenagers, all hands and quick breaths and eager mouths. When Cal's phone buzzed across the table, he waved it off, but Edie pulled back, nudging her head in its direction.

"You can go ahead and grab that," she said.

"Whatever it is, it can wait."

Cal went in for another kiss, but Edie blocked him, two hands splayed across his chest. "Cal, we can't just make out all day."

"We absolutely can make out all day. In fact, I think that's the perfect way to spend our afternoon. I'm going to clear my calendar."

Edie giggled at that. It did sound like an enticing use of their time, but not a particularly productive one. "You have to paint. I don't want to distract you from that."

"You're not a distraction, Edie. You're an inspiration." He glanced at his phone, satisfied that the text didn't need his immediate attention, and then picked up his brush. "Want to paint with me?"

"Seriously? You're sure I won't completely ruin it?"

"You can't ruin this one. It's not possible. It's called Stars Crashing. Just from the title alone, you can probably tell there's a lot of freedom in it."

They painted for the next hour, Cal mostly, with Edie following behind with a sweep of her brush when she saw a place that needed to be covered. Sometimes Cal would take her hand into his and guide her strokes. He moved with abandon, never second guessing the placement of his brush on the canvas. When he let her take the lead, Edie hesitated.

"Aren't you worried I'm going to do something to wreck all the work we just did?"

"No. I'm not. What's the worst that could happen? I have to paint over it?"

Edie brought the end of the brush to her lips and tapped it like a pencil. "When you put it that way, I guess it's not so scary."

"Not scary at all." He stepped back and watched her blend a canary yellow dollop of paint with a touch of tangerine, mixing them together on the palette. "I like painting with you, Edie. Maybe sometime you'll even let me paint you."

"Paint me as in paint *me*?" She laughed aloud at the thought. "Or paint my likeness?"

"Your likeness," Cal answered. "But painting you might be fun, too."

Reaching around, he grabbed the nearest brush. With a devilish smirk and a flick of his wrist, he sent a spray of blue paint splattering across her blouse. Like a child caught with his hand in the cookie jar, Cal froze.

"You seriously did not just do that." Edie looked down at her top, at the fresh droplets of paint clinging to the fabric. It wasn't a blouse that she had been particularly fond of, so there was no issue there. But she'd been caught off guard. She hadn't even planned on painting today. She certainly hadn't planned on wearing it.

Cal stood stock-still, waiting for her response. When she offered a meek smile, that was all the permission he needed.

It became an all-out paint war, a kaleidoscope of color showering through the air like confetti.

Edie raced to hide behind a blank canvas propped on an easel. She loaded her brush with fresh acrylic from tubes she'd quickly gathered from the long work-table and then peeked her head out to survey the scene. Before she could take in her surroundings, she was met with a fresh smattering of paint across her cheek.

She shrunk behind the canvas again, panting and out of breath. "Not fair!" she called out through a fit of laughter. "You've got like three brushes in your arsenal. I only have the one."

"I'd be happy to share, but you'll have to come out from behind there and take it from me," Cal taunted, like they were playing a game of childhood tag.

Taking one tube of hunter green paint into her grip, she twisted off the cap, sucked in a huge breath, and spun out from the makeshift bunker, readied to fire. Instead, she collided with Cal's chest, smacking straight into him.

"You're not great at this, Edie." He drew a slow line from her forehead to the tip of her nose with his brush. The cold strip of paint on her skin made her shiver, but when Cal took her chin between his fingers and lifted her mouth to his, that shiver branched out to every limb. He kissed her softly and sweetly, and her knees turned to mush.

"We've made a huge mess." Edie pulled back and looked around the room. "I'll help you clean up."

"There's not much to clean up, really. That's the perk of having a studio designated solely for painting. This is what it was made for."

"For having paint wars with your girlfriend?"

Cal wobbled his head back and forth. "That wasn't something I've ever done in here. I've actually never even brought any of my girlfriends into my paint studio before. You're the first."

Edie knew she should've received it as the compliment Cal probably intended it to be, but after the conversation with Ben that morning, she couldn't settle fully into it.

"Cal, you know you can keep this space to yourself, right? This is your creative space, and that's something special. Sacred, even."

"I'm happy to share it with you, Edie. I *want* to share it with you."

"I just need to make sure I'm not pushing myself into a part of your life where I don't belong." Edie placed the paint tube on the table and looked up at Cal.

His brow lowered tightly over his eyes as he explored her face. "What would make you think I don't want you in this part of my life? I sure hope I haven't given you that impression."

"No, you haven't. Not at all. But I've watched too many relationships fail because they didn't communicate these things clearly, and I don't want ours to start off that way. I want to do things right."

Taking up both of her hands into his, Cal leaned forward when he said, "So do I, Edie. I want you in this part of my life. I want you in every part of my life," he said as he dipped his head for another kiss. "Which is why I'm hoping you'll agree to have dinner with me this Saturday."

That was an easy answer. "Absolutely. Anything special?"

With a strained, noticeably apprehensive look, Cal said, "Yes, actually. It will be with my parents."

CHAPTER TWENTY

"When did she say she would come back for us?"

Tabitha searched her brain to remember what the young woman had told them before she'd left, but she hadn't been paying much attention. "I don't know. Twelve minutes, maybe?"

"I don't think I'm going to make it," Camille yelped in a tone which showed she wasn't entirely joking. "I guess this is it. This is where I die, ladies. In a trough of slop. I was hoping for a much more glamorous ending than this. This is right up there with Elvis dying on the toilet."

"It's not that bad." Edie spoke loudly over the hot running water that sanitized the tubs between them. "I thought it would be a lot worse."

"I feel like I'm literally being suffocated," Camille groaned. "With pig poop."

"We've been over this, sis. It's imported pig poop. From France." Tabitha snickered, but her sister wasn't having any of it.

Camille wasn't completely alone in her discomfort. There was an off-putting heaviness from the mud and how it spread over every inch of her body, like a weighted blanket. Tabitha had hoped she would at least be able to wiggle her toes or swish her arms side to side, but the hot mud molded around her frame like a plaster cast. It didn't allow for even a fraction of movement. Even her breaths felt strained as her chest struggled to rise and fall under the thick sludge.

"This goes straight onto my list of *Things I'll never do again*. Right under Mark's name."

"Camille!" Edie shot her friend a scandalized look.

"Oh, come on. Don't be such a prude," Camille quipped. "Of the three of us, you're the only one getting any sort of action, anyway."

"I'm not getting any action. Cal and I have only kissed."

"Still, that's infinitely more action than I've seen in the last few years. In fact, this mud is becoming much more intimate with me than Mark ever has." Camille's mouth contorted into a grimace. "Is there a reason we couldn't have worn our swimsuits?"

"They said the mud would stain it. And that it's supposed to be a more immersive experience if you don't have those extra layers between you and the mud," Tabitha explained to her sister. "The website said there are some healing elements or compounds or something that I don't quite understand that are found in this particular type of mud."

"If the woman with an M.D. behind her name doesn't understand it, then it certifiably cannot be understood."

Tabitha snickered. "All I'm saying is there might be some benefit to just relaxing into the discomfort in hopes of getting something out of the experience."

Edie and Camille openly stared at Tabitha and even though only their faces peeked out above the mud, it was all the body language she needed to read.

"Fine. I get it. I should take my own advice?"

"Yes, you should," Camille said, firmly. "Try to get something out of this retreat experience. We're almost a week in. What do you think so far?"

The last couple of days had been the best yet. She'd started and finished a new medical drama novel by her favorite author, all while working on her tan by the pool. The three women went to happy hour at the Villa's bar two nights in a row and Tabitha discovered a new drink, The Beached Whale, that she ordered both times. She'd been able to run each day, and even took a refreshing nap yesterday.

Much to her chagrin, Tabitha had to admit, the Villa was a beautiful escape.

"I'm enjoying myself," she confessed, then quickly shut her eyes so she didn't have to witness her sister gloat.

"I'm enjoying myself, too," Camille agreed. "Well, I'm enjoying everything except for this mud bath. This is terrifying."

"I thought you were the one who was so gung-ho about it, Cam," Edie pointed out.

"I was intrigued. But I've been intrigued by a lot of things these days and all have let me down."

Tabitha didn't have to pry to know her sister was referring to Foster. She'd been startled at how quickly they'd connected and also how quickly things had dissolved before there was even a chance to explore what might have been. Tabitha shouldn't have been surprised, though. Camille was like that. Passionate and all-in, sometimes without even thinking about the consequences of those hasty decisions. It was why she'd jumped into her receptionist job right after Mark had left her. One day over coffee, she'd mentioned to Tabitha that she should probably get around to looking for work, and the next day she had a job. When Camille set her mind to something, there was little that could pull her away from seeing it to fruition. She had decided she was done with Foster, so that was the end of that.

"I'm really sorry about Foster," Edie said, picking up on the same undertones in Camille's statement. "He really did seem like a good guy."

"He might still be a good guy," Tabitha offered. "Just because there's a blemish on his past, that doesn't mean you totally need to write him off."

"But I do." Camille shimmied lower into the mud

so it reached her earlobes. "After everything with Mark, I just can't be with a man I don't fully trust. At this point in my life, I'm not looking for complicated."

"Amen to that," Tabitha agreed. "Not that Ben was all that complicated, but you know." She tried to shrug, but the mud made it difficult to do so.

If Camille and Edie were attempting to be sly in their exchanged glance, they'd failed miserably.

"What?" Tabitha's voice was clipped. "What's that look for?"

"There was no look." Camille cleared her face of her wary expression.

"Yes, there was. I saw it. What are you two not telling me?"

"It's nothing, really," Edie tried to say convincingly. "Seriously."

"If I didn't have about a hundred pounds of mud on me right now, I'd march over and shake it out of you both. I can tell you're keeping something from me."

Camille and Edie traded another look, then, like they'd agreed on something using only their eyes to communicate, Camille finally said, "I just think Ben might be more complex than you give him credit, Tab. That's all."

"O-kay." Tabitha drew out the two syllables in the word. "But why would you say that? What makes you think so?"

"You know the other morning when you went out

for a run and he stayed behind to shower? Well, Edie and I had a pretty candid conversation with him and he opened up a lot about your marriage and how things ended and his part in the whole thing."

If Tabitha could've willed the mud to swallow her up at that very moment like a pit of quicksand, she would've welcomed it. She had a horrible sinking feeling in her stomach, a twinge of betrayal that roiled within her. "You talked about me? With Ben?"

"It wasn't like that, sis. I just asked him why he'd gotten into running and that opened up—"

"A huge can of worms?" Tabitha finished for Camille.

"No. Not at all. I think you'd be surprised to hear some of the things he told us."

Edie gave Tabitha a soft look. "He really does care about you, Tab. And I think he realizes he didn't try hard enough to understand you when you were married."

This was a lot. It felt like the longest twelve minutes of Tabitha's life, and it was no longer just the crushing weight of the mud that made her feel like she couldn't breathe.

"When are those ladies going to come back to get us out of here?"

"Fine. I get it," Camille said. "We don't have to talk about it right now. But I think it's worth having a conversation with Ben at some point. Maybe it'll provide some closure for both of you."

"My closure took place when I signed the divorce papers."

"Okay, maybe. But I don't think that's true for Ben. Talk to him, Tabitha. It could be a really good thing."

WATER PELTED down on her shoulders, hot, stinging beads that were just barely tolerable in temperature. Steam fogged around her in an opaque white haze. Tabitha rolled her neck. She'd been excited about Casey's coffee shop gig all week, even with the knowledge that Ben would be there. But now, with this new information and the feeling that everyone was in on something she wasn't, she couldn't stomach the thought of seeing her ex again.

Things had been comfortable the other night when he'd stayed while Edie had her wedding photography consultation. It was nice, even. Tabitha knew how much Casey wanted his parents to get along. That evening proved it was possible, and that felt like a giant leap forward. Thoughts of shared holidays or important occasions celebrated together again didn't seem as farfetched as she once felt they would be.

But all of that was different now. Ben had opened up—about God knows what—to her sister and her best friend and something about that didn't jibe with Tabitha.

She stayed in the shower until her prune-like

fingers and toes demanded she shut the water off. Even then, she remained in the lingering steam a moment longer and tried to gather her composure. Tonight was about Casey. It certainly wasn't about her. She'd have to get over her hang-ups with Ben and just let the night be the celebration it was intended to be.

She tried on three outfits, even the dress she'd purchased with Camille and Edie at Monarch's before the trip. It felt fancier than your typical coffee house attire, so she slipped that back onto the wooden hanger and left it in the closet for another time. Finally, she decided on a pair of dark denim jeans and a lightweight blue knit sweater. The temperatures had recently been dipping in the evenings, and she knew Curly Joe's had a large outdoor seating space where they usually set up their musical talent. It might be cold out, but the sweater would keep her plenty warm.

At a quarter to seven, Tabitha said quick goodbyes to her sister and Edie, both of whom were a mess of tears in the living room. Whatever sad movie played on the television had turned them into emotional, blubbering messes, and Tabitha was grateful she had other plans. Crying on the couch did not seem like an enjoyable way to spend a perfectly good evening.

She fired off a text to Casey before getting into her car, wishing him luck and telling him she would be there in fifteen. It was a fast drive to the coffee shop, and Tabitha was pleased to see the limited availability for parking already. That had to be a good sign, she thought. Casey had sent her a screenshot of the promotional poster he'd been hanging around town over the last week. She hoped it would draw a crowd, and to her delight, it looked like it had done just that.

Tabitha's heart swelled. This was her son's dream: to make music and share it with others. She was grateful to experience it with him and happy he wanted her there. After circling the block three times, Tabitha slipped into a space across from the shop, angling her vehicle into the vacant parallel spot.

"Nice car," a young man around Casey's age called out as soon as she opened the door.

"Thank you." Tabitha always felt strange accepting compliments on behalf of her vehicle. After all, it wasn't like she'd had any part in engineering or designing it. All she'd done was sign the check that allowed her to park it in her garage.

"You must be loaded to be able to afford that," he snickered as he paced down the sidewalk, neck still craned Tabitha's direction.

Tabitha ignored that last comment. It was one she'd heard before, but she never dignified it with a response. She was entitled to spend her money however she pleased and didn't need to answer to anyone, let alone complete strangers. Her mortgage was paid off, her son's education paid for, and her credit cards never held a balance. She was responsible with her money. That afforded her the opportunity to purchase items that others would consider a luxury.

Plus, she really liked how fast the car drove. That had been the major selling point. The adrenaline rush was the same sensation she felt when she slipped on her medical coat. She couldn't explain it, but she figured she didn't need to. The car belonged to her, and she was certainly allowed to enjoy it.

Slinging the strap of her purse over her shoulder, Tabitha glanced both ways before she crossed the busy street. She lifted a hand, thanking the cars that slowed for her in the crosswalk. She could already hear Casey speaking over the microphone, greeting those at the café that had come out to listen to him play. He must've said something funny, because a swell of laughter filtered out in the evening air. It made Tabitha beam. Her son was totally in his element.

The coffeehouse was packed, not an empty table in sight. A line at least ten people deep zigzagged out from the counter, weaving through the tables in the tight space. There was a steady hum from the espresso maker and the barista's booming voice would call out a name every minute or so, straining to be heard over the chatter in the shop. In any other situation, one might find the commotion stressful, but Tabitha felt the energy in it all, a frenetic and exciting buzz that emanated from every square inch of the room.

She folded her arms and stepped closer in the line.

"Decaf medium roast coffee for Ben!" The barista

deposited a cardboard cup onto the counter. "Order for Ben?"

Like he'd had his lottery number called, Tabitha's ex-husband rushed up to the counter, swiveling around tables and chairs and apologizing to patrons he accidentally bumped into on the way.

"Thank you," he said to the young man as he took his cup. When he turned around, he locked eyes with Tabitha across the room.

Ben lifted his cup like a greeting.

Tabitha returned it with a wave of her hand, but hers was less enthusiastic.

"I've got a table outside if you'd like to join us," he hollered from halfway across the coffeehouse. "I don't think there's an empty seat left."

"Okay, thank you," she said, not that it would be her first choice. But Ben was right; there wasn't a vacant seat in the place. "I'll be out after I order my drink."

Ben flashed a smile and then wove his way through the shop toward the back patio. Tabitha couldn't help but follow his movements.

When he held the door open for a young mother struggling with an umbrella stroller and a small child who was doing everything she could to tumble out of it, Tabitha's gaze held tightly to Ben's face and the sweet expression that covered it. Camille was right. Ben was noticeably different, both in his demeanor and in his actions.

By the time Tabitha made it up to the counter to

place her drink order, Casey had already started in on his first song, a cover from a favorite rock band of his youth. Tabitha hated to miss any part of his set, but this particular song she'd heard a million times over, and admittedly, it wasn't one of her favorites.

Despite the large crowd, the coffeehouse employees had everything down to a science, cranking out drink orders left and right like an espresso assembly line. Thankfully, Tabitha only missed Casey's first song. She took her chai latte from the counter, thanked the barista, and slipped the drink into a cardboard sleeve before making her way outside.

To her surprise, the patio was even more congested than inside the shop. Extra folding chairs filled what would've been empty spaces between bistro tables. There was even a front row created with a line of a dozen chairs. Tabitha recognized many of the faces of Casey's friends from high school and college, and when she saw Hannah, front and center, Tabitha smiled. In her last conversation with her son, he'd expressed how busy his girlfriend's schedule had become, so it was nice to see that Hannah made it a priority to come out and support Casey at his show.

Scanning the area, Tabitha located Ben near the back corner of the patio, an empty chair to his left and a woman in scrubs with puppies printed across them to his right. Like he'd been keeping an eye out for her, Ben stood and waved, just to be sure Tabitha saw him. She took a deep breath and walked over.

"Saved you a seat," he said as he pulled out the chair for her. He waited for her to slide in.

"Thank you." Tabitha sat and placed her chai on the small table. She curled both hands around the cup. "I hadn't realized it would be so crowded, but I'm sure glad to see it is. This is quite an impressive turnout."

"That's what I was just telling Donna." Ben took his seat between the two women. "I've never seen this place so full. Good for Casey."

The woman looked closely at Tabitha, a too-forced smile fixed on her mouth.

"Where are my manners?" Ben blurted. "Donna, this is Tabitha, my ex-wife. Tabitha, Donna."

Tabitha extended a hand across the table. "Nice to meet you, Donna."

"You as well," Donna said, but nothing in her tone indicated she meant it. She didn't come across as rude, but apprehensive. "Wow. Casey sure does look like you."

"You think so?" Tabitha pulled her cup to her lips, grateful to have something to busy her hands. "Everyone always says he favors Ben."

"Maybe in his eyes, but he has your coloring and bone structure, for sure." Donna lifted her mug, but then set it back down without taking a drink from it. "I'm sorry. That was probably weird of me to point that out."

"It's not weird," Tabitha assured, but she did think it was, just a little. "It's actually nice to hear because

Ben and Casey have always been two peas in a pod. Like father, like son and all. I'm happy that maybe Casey does take after me a bit."

"We might be a lot alike, but we all know he doesn't get his musical talent from me," Ben said.

"Doesn't get that from me either." Tabitha laughed. Neither she, nor her ex-husband, had a musical bone in their body.

"Nope. That he doesn't." Ben joined her in laughter.

Across the table, Donna giggled nervously. "I'm not musical either," she offered, but it fell flat amongst the shared moment between the exes.

It was as though a myriad of memories passed back and forth on each laugh, all the times Ben and Tabitha had belted out radio tunes in the car, back when Casey would firmly cover his ears, blocking their noise. She thought back to the time she sang a lullaby to her infant son, and it made him cry all the more. That was something Ben and Tabitha would always have in common—their uncanny ability to butcher a good song.

"I hear you're joining him for a duet a little later on in the set." Tabitha nudged her chin toward their son, who was currently in between songs, chatting with a friend in the front row. She gave Ben a mischievous grin.

"Not unless Curly Joe's has hopes of receiving a noise violation from the county. I sing about as good as a dying goose," Ben said, the chuckle that followed this statement even heartier than the ones before.

"We had one of those at our clinic today!" Donna interjected, a little too excitedly. It was glaringly apparent she was trying to wedge herself into the conversation, and Tabitha felt terrible about that. Not only had she seated herself at their table, but she'd stolen Ben away from whatever conversation they'd been having earlier. Then she'd continued to inadvertently shut Donna out by teasing Ben about his singing. That just wasn't fair.

"Ben says you're a vet tech?" Tabitha angled toward Donna and attempted to right her wrong. "That must be interesting."

"Oh, I just love it. Not a lot of people can handle the blood, you know. Luckily, it doesn't bother me. The real life-or-death emergencies are the most exciting, if that doesn't sound completely awful to admit. We see lots of cats and dogs, but occasionally, we'll treat livestock and other critters. It can be pretty fast-paced, but I thrive in that environment."

"Tabitha knows a little about that." Ben nodded his head toward his ex-wife. "She's a trauma surgeon. World renowned."

"I'm not world renowned."

"The best in Southern California, at the very least."

It had been the first time she'd ever heard Ben compliment her in that way. The glint of pride that twinkled in his eye made her stomach clench.

"Oh, wow." Donna shrunk back in her chair. She fiddled with the handle of her mug, spinning the cup around in circles. "Well, that's definitely more important than what I do. I just get to assist in surgeries with animals. I can't even imagine operating on people."

"It's not more important than what you do, Donna." Tabitha hated this sort of comparison and wished Ben hadn't mentioned anything. "Just different. I, for one, would have no idea how to deal with a goose."

"Well, you treat them just like you would any other sort of feathered creature. Sure, they've got longer necks, but that's not really a big deal. The goose who came in today was struck by a baseball over on the little league fields off Hampton Street. Dropped right out of the sky like a popped balloon." Donna's eyes lit up when she talked about the ailing bird. "He's got some internal bleeding that they're still trying to locate the source of, but I'm hopeful he'll make a full recovery."

"That certainly is good news." Tabitha offered Donna a warm smile. She really did seem like a lovely woman, and based on the affectionate look she gave Ben, Tabitha figured she did care about him. Ben deserved that.

Tabitha tried not to let her gaze linger when their hands slipped together under the table, joining there and resting on Ben's knee.

"Looks like he's starting up another song," Ben

acknowledged. His thumb rubbed against the top of Donna's hand.

Tabitha turned in her seat so she could face Casey straight on. Plus, she felt like she should let Ben and Donna share their intimate moment together. They didn't need Tabitha staring at their hands while she tried to remember the last time she and Ben had held hands in public.

Tabitha wasn't sure they ever had.

When Casey strummed the first chord on his guitar, Tabitha's breath quickened. Her heart recognized the notes immediately. It was her favorite song he had ever written, one he titled *On Bird's Wings*. He'd first penned the chorus as a young boy, adding to it each year until—when he was a high school senior —he had finally completed it.

It was the story of a young bird and his mother, detailing his struggles to jump from the nest out of fear of crashing to the earth below. There was a line in the song where the mama bird said, "There's no need to worry, even though you may be small. I'll be right there to catch you; my mighty wings will always break your fall." It consistently brought Tabitha to tears. She knew the verse wasn't coming until later in the song, but she prepared herself, snagging a napkin from the dispenser in the middle of the table, ready to blot away the inevitable tears that would flow.

Tabitha had always wished the song was about her, but she knew it wasn't. She wanted so badly to be the sort of mother who was there for every heartbreak, there to pick up the pieces when things fell apart. She wasn't. In fact, she sometimes felt like she caused those pieces to crumble in her son's life, her absence from things like plays or games or school ceremonies chipping away at his spirit piece by piece.

Of course, Casey had never said that, but it didn't change the truth in Tabitha's feelings.

Her heart sped up in anticipation of those final lines. It rang in her ears so loudly she almost didn't hear the altered verses. It took her a moment to let the new words seep in, but once they did, the tears came even faster than anticipated.

"Don't you ever doubt my love, my dear son. You and me, we may love a little differently, but on mighty wings, we will forever soar as one."

If she had falsely projected herself into this new version of the song, it couldn't be helped. The thoughtful look Casey cast her direction as his pick plucked out the final notes made her chin tremble while she fought back the tears. When he mouthed, *Love you, Mom,* from across the patio, Tabitha nearly lost it. It wasn't a phrase they said much in their family, not that they didn't feel it.

Between the song and the quiet declaration, Tabitha felt like a ball of yarn come undone. All the emotions she'd kept so neatly bound up suddenly unrolled and tangled out in a million squiggly directions. Her composure was completely lost.

Then, just as she scolded her quivering lower lip

with a firm bite, she felt a warm hand come down on her shoulder. Ben's hand.

He leaned close to her ear and said, "I know sometimes you doubt it, Tabs, but you were always there for him in all the ways that mattered." He gave her shoulder a quick squeeze. "And you were there for me, too. I just couldn't see it then."

CHAPTER TWENTY-ONE

*C*amille sat at the bar and checked her watch like she was waiting for her favorite store to open. Edie was supposed to meet her for their newly minted happy hour routine, but she had texted earlier and said she would be running late. Apparently, there was this thing called *golden hour*, and it was a photographer's favorite time of day. Something to do with lighting and shadows and the slant of the sun. Camille told Edie it was fine and to join her whenever she could.

She didn't mind the time alone. The bar at the Villa was beautiful with a long moon-shaped granite counter and tall barstools with comfortable leather cushions on the seats. There were two large flat screen televisions flanking a mirrored wall that housed every label of liquor one could imagine. Plus, the bartender, Kyle, was easy on the eyes. He'd just given Camille a complementary order of ahi poke that had been prepared by the kitchen by mistake.

She'd be just fine enjoying her free appetizer while catching up on the local news. Other than a handful of sappy movies, Camille hadn't really spent much time in front of the television since arriving at the Villas, and she felt out of the loop when it came to current events. So she munched on a crispy wonton chip and swirled her lemon drop as she read the subtitles that scrolled along the bottom of the screen.

There had been a shark sighting off the coast about thirty miles north of Seascape Shores. It sent the locals into a tizzy, despite the fact that it hadn't harmed anyone and was spotted by a surfer who couldn't really describe anything beyond the shark having a "totally gnarly fin." An electronic waste recycling event was scheduled for the following Saturday at the First Baptist Church of Seascape Shores as a fundraiser for the youth group's trip to Mexicali. There was an upcoming bridal expo at the convention center and a mobile dental clinic for seniors and a free pancake breakfast down at the Moose Lodge. Nothing of any relevance—or interest—to Camille. Slow news day.

She twisted the stem of her martini glass, mesmerized by the sugar crystals on the rim that caught the light. Lifting the drink to her mouth, she took a sip. When she saw Mark's face flash across the screen in her periphery, she stiffened.

"Can you turn it up?" Camille flapped a hand at

Kyle, who was mid-shake, mixing a martini above his shoulders like it was a musical instrument. "The TV. Can you unmute it?"

"Oh, uh, sure." Kyle set down the shaker and wiped his hands on a towel tucked into his apron, then spun around as he tried to locate the remote. "It's around here somewhere."

"Right there." Camille pointed at the remote, which was placed next to an empty water pitcher.

"Oh! There it is."

With a click of the button, the sound switched on, just in time for the anchorman to say, "Our congratulations go out to Senator Todd and his wife Stephanie on their recent pregnancy announcement. This will be the Senator's first child, a son, with an expected due date in late November. Looks like the Senator will have quite a lot to be thankful for this year."

Camille's martini slipped through her fingers like sand through an hourglass. It shattered noisily, shards of glass skittering across the counter.

Within seconds, Kyle was there with his towel. "No worries. Happens all the time," he said, but Camille hadn't apologized. She hadn't done anything other than gape at the screen, which had now transitioned to a blaring used car commercial. "These glasses aren't as expensive as they look."

"Oh." She broke from her glazed-over stare. "I hadn't realized...I mean...I didn't mean to..." Shoving her hair off her face, she shook her head like a twitch and shut her eyes hard before reopening them. "I'm so sorry. I really didn't mean to do that. They said his first child..."

"Like I said, happens all the time. Usually at a few more drinks in, but no judgment here."

"Guess I'm all butter fingers." Camille wiggled her fingers in the air.

"How about I make you another?" Kyle gave the counter one final swipe with the rag. "On the house."

"I think I should probably stick with water."

"Well, where's the fun in that?" a voice Camille had come to recognize all too well said at her side. "Mind if I join you?"

"First lounge chairs and now barstools?" Camille looked at Foster for longer than she needed to before shrugging and saying, "Fine. Go ahead."

He slid out the stool and lowered onto it, but was hesitant. "You sure I can't buy you a drink? You look like you could really use one."

"I could use a lot right now, but a therapist would probably be at the top of that list, not alcohol."

Foster's expression softened. "Anything you want to talk about? I'm not a therapist, but I raised three girls, so I've gotten really good at listening."

"No." Camille closed her eyes again. Everything felt heavy. Her head. The air. Her heart. "I'd rather not talk." Then, glancing over at Foster, she added, "But thank you."

"Do you mind if I sit here and get myself a drink while we don't talk?"

She snorted. "That would be just fine."

Foster ordered an old fashioned for himself, and despite Camille saying a glass of water would suffice, he requested a Diet Coke with two cherries for her. He must've been paying attention when they went out for sushi. The gesture was small, but thoughtful.

Camille could usually fill a lull in a conversation with a million different topics, but at that moment she had nothing, nor any desire to search for something. An image of her ex with his new wife was often enough to turn her stomach, but the words that had accompanied tonight's photo stole her breath.

Of course, it had crossed her mind that they might decide to start a family. Men had that luxury, she supposed, the ability to procreate much longer than their female counterparts. Stephanie was young. It wasn't surprising that she wanted to be a mother.

That wasn't what almost knocked Camille off of her barstool. Some small, secret part of her even felt the slightest morsel of happiness for them. Finding out you were about to become a mother was a joyous celebratory event. But the overwhelming part of Camille, that part felt nothing but grief, a mourning deep within her that would never be complete.

"*This will be the Senator's first child, a son,*" she repeated the exact words from the television segment. "This isn't his first son."

Yes, it was his first child with Stephanie, but Mark already had a son, and even though Patrick was no longer with them, his precious life should never be diminished in that way. It broke Camille's heart on such a level that it felt like the shattering of her soul.

She folded her arms on the counter and dropped her head down, a shuddering of sorrow bursting out in a cry she tried unsuccessfully to keep muffled. Other than Kyle and Foster, the bar was empty. But even if she had been surrounded by a thousand people, it wouldn't have changed things. She just couldn't keep it in.

"Oh, Camille." Foster placed a hand on her back and rubbed a slow circle between her shoulder blades the way a parent would with a sick child. "I'm so sorry."

She shook while she cried, her tears soaking the fabric of her sweater pressed up against her eyes. Minutes that felt like hours passed before the wave of grief that had swept Camille out into a sea of emotion returned her back to the shores of reality. Sniffing, Camille wiped her face with the inside of her sleeve and sat up straight. Composed herself. Her eyes burned and her mouth felt like it was stuffed with cotton balls.

"I wish I could help you," Foster said, his hand still in place. It felt warm against her back. Comforting. He searched out her eyes with his piercing gaze, but there was nothing intimidating about it this time.

Camille shrugged. "Some things just can't be helped."

"I'm not good at feeling helpless. I like fixing things. That's always been my biggest fault." Foster pulled his hand from her back and took hold of his drink. He swirled the amber-colored liquid in the tumbler and ice cubes clinked against the glass. "It's gotten me into trouble in more ways than one."

"If there was a way any of this could be fixed, I would welcome it. This is just one of those things that can't be, unfortunately."

"And you're sure you don't want to talk about it?" He drew in a sip of the old fashioned and breathed out through the burn that followed the sharp swallow. He hit his chest with a fist and cleared his throat. "Wow, that's really strong."

"The only way Kyle knows how to make them." Camille tugged a cherry from its stem with her teeth and crunched down. "I don't think I want to talk. I don't know. Maybe I do."

Camille knew talking through it would be the only way to process it. That's how it always worked. And for that very reason, she was a proponent of therapy and counseling. But Foster shouldn't be the person to share this with. There were far too many unknowns in this new but complicated friendship. Some things needed to be guarded, and her son's memory was something she would protect with all her being.

"If you don't want to talk, maybe you'd like to listen?" His lifted brow, along with the soft lilt to his tone, made Camille's heart do a double take. The wall she had so quickly constructed between them when she'd learned of his past didn't fully come down right then, but she suddenly felt willing to peek over the top of it.

"I can listen," she said. She turned in her chair to face him and give him her full attention. "I'd like that, actually."

Foster nodded, seemingly pleased. "So, you asked me the other night about the reason I'd gone to jail."

Camille perked up. Not where she thought the conversation was going. "Yes."

"I said earlier that my desire to fix things has gotten me into trouble. In one specific instance, it landed me behind bars."

"Foster, you really don't need to tell me what happened. I know I had asked about it the other night, but it's none of my business."

"I understand that. You're right. It's not. Just like whatever you're going through isn't any of my business. But I want to tell you about this, Camille." He paused, took another drink, and continued, "I told you my wife left me when my kids were young. What I didn't tell you was that she left me for my brother."

"Ouch," Camille interjected with a groan. The women at the salon had mentioned it, but Camille wasn't sure how much of their gossip was actually true.

"I know, right? Camille, the guy is a loser and I'm not saying that because he stole my wife. Jim was always troubled, even as a kid. He moved out when he was fifteen. More like he was kicked out, really. He'd gotten into drugs and drank heavily.

Failed all of his classes and just ran with the wrong crowd.

When Darla and I had been married for about ten years, he came by our place one night, looking for somewhere to crash. Something about being on the run and some mistake he'd made. He needed to lie low for a couple of days. All I knew was that I needed to protect my new family from my old family. I told him he wasn't welcome and to never come back. The kids were so small then. I didn't want them around any of that.

Little did I know, Darla began sending him money each month. She felt bad that Jim's own family had rejected him and thought I'd done him wrong in sending him away. She sent money for two years before I found out. And it was more than just money, Camille. They had corresponded and started up a relationship. When I discovered what had been going on, I told her he wouldn't be getting another dime from us. That all communication needed to stop. That's when she ran off with him."

"Foster. That is a lot. I can't even imagine."

"It was a lot," he agreed. "The worst part was, Darla didn't want to have anything to do with the kids after that. Our custody arrangement allowed for weekend visits on her end, but she would always have some reason she couldn't take them. It went on like this for years. Then, right around the time the twins turned sixteen, she suddenly started showing interest in them again. She wanted to right some of her wrongs and that began with being more intentional in her relationships. Being more of an active parent in their lives."

"That's noble, I suppose."

"Sure, if it wasn't a self-serving lie." Foster stroked his jaw. "She didn't care about Becca and Danny. She was just happy that she finally had transportation to and from her drug deals. Both her license, as well as Jim's, had been suspended. A DUI or something. The kids didn't know that's what they were doing, of course. But the night Becca came home and told me the area of town she'd driven her uncle to and how she was nearly carjacked while she waited for him was the night of my arrest."

Camille brought her hand to her mouth. "Oh, Foster."

"I told him if he ever placed any one of my children in harm's way again, I would kill him. And I meant it. Then I let my fists show him just how serious I was," Foster retold the memory. "He was in the hospital for three weeks. I went to jail for two years. It was awful and I'm not necessarily proud of what I did, but honest to God, Camille, I would do it all over again if I had to. I'd do anything to protect my children."

"Why are you telling me this? You don't have to share all of this with me, Foster. I mean, I'm glad you want to, but it must be painful to talk about."

"It rips me up inside to even think about it, much less talk about it. There's no question about that. But it's part of my story, even if it's ugly." Foster threw back the last swallow of his drink. When he set the empty glass on the bar, he turned in his seat so he was face to face with Camille again. "The love a parent has for their child is unlike any other love. You are entitled to feel that love and carry it with you forever, Camille. I'm sorry if it feels like your ex-husband has taken that from you."

"It feels like he's taken *everything* from me." Camille lifted her hand and wiped her eyes with the back of it. Salty tears curved down her cheek, her jaw. She sniffed and blew out a breath. "I know it was probably just some stupid mistake on the journalist's part, but when they said Mark was expecting his first son…I don't know…It just felt like Patrick had been erased. Maybe even replaced."

"Mark can't do that, Camille. Don't give him that power."

"Well, he's replaced everything else. I guess it was just a matter of time until this happened." Eyes closed, Camille shook her head. "I'm so sorry, Foster. I'm sorry I doubted you and I'm sorry I had my friends over the other night to spy on you. I think I had you all wrong."

"So that's what the entourage was for?" He chuckled, nodding. "It's all making sense now."

"I've got some major trust issues, as you can plainly see."

"I've got my share, too, Camille. Believe me." Foster turned back toward the bar and flicked a finger in the air to beckon Kyle over. "Can I get another?" he asked. "Want another soda?"

"I'm good. But thank you." She smiled at Foster.

Sure, he was complex, but the same could be said for herself. For several quiet moments, she found herself staring at the planes of his face, his sharp jaw that she'd noticed he tended to stroke when lost in thought. The smile lines around his mouth were deep and that made her hope Foster's life ultimately contained more happiness than sorrow. It was no secret she had been drawn to him from the instant they'd met, but now they had connected on a level she hadn't anticipated. Camille found herself feeling something for Foster that she hadn't felt in a long time.

"Foster?" she said, suddenly emboldened by the revelation. "I think I really like you."

"Yeah?" Angling back toward her, he dropped a hand on his knee and said, "That's nice to hear because I think I really like you, too, Camille."

"Would you want to go out on a date sometime? One that doesn't involve spying or crying or anything weird? Just you and me getting to know each other."

He beamed, those laugh lines creasing firmly into his cheeks. "I would like nothing more."

CHAPTER TWENTY-TWO

"*T*hey are going to love you." Cal draped his arm possessively over Edie's shoulder.

The Seascape Shores Country Club was upscale, with a prominent water feature in the center of the roundabout and thin Italian cypresses lining the brick walkway like soldiers at attention. Edie tried to negotiate the bumpy path in her high heels, but found herself clinging to Cal's side to keep from tripping.

"You have nothing to be nervous about," Cal said, patting her arm.

That assurance did little to squelch Edie's rising anxiety that bubbled within her like a geyser about to blow. The last time she'd met anyone's parents was after she and Evan had already eloped. He had brought her home for Christmas dinner, but by then, his parents' approval was more of an added bonus than a necessity.

Things were different with Cal. They were just

starting out as a couple. Meeting his parents felt like something that should take place many months out, or maybe not even at all. Definitely not this early on in their new relationship.

"I'm not nervous," she fibbed. Her ankle twisted, and she gripped onto Cal's arm to keep from falling flat on her face. "I'm excited."

"You're lying," Cal said. "I can tell you're nervous because you have the same look on your face that you did that first day I took your camera from you and looked through your images. You have this tell—you nibble on your bottom lip. It's crazy sexy, but I feel bad even saying that since I know you only do it when you're really uncomfortable."

Edie released her lip from between her teeth. "I don't do that."

"You do. And I kinda love it." Cal hauled her close and nuzzled her neck, leaving a too scandalous for public kiss there. "But I'm serious, Edie. They are going to adore you. Just like I do."

Cal was about to reach for the handle when a statuesque doorman opened it for them. "Good afternoon, sir." He stiltedly turned toward Edie. "Ma'am."

Edie wanted to groan. Ma'am always sounded so old, a title earned by a tiny, frail woman knitting in her antique rocking chair.

"There they are."

Cal motioned across the restaurant toward a couple seated at a table with an expansive ocean view. An open bottle of white wine rested in an ice bath just off to the side and a tower of oysters was placed in the middle of the table like a shellfish centerpiece.

Cal's parents stood when they saw their son approaching.

Edie plastered on her practiced smile. "Here we go," she mumbled under her breath.

"Mom." Cal gave his mother a swift kiss on her cheek. The woman was sophisticated with her blunt-cut, silver bob and black-rimmed glasses that rested on a pert nose. Her black dress was more tailored than the one Edie wore, like it was made with her exact measurements in mind. She leaned into her son's kiss.

"Hello, Callum." Her eyes flicked Edie's direction. "This is your girlfriend, I presume?"

"Yes, ma'am," Edie said, silently scolding herself for using the term she hated so. But this woman definitely demanded a formal introduction. She certainly wasn't the sort you addressed by first name. "It's a pleasure to meet you."

"Likewise."

Cal's mother was intimidatingly tall, which made her look down her nose, even if that wasn't her intention.

"Dad, this is Edie." Cal turned toward a man who was a little shorter than he, but who shared his crop of blond hair and light eyes. He wore a three-piece suit with a bow tie snug up against his collar. Though he came across as less formal than his wife, he still held an air of pretentious sophistication that made Edie feel absurdly out of place.

"Nice to meet you, Edith," he said, taking her hand in his. "I'm Craig."

"It's Edie, actually," she said and instantly felt foolish for the correction. "I mean, my given name is Edith, but I've always gone by Edie."

"I'm surprised you haven't switched back to Edith yet," Cal's mother noted aloud as she took her seat next to the window. Cal pulled out the chair across from his mother and Edie lowered into it. "Now that you're obviously a grown woman. When I was in college I decided to go by Ana instead of Annie. It was time to grow up and be taken more seriously."

"Edie suits her perfectly," Cal said, squeezing Edie's knee under the table after taking his place. "I hope you two haven't been waiting long."

"Only a half hour," Ana said. "We had the waiter put the wine on ice so it wouldn't get warm."

"Sorry. There was more traffic on the five than I had accounted for."

"Always is, son." Craig spread his white cloth napkin across his lap and directed his gaze toward Edie. "So, Callum says you're an artist, too?"

"Struggling, but yes."

"Because the world needs more struggling artists," Ana muttered behind her glass of chardonnay.

"Edie is being modest. In fact, I haven't told you this yet,"—Cal turned to Edie—"but I already have an offer on your starfish image. I showed it to an interior designer friend of mine and she's got a client with beachfront property who wants it printed large on canvas. They want to talk to you about creating a whole series. You're going to love what they're willing to pay, too."

"You photograph sea creatures?" Ana asked, but it sounded like a judgment rather than a question. "How…charming."

"Edie's work is phenomenal. It's only a matter of time until she becomes a household name."

Cal was talking her up. She knew that. But Edie still felt the compliment in the form of a light flutter in her stomach.

"Have you always been a photographer?" Ana cocked her head in the most bird-like way. "Or have you ever had a real job?"

"I was a preschool teacher when my daughter was young, but after my husband passed, I decided to stay home with her."

"You were a stay-at-home mom?" Ana seemed surprised. Her eyebrows lifted on her smooth forehead. It was the first time since joining the Burton's at the table that Edie sensed any hint of approval. "I was, too. Personally, I think there are too many working mothers these days. Children are suffering because their mothers just aren't around. It's going to have detrimental effects on future generations, I'm sure of it."

"Some of the best mothers I know actually work

full time." Edie couldn't let Ana's ignorant statement go unchecked.

Craig and Ana exchanged a look, the kind that married couples used to communicate without words.

"Should we order?" Cal searched the table for a menu.

"Already did, son. We'll all be having steak and lobster." Craig lifted and threw back an oyster in one swallow.

"Oh, okay. Edie isn't really a big shellfish fan."

Edie jabbed Cal with the point of her elbow. "It's fine," she whispered.

"You don't like lobster?" Ana looked appalled, like Edie had just admitted to murdering puppies in her free time. "Or you've never had it?"

"I've had it. It's just not my favorite, that's all."

Mouth pinched, Ana nodded. "I see."

Scooting closer to Cal, Edie slipped her arm within the crook of his elbow. She had been nervous that Cal's parents might not like her. It had never occurred to her that they would be repulsed by her. But the look of pure disgust that Ana had no shame displaying took things to an entirely new level, a territory that made Edie's chest burn. Like he was her security blanket, she gripped tightly to Cal.

"Two lobsters for me then," Cal said, giving her the sweetest look.

"So, you two met at Cal's studio?" Ana asked Edie directly.

"Yes, a little over a month ago. I was photographing a bird outside—"

"Craig, dear, is that the McPhersons?" Ana sat up in her chair, looking over the top of Edie's head. "I'm surprised to see Mona out and about so soon after her surgery."

Cal looked over his shoulder. "Surgery? Is everything okay?"

Edie tried not to be rattled by the rude interruption.

Ana pointed to her nose. "She had a little work done. But rumor has it, it was terribly botched." Her gaze fell back on Edie. "I'm sorry, Edith. You were saying you were photographing a dog?"

"A bird. I was photographing a hummingbird outside Cal's studio—"

Cal's buzzing phone interrupted her this time. He looked down at the incoming text, then up at Edie with apologetic eyes. "This is the dealer I've been playing phone tag with for the last week. Do you mind if I call him real quick? I don't want to miss him again."

"Of course not," Edie said, but every bone in her body wanted him to stay right there at her side.

He gave her a quick kiss before standing. "I'll only be a second."

With Cal now gone, Edie steeled herself, readying to be fed to the wolves.

The three sat in stifling silence for a long beat

before Craig said, "I was quite surprised to hear that Cal was dating—"

"Someone older?" Edie asked before Craig had the chance to, hoping she could own the truth before he had the opportunity to turn it into an accusation.

"No." Ana's face didn't move. It was like she was made entirely of plastic. Maybe she was. "I think my husband was going to say he was surprised Cal was dating so soon after calling off his engagement."

Edie stiffened.

"Of course, you knew that he was recently engaged, didn't you? Canceled the wedding just about a month ago," Ana stated. "Surely that's something you have discussed."

Edie cleared her throat with a soft cough. "No. I didn't know that."

"He didn't tell you that he and Nora only recently split? I'm surprised that didn't come up, what with you two being so close and all."

"I never asked," Edie said, as though that was a valid reason for her lack of knowledge.

"How would you know to ask?" Ana asked.

Craig slurped down another oyster.

Edie's stomach churned.

"It's really a shame you don't like seafood. The lobster here is just superb." Ana changed the subject like the conversation wasn't one worth continuing. Like it hadn't pulled the rug completely out from beneath her son's new girlfriend.

The room began to sway. Edie's vision narrowed,

blackening at the edges. Her ears started to ring, a trill that swallowed up all sound within the restaurant. She thought she saw Ana's mouth moving, but the words didn't reach Edie's ears.

"Excuse me for a moment," Edie announced. She didn't wait for a response. She stood and rushed through the restaurant, heading toward the country club's grand entrance. Her shoulder collided with the man stationed at the doors. "I'm so sorry," she blurted, disoriented and stunned. She burst through the door, doubling over once on the other side.

Heaving breaths had her gasping for air. She felt like she was hyperventilating.

"Can I call you right back?" Cal had his phone to his ear when he caught sight of Edie on the front step. "I need to go."

Struggling to stand, Edie braced herself against the long brick wall.

"You were engaged?" She spat the words once he was within earshot.

It all made sense now. The bare walls in his house. The table that had never been assembled. She figured it was a bachelor pad, but she hadn't realized it had only recently become one.

"I was engaged," Cal confirmed. "But I'm not now."

"But you *were* engaged when we first met, weren't you?"

Cal's Adam's apple lifted with a drawn out swallow. "Technically? Yes, I was. But only because I hadn't officially gotten the ring back. Things had ended between us long before that. You have to believe me when I say any sort of romantic relationship had been over for months."

"Why does all of this feel like a lie?"

"I'm not lying to you, Edie. I promise. I wouldn't do that." Cal went to reach for her, but Edie recoiled, pressing further against the brick wall to reclaim her space. Cal's face fell.

"You said I was the first woman you took to your studio. You said it had been a long time since you'd kissed anyone. Why did you tell me those things?"

"Because they were true."

"But until a month ago, you were engaged to be married to someone else!" She hadn't meant to shout, but she couldn't keep her volume in check. "You mean to tell me your fiancée never came to your studio to watch you paint? I'm finding this all very hard to believe, Cal."

"It might be hard to believe, but it's true. Nora hated that I was an artist. Like my mother, she didn't think it was a real job. She never supported me in that way."

"Cal, this is too much to take in."

Cal looked like he'd been punched in the gut. "Edie, I probably should've said something to you sooner, but you have to believe me when I say my relationship with Nora was over long before we officially called off the wedding. And definitely well before you and I met."

"But that doesn't change the fact that you were engaged until very recently, Cal." Edie's jaw clenched so hard she feared she'd crack a molar. "And it doesn't change the fact that I'm your rebound."

Even though she tried to struggle free from his grasp, he grabbed onto her hands and drew them up to his chest. She could feel his heart racing against her fingertips, an erratic rhythm that felt out of control. "You are *not* a rebound, Edie."

"How can you say that? That's exactly what I am. Isn't it just a little convenient that your fiancée wasn't supportive of your career as an artist, and here I am, an artist myself? Someone who shares your passion and fills the void your fiancée couldn't?"

"I'd call it coincidental, not convenient."

"Call it what you will, but you're not who I thought you were."

"Who did you think I was?" He wouldn't release his hold on her hands, even when she tried to tug them back.

"I thought you were honest and sincere and that you truly cared about me."

"And all of those things are somehow now untrue because you found out that I had been engaged? I think you're making this into something bigger than it really is."

"It is big." Edie paused, knowing her feelings were valid, and that she had every right to express them. "And it feels like those things are now untrue."

"Truth doesn't change based on feelings." The

wounded look on Cal's face made Edie's mouth go dry, like she'd swallowed a handful of gritty sand. Her eyes burned around their reddened rims. "I'm still all of those things, Edie. I'm the same man you fell for. Would you rather I marry a woman who never really loved me? Because it feels like I'm in a lose-lose situation here. You're upset that I was engaged, but you're not happy that I broke it off, either. I believe I did the right thing by putting an end to an unhealthy relationship that hung on for far too long."

"Of course I wouldn't want you marrying someone who was all wrong for you," Edie conceded. "I just wish it had happened before I came along. It feels like I'm the reason you finally cut ties and I don't want to have that sort of responsibility. Your parents don't take me seriously and now I know why. I'm the woman who ruined your future. Of course, they would hate me."

"Nora is the one who ruined that particular version of my future, Edie." The sheen in Cal's eyes and the quiver of his voice made Edie's knees feel like they were about to give way. She stood straight and locked them tight. "You're the one who made me realize I wanted a different future altogether."

"I think I need to go."

Cal's stricken gaze wouldn't release hers. Edie had to turn her head to break the agonizing connection.

"I understand," he said finally, his voice filled with substantial regret. "I can take you home—"

"No, Cal. It's okay. I'll arrange for my own ride."

Edie needed space. The confines of a shared vehicle wouldn't afford her that. She needed to get her distance. "Would you mind apologizing to your parents for me?"

"Edie, please believe me when I say I'm really so sorry I didn't tell you about Nora earlier. I hope we can move forward from this. You've come to mean so much to me. I need you to know that."

"I'm going to need some time, Cal." Edie looked up at the sky, at the clouds that tumbled in like a dreary, gray cloak. She felt the weight of the air around her as a heaviness in her heart. "I think it would be best if we stopped seeing each other."

Cal looked like he'd been slapped. "If that's what you need, Edie, then I will respect that. Of course," he said, but nothing in his body language matched those words. "But please know that when I look at my future, I still see you in it. That's not going to change."

Edie held back tears when she said, "It might have to."

CHAPTER TWENTY-THREE

Tabitha handed her best friend another tissue from the half-empty box.

"I'm swearing off men forever." Edie blew loudly into the Kleenex, crumpled it up, and tossed it on the coffee table. It landed at the peak on the mountain of tissues already discarded there.

"Ugh. I'm so sorry, Edie." Tabitha consoled. "I, for one, can honestly say I didn't see that coming at all."

"Right? But really, it's just my luck. I don't date for nearly two decades and when I think I've finally found what appears to be the perfect guy, he's engaged!"

"But he's not engaged." Camille plopped down onto the empty loveseat. "Didn't he call off his wedding? Am I missing something here?"

"Yes, he called off the wedding. But he was definitely still engaged when we met."

Camille bit off the corner of a chocolate chip cookie and spoke with her mouth full.

"Sure, but that's not really his fault, right? It's not like he was planning to meet you when he did."

"Can't you just let me have a sufficient pity party?" Edie slumped her head onto Tabitha's shoulder. "And pass me those cookies. Cookies are required."

Camille grabbed the plate and held it out for Edie to take a handful of the freshly baked treats. "If you want to wallow, by all means, wallow. But I don't necessarily think we should penalize Cal for being engaged at one point in time. It's not like he can change his past."

Both Tabitha and Edie's heads swiveled in Camille's direction, almost in slow motion. "Um, isn't that *exactly* what you did with Foster?"

"Yes, it is. And you should learn from my mistake. I have. In fact, I've learned so much that I now have a date with him next week."

"You are going on a date with Foster?" Edie shot upright. "How and when did this happen?"

"Last night, at the bar. You know, when you stood me up because you had to photograph the ocean during bronze hour."

"Golden hour."

"Same difference. He bought me a soda, we got to chatting, and he came clean about his conviction. Turns out, it's not something that's a deal breaker for me."

"Well, Cal's engagement is one for me."

"And that's perfectly acceptable, Edie." Tabitha was glad to hear that her sister had been able to move forward with Foster, but she felt Edie was entitled to take a step back from Cal, if that's what she needed. "We all process things differently."

"And what about you, sis? How are you processing the fact that your ex-husband is still in love with you?"

Tabitha shot Camille a horrified look. "Ben is not in love with me! That's crazy talk."

"Okay, maybe he's not in love with you, but it's clear he still loves you."

"He's got a girlfriend, and she seems wonderful. I met her at Casey's coffeehouse gig. She seems to be a great fit for Ben. Very sweet and kind. I'm happy for them."

"A girlfriend? That's nothing. Cal had a fiancée, and that didn't stop him from falling for Edie." Camille swiped a spot of melted chocolate from her upper lip with a finger.

"Camille! You are terrible at this whole consoling thing!" Edie launched a throw pillow at her friend. "Seriously. I'm devastated over here."

"I'm sorry, Edie. I really am. I hate to see you this way. But I think if you still have feelings for Cal, then you shouldn't be so quick to dismiss that. Maybe in time, you two can work things out. Talk it through."

"Maybe, but for now I've got my girls, and that's all I need." Edie gave Tabitha a squeeze. "And these cookies. I think the cookies are what I'm going to miss the most about this place when we leave. They are heavenly."

"I don't even want to calculate how many more cookies we'll consume in the time we have left here," Camille said. "Or how many calories that equates to."

Tabitha sat quietly a moment while Edie and Camille threw around the idea of asking the staff for the recipe. While she could tell the others were happy with the time they had remaining at the Villas, Tabitha couldn't say she shared that sentiment. She was eager to get back to work. She missed it more and more each day.

She sincerely worried her skills would suffer due to her prolonged absence. She felt like an old, un-watered plant discarded on the shelf and feared she'd already begun to wither and shrivel up. That couldn't be what Chief Houston had in mind, right? He'd said he wanted her to come back at the top of her game. If that was truly his desire, then why didn't he send her on a learning fellowship or a sabbatical where she could further hone her surgical skills? Why a retreat that did nothing but pamper and spoil? Sure, to some it might feel like a reward, but Tabitha couldn't tamp down the thought that it was actually a punishment.

She would come back rusty and out of practice, and then they would have every reason to let her go. Cut her loose.

Like a final puzzle piece slipped into place, it all came together.

This retreat was just the start of her slow and

eventual exit from the hospital. The revelation made her sick.

She gently slid out from under Edie's shoulder. "I think I'm going to go for a run."

"What about our massages at two?" Edie looked up with concern in her eyes. "You'll be back in time for them, right?"

"I'll try. But if I'm not, you can go without me."

"Are you sure, sis?" Camille asked. "Your masseuse's name is Ricardo or Paulo or something exotic like that. I really don't think you're going to want to miss it."

Tabitha already had her shoes laced up and her hand on the door handle. "I'll do what I can to be back by then."

JUNE GLOOM. It was a term used by the locals to describe the Southern California weather pattern this time of year, but it could've equally defined Tabitha's state of mind. Hazy. Clouded. A layer of mist that never seemed to burn off. Even after six miles, her fog hadn't lifted.

Today, she ran up the coast. She hoped the change in sights, sounds, and terrain would help her focus on something other than the thoughts playing in her head on repeat. The ones that told her she wouldn't have a job at Seascape Shores General after her month off. The ones that said she had already peaked in her career. It made her question every procedure that ended with a flat-lining patient on her table. She felt her career had somehow become the summation of her mistakes.

The landscape was different here, rockier than opposed to the fine, smoother sand by the Villas. She could feel the stones under the tread of her shoes, little lumps that pushed against her soles. She had to pay more attention to the landing of each footfall, but Tabitha welcomed that.

Seagulls soared overhead, zigzagging across the skies like wayward kites in a storm. Offshore, Tabitha could see a lone sailboat bobbing on the water's surface. She squinted her eyes as she tried to make out the name written in chipped paint along the side.

"The Getaway," she read aloud. It was a sloop-rigged boat, just like the one her parents had once owned.

She hadn't changed running speed, but her breathing picked up.

As a child, that sailboat brought her so much joy. She loved setting out on the water with her parents and her sister in their boat, a packed lunch and a classic novel that her mother had every intention of reading to them tucked into a picnic basket. Those books were never cracked open. Instead, their mother would weave her own tall tales, narrating fantastical stories that had her daughters hanging on every word. She always did voices, giving each character their own distinct dialect. Tabitha loved that the most. Her mother made everything come alive.

Tabitha couldn't keep the smile from her face as she tracked the sailboat across the water. It was a well-loved vessel, in need of some obvious refurbishment, but evidently still seaworthy. She wondered what memories were made out under that particular set of sails.

She continued her run, knowing full well she would never make it back in time for their afternoon massages. That was fine. For Tabitha, using her muscles was more relaxing than having them massaged. The thought of a stranger's hands working out the kinks in her shoulders made her shudder. She'd never been one for physical touch and certainly not from a man she'd only just met.

Following the ragged curve of the coastline, Tabitha negotiated the thin strip of sandy beach. When she jogged around the bend, she startled when a row of three houses came into view. They were visibly neglected, battered from years of salty sea wind that peeled their paint and weathered their exteriors. And just off to the side, peeking out from the tall wheat-gold reeds, was a carved wooden sign. Tabitha jogged over and swept back the stalks concealing the words.

The Getaway.

Then, underneath the name was a flimsy piece of cardboard, tacked on by a single long nail. In barely legible penmanship, someone had written *For Sale. Call*

Skip. 555-243-5270.

"THANK you for coming out here to meet me."

Tabitha rose from the lookout bench and walked up to the car.

"Not a problem at all. I'm just as intrigued as you are. Sounds like it's a For Sale by Owner sort of thing. I couldn't find the listings anywhere online or in any of our databases," Ben said. He walked toward Tabitha and halted before ultimately going in for a hug. "You don't normally run up this way, do you?"

"No. I've been running south on the beach, but today I needed a change of scenery."

He offered her a small smile. "Well, when I called that number, an answering machine picked up. It was a man—older, I'm guessing—and he said chances are he's out sailing, so anyone who is interested in viewing the place can just let themselves in."

"I'm pretty sure he *is* out sailing. I think I saw his boat about a mile offshore. It had the same name as the homes: The Getaway. Do you feel comfortable checking out the properties without him being there?" Tabitha wasn't sure if that was the norm.

"Of course. I do it all the time. Owners typically aren't present during a showing, anyway."

"Okay, then. Let's take a look. They're just down this path. It's a bit steep, but there are old railroad ties wedged into the bluff to create a makeshift staircase. Just watch your step."

"I think I can manage," Ben said at her back. She could hear the smile in his voice.

Tabitha didn't know why she felt so drawn to this place. She wasn't in the market to buy and even if she were, she wouldn't be looking this far from the hospital. Even still, it felt like a siren call she couldn't ignore. Like an old memory resurfaced.

"This view is phenomenal," Ben said as they approached the cliff house.

He was right. The miles of untouched beach that sprawled in either direction of the houses made it feel like a private oasis. This space felt like more of a retreat than the Villas ever had to Tabitha. The remoteness and the lack of people were much more her speed.

They descended a long walkway and when they got to the front door of the first house, just as Ben had suggested it would be, they found it unlocked.

"Hello?" Ben called out upon stepping into the foyer. "Hello? Anyone home?"

His greeting was met with silence.

"Should we take off our shoes?" Tabitha asked.

"No, I don't think that's necessary," Ben said, looking around. "Usually there's a note if that's what the owners prefer."

Tabitha hung back, unable to shake the feeling that she was snooping where she shouldn't be.

"It's really okay that we're here, Tabs. I do this all the time."

"And don't you feel like you're invading someone's privacy each and every time?"

"No. Not really. I mean, if you have a property on the market and you're hoping to actually sell it, then you have to be willing to flex a bit when it comes to letting people in to look around."

"What if you don't actually want to sell it?"

The raspy voice made Tabitha shoot sky high. She grabbed onto Ben's arm before her legs gave out from underneath her.

"Sorry 'bout that. Didn't mean to startle you." A pudgy man with snow white hair to his ears and a thick, full beard of the same color slipped off his windbreaker and hung it on a hook just inside the front door. He tugged off a yellow sailor's cap and placed it next to his jacket. "You just about came out of your skin there, dear. I thought I might have to scrape you off the ceiling."

"I'm sorry." Tabitha reclaimed her composure. "I didn't think you'd be here. I thought I saw your sailboat out on the water just a little bit ago."

"That you did," the older man replied. "Came in for a bite to eat. My stomach was growling louder than those waves. Couldn't ignore it any longer. Can I offer you anything?"

"No." Tabitha felt like she had been overstepping before, but now, with the owner of the home standing right in front of them, she was even more certain she'd trespassed in an area she had no right to. "We should really get going."

"But you just got here. Figure you should look around before you head on out like that. That's what you came for, right? To check out the property?"

"It's really okay—"

"I'd actually love to take a look around, if you don't mind." Ben handed the gentleman his business card. "Ben Parker. I'm a realtor with Seascape Shores Realty."

"Name's Skip."

The man shuffled through the entry toward the kitchen with a certain stride that commanded they follow.

"Nice to meet you, Skip. I see that you're selling on your own?"

"I've had that old *For Sale* sign out there for a few months now. You're the first to bite. Probably the first to even see the sign, really. I need to get to trimming those reeds. They've gotten ugly and overgrown, kinda like me." The man yanked on the handle to the refrigerator and pulled out a packet of bologna from within. His hands trembled as he separated a paper plate from its stack, and when he reached for the breadbox to grab two slices, he had to pause to take a breath.

"So you're not actively advertising?"

"Son, at my age, I'm not actively doing much of anything these days." His gaze, shrouded by fuzzy eyebrows, looked out toward the water just feet from the wall of windows. "Not much other than sailing, but that's not an activity. That's a way of life."

"My parents used to sail," Tabitha said. Ben looked over at her like he was surprised by the disclosure. "They had a boat similar to yours."

"That so?" Skip slapped a folded slice of bologna onto the bread and then ripped off a large bite with his teeth. "What about you? You ever get out on the water?"

"I don't have much time these days. Plus, I think I do better with my feet on solid ground."

While Skip and Tabitha chatted, Ben took the liberty of looking around the house.

"What are you asking?" he asked once he'd come back down the stairs to join them in the kitchen again.

"Oh, gosh." Skip shook his head and wiped his mouth with the back of his hand. "I haven't even thought that far ahead to tell you the honest to goodness truth."

"That's probably something you should think about, Skip. It's usually the first thing a buyer looks at when narrowing their search. Price, location, square footage. Things like that."

"Well, like I said earlier, my heart's not one-hundred percent into selling. Truth be told, my heart hasn't been one-hundred percent into anything since my Gertie passed."

Tabitha's heart sank like an anchor thrown overboard. "I'm so sorry to hear that."

"It's been three years, so it's not like its headline-making news. But she was the heart of this whole operation and without her, it just doesn't seem worth continuing. Without the income, I can't afford to stay here much longer."

"When you say operation, what are you referring to?" Ben crossed his arms over his chest and leaned against the kitchen island, head cocked. Though she fought to fully admit it, Tabitha thought he looked quite handsome in his flat-front gray slacks and light blue collared shirt tucked in. He was sharp and put together in a way she'd never seen.

"Well, sweet Gertie and I used to run a little sailing company. We'd have guests come out to stay, and we'd take them out for an afternoon on the seas. Nothing big or too commercial, you know. Usually just families visiting the area who wanted a chance to leave the shore and experience all the wonder the ocean had to offer."

"And you don't do that anymore?"

"Nah. Gertie was always so good with people. Everyone loved her. She could make a stranger feel like a long-lost relative within minutes of meeting. Me, well, I just don't have that gift. I tend to keep to myself."

Tabitha looked at Ben, noticing the compassion in his eyes. "If you sell, where will you go, Skip? Do you have family you can stay with?"

"Gertie was the only family I've ever had. We weren't blessed with children, you see. But my Gertie never complained, even though I know it broke her heart. She'd always say our guests were our family and how rich it was for us to have a new family arrive each and every week. I don't know if she truly believed it or not. But she was good at convincing me she was happy, even if she wasn't."

"I'm sure she was happy," Tabitha assured. "How could she be anything but? It sounds like you created a beautiful life together."

"It was a beautiful life. Sometimes I'm not sure why I'm the one who gets to continue living it, though. Gertie was a good woman, and she deserved more than the years she was given." A mist came over Skip's eyes. He yanked a blue bandana from his back pocket and blew his nose into it loudly. "Cherish every moment you've got with the ones you love." His gaze switched back and forth between Ben and Tabitha. "You never know which day might be your last."

Tabitha contemplated correcting Skip, as he had obviously misinterpreted her relationship with Ben. But before she had the chance to, he added, "And never spend a day doing anything but what you absolutely love. Find work that fulfills you and you'll never feel like you're actually working. That's what our little sailing business has been for me. Prosperity with a purpose. It breaks this old man's heart that it's forced to come to an end."

"But what if it doesn't have to come to an end?" Tabitha asked. She couldn't stand the thought of this sweet man giving up what appeared to be his life's greatest calling.

"I can't run this place on my own anymore. One rundown house is too much, let alone three. And I don't have any family to pass the property down to. The only solution I can see is to throw in the towel and hang up my hat. It's been a good run and I'm blessed to have been able to share the seas with so many people over the years. It's a bittersweet goodbye, but one that has to happen."

Though she'd only just met him, Skip had a kindred familiarity that Tabitha couldn't shake. He'd said Gertie had the gift of easy relationship, but Tabitha felt the same could be said for the man standing in front of her. He'd opened up to her within the span of ten minutes and she suddenly felt a deep, even if unfounded, responsibility to help him out in one way or another.

"What if you could find someone to help you run the property? Someone to coordinate reservations and handle correspondence with the guests? Someone who could cook and clean and deal with the ins and outs so you could focus on your sailing expeditions?" Tabitha suggested, the idea unfolding as she presented it. "How many rooms do you have in this particular house?"

"Five total," Skip answered. "Three upstairs and two down."

"If you used one of those rooms for yourself and then had the other for a live-in helper, that would still leave three separate rooms available to rent just in this house," Ben suggested. "I think you could easily sell the two remaining homes, if you're open to that. There might be a way to make this pencil without having to sell it all, Skip."

A spark of joy that had been absent from his eyes lit anew in unison with the cautious smile that lifted the corners of Skip's large mouth. "I wouldn't have to sell the Getaway House?"

"I don't think you would," Tabitha affirmed.

"But where would I even find someone who would want to do that? To help me keep the business afloat?"

"You know?" Tabitha began, "I think I just might have the perfect person."

CHAPTER TWENTY-FOUR

"*I*'ve never been house hunting on a first date before."

"It's not house hunting. More like job seeking." Camille picked an imaginary piece of lint from her black pants and then pulled at the seatbelt that cut across her shoulder. She usually wasn't one to fidget, but it couldn't be helped. "Tabitha said she found an opportunity that might be right up my alley."

Foster's pickup truck coasted along Highway 1, following the bending stretch of road that hugged the California shoreline. With the windows down, the salty ocean air swirled throughout the cab, making Camille shiver.

"Cold?"

"Actually, I am a little, but the sea breeze is too nice to roll up the windows."

Keeping one hand on the wheel, Foster bent forward to tug his arm out of a coat sleeve, then switched hands to pull the other free. "Here. Put this on."

The denim jacket held a musky scent, a woodsy mix of spice and pine, like he'd splashed a modest dose of cologne on his neck before slinging it on. It instantly provided the warmth Camille craved. "Thank you. Much better."

"Not a problem. So, what is it exactly that you do for work?"

"As of right now, nothing."

"That's right." He glanced her direction, his head nodding slowly as he recalled their poolside conversation. "I remember you saying something about never settling with your job again. So I take it, whatever you did before wasn't your life's ambition, huh?"

"Not even close. I was a receptionist at an accounting firm. Not that it wasn't a fine job, because it was. Good hours and decent pay. Just not what I was born to do, you know?"

"I totally get it," Foster said. He squinted through the windshield. "Remind me the address?"

"325 Getaway Cove, Highway 1. Just a half mile up, I think."

"So tell me about this opportunity we're checking out."

"I don't know much, other than it involves an old sailor and something about a potential bed-and-breakfast. One that could use some construction help. That's why I brought you along."

"I do know a thing or two about construction."

Foster pointed to a lookout just off the side of the road. "Looks like this might be it?"

"The Getaway," Camille read aloud from the placard at the edge of the bluff. Foster directed the car off the highway and into a small gravel lot, then shut off the engine.

"This has to be it. I don't see any other houses for miles."

Camille unhooked her seatbelt and opened the truck's door. It squealed loudly on its hinges, begging to be oiled. Something about the truck's age made Camille smile. She liked the thought of Foster tinkering around under the hood, changing the truck's oil, and doing other manly things that her ex had always paid someone else to do.

"Sorry. I really need to get some WD-40 on that door." Foster came around to her side of the vehicle to close the door behind her. "Truth be told, I don't have a lot of passengers in this truck, so I tend to forget that it squeaks like that. Doesn't get opened much."

"It doesn't bother me one bit." If anything, that Camille was the only one to recently share the cab with Foster only made her like him more. "Wow, Foster." She grabbed onto his elbow. "Look at that."

From their cliff lookout, they had a front-row seat to the most spectacular show she'd seen in ages. Blazes of orange, pink, and yellow flared out from the setting sun like a brilliant halo as it slipped into the ocean's crisp horizon. The fog had finally lifted only an hour before, and it had cleared out just in time for this exquisite display.

Camille could feel the warm reflection of waning daylight on her skin. "I think this is called golden hour," she whispered to Foster. His mouth was agape in awe. "That's what Edie calls it."

"I can certainly see why. It looks as though the sun has left a golden kiss on everything its light touched."

Camille looked up at Foster.

"What?" He shrugged his shoulders to his ears with his hands shoved deep into his pockets.

"That was certainly poetic. Especially coming from a construction guy."

"Oh, Camille." He bumped her playfully with his broad shoulder. "I'm so much more than just a construction guy. You'll soon see."

She didn't know if it was the fact that she was already wrapped up in his jacket like an embrace, or if it was the husky, flirtatious tone of his voice, but if Foster had leaned over and kissed Camille in that moment, she wouldn't have protested. She would've gladly welcomed it.

She was thinking through just what that might feel like, to be kissed by a man like Foster who was thoughtful, yet exceptionally masculine, when he grabbed onto her arm and beckoned her forward.

"Let's go check this place out before it gets too dark. The path down to the houses looks a little dicey and I don't see any sort of lighting or railing. Hold my hand?"

"Absolutely!" Camille blurted with a touch too much enthusiasm.

Foster chuckled. "You said the house might need some work, but I think the first improvement should be this pathway. It's a lawsuit waiting to happen."

Foster was spot on in that observation. The Getaway homes were located on the water, but the only way to access them from the road was to scale an almost vertical, craggy bluff, one without any sort of secure footing. At one point in time, someone had used large beams to create stairs into the hillside, but they were rotted and loose and offered little in the way of stability.

"This does seem pretty dangerous." Camille's stomach went weightless as she unexpectedly slipped, skidding forward like she had roller skates on.

Foster jerked her near. "Careful, there," he breathed hotly against her cheek. Their bodies pressed intimately close. Man, he smelled even better than the jacket.

Camille gulped. "Thank you," she said in a wobbly voice.

"Anytime." Foster shot her a coy grin that made Camille's stomach feel even lighter than before.

They made it the rest of the way down the hillside without incident, both to Camille's relief and disappointment. She wouldn't have minded another up-close-and-personal moment with Foster. She even contemplated the ways she could get him to pull her close again. What on earth was going on with her?

Just as Tabitha had noted, the homes were in need of visible repair, but there was an ocean-tattered familiarity that pulled at memories from her youth. A modest, shabby sailboat docked along the shore and an abundance of reeds grew along the beachside property, making it feel like a dense jungle. Lifting a hand to knock on the front door, Camille took a steadying breath.

"Here goes nothing," she murmured.

Tabitha had implied this could be a fantastic opportunity for Camille, but it felt almost too good to be true. After all, Camille hadn't even begun her job search. That something like this—a chance to live on the very ocean her parents used to sail upon—would just fall into her lap seemed like a fanciful dream, not reality.

"You must be Camille." An elderly man appeared behind the door. He stood in the doorway, taking up much of the frame. In his youth, he likely had a commanding presence, but the years had rounded his shoulders and hunched his stature, withering him into a smaller version of his former self. He stretched out a quivering hand. "Skip Hartley."

"Hi, Skip." Camille took hold of his hand, surprised by the rough, leathery texture and assertiveness in the shake. "You're right, I am Camille. And this is my friend, Foster."

"Nice to meet you, sir." Foster went in for a handshake.

"Well, come on in off the stoop, you two. We don't want to let the seagulls in."

Foster bent toward Camille's ear and whispered, "Is that a thing?"

"Not sure," Camille snickered.

"Your sister says you're looking for work," Skip spoke over his shoulder.

Camille didn't care for the way that sounded. It conjured up sad visions of sitting on the street corner, cardboard sign in hand, tin cup filled with loose change at her side. "I'm looking for a change in profession, yes."

"Good, good. I've made some tea." Skip motioned for them to follow with a wave. He led them through the house and tipped his chin toward a folding card table placed in the nook of the kitchen. "Have a seat and I'll pour you both a cup."

Foster scooted out a chair for Camille and then took the one right beside her. "I see what Tabitha means about this place being a fixer upper," he said quietly, glancing around to take in their surroundings.

The house had great bones, but the interior left much to be desired. Like Skip, Camille figured it was something truly grand back in its prime, but the recent years hadn't been very kind. Layers of dust, fading wallpaper, and 1980s oak dated the décor. But all of that was purely cosmetic and easy enough to fix.

"Honey lavender," Skip said as he lowered a cup and saucer in front of Camille. The ceramic rattled with his trembling movements. "I hope that's okay."

"My favorite," Camille noted. She breathed in the floral-scented steam that curled up from the cup in wisps. It smelled delicious.

"It was my Gertie's favorite, too," Skip said. "Let's get right down to it, Camille." Skip plopped into his chair with a huff. "I'm gonna need help if I have any hope of keeping this place. I've got a humble sailing business, but a day trip here and there isn't going to keep the lights on. I need someone who can generate more interest in my little endeavor. Your sister seems to think we can fix this place up and get some of the rooms rented out. Gertie used to be in charge of that sort of thing. I wouldn't even know where to start."

"I'd actually start by replacing that pathway down to the house," Foster interjected. "Decking with a railing would be safer than what's currently there and it would be easy enough to install."

"Is that the sort of thing you're good at, son?" Skip asked with a voice full of hope.

Camille got the sense Skip thought his two visitors were there to save him and she feared she wouldn't be able to live up to that lofty expectation.

"It's the sort of thing I'm great at. I've been in construction since the time I could swing a hammer."

"Good, good." Skip turned his attention to Camille. "And I hear you're good with people?"

"I don't know about that," Camille replied. Just what had her sister said?

"She's great with people," Foster corrected. "The best. People person extraordinaire."

"All I'm good at is navigating those ocean waves," Skip said wistfully, his gaze flickering out the window beyond. "If I could live out there, I would. But this is a good second choice, I suppose."

"This place is amazing, Skip. I think with a little updating, it would be a very sought after beach rental. Getting people here wouldn't be an issue at all. I know several rental websites where we could list it. We'd need to stock up on things like linens and towels and the sort, and you'd have to decide if you want to provide meals to your guests, but those are all details that could be worked out further down the line."

"Well, I do like you, Camille. You've got the job if you want it."

Camille stiffened. The cup she had just lifted to her lips shook with her jolted surprise. "Wouldn't you like to see some references first? Maybe think it over for a few days?"

Skip looked Foster square in the eye. "Is she an honest woman?"

"Yes, sir. She most certainly is."

"That's a good enough reference for me. You're hired, Camille. Feel free to poke around the place and pick your room. Mine is the one down the hall since I don't get up and down the stairs as easily anymore. But the rest are up for grabs. Welcome to The Getaway House."

"THAT WAS the strangest job interview I've ever been on."

"I'm still trying to decide if I should be concerned that another man just asked the woman I'm currently on a date with to move in with him."

Camille waggled a shrimp tail at Foster. "Skip's harmless." She tossed the shell onto the growing pile on her plate and took another jumbo shrimp from the appetizer tray. This was totally her kind of restaurant: all-you-can-eat shrimp with endless Caesar salad and garlic bread. When Skip had suggested it, she felt herself fall for him even more. "Unless he's not harmless. I mean, I don't really know the guy at all, do I?"

"For all we know, he could be a convicted felon."

Camille groaned.

"Too soon?" Foster shed a devilish grin and plunged a shrimp into a ramekin of cocktail sauce before taking a bite. "It might be worth doing a little research, though. Especially if you do have plans to live with the guy. You've done research for far less important relationships."

"What makes you think I didn't hope for something more?"

Foster looked up from his hands, which had been busied with shrimp peeling. "With me?"

"Yes, with you, silly. Please don't tell me I'm the only one who felt a connection when we met at the pool."

"I felt a connection, absolutely, Camille. That's really why you looked me up? I thought it was something about overhearing salon gossip and wanting to know if it was true."

"Well, yeah, I wanted to know if it was true because I was interested in you."

Foster fought a smile. "So tell me a little more about you. Since we're out on a date, let's treat it like one. Get to know each other and all that."

She fiddled with the napkin in her lap and flicked off a piece of shell that had landed there. "You already know about my ex-husband, Mark. We were high school sweethearts and were married twenty-five years before he decided to upgrade to a newer model."

"No such thing."

She knew he was trying to be nice, but she'd come to terms with her reality long ago. "Oh yes, there definitely is such a thing, and I've seen her. Stephanie's almost half my age with much newer parts—some I think she might've even paid for," Camille said with a snicker.

"I don't think you're giving yourself enough credit, Camille. You're a very beautiful woman."

Camille's gaze lifted to Foster's. "You don't have to say that. I realize I set you up for it."

"I'm not the sort of man to say things that aren't true."

All of her life, Camille had felt like a distant second fiddle to her sister, who was not only stunning, but had the brains and prestigious career to match. To Mark's new wife and now his growing family. She was ever the supportive friend and sister and it was a role Camille was glad to play. But the intensity in Foster's eyes, and the way his expression didn't falter when she challenged him with a questioning look, confirmed his statement. He really meant it.

"You're acting like no one has told you that before," he said.

"Because it's been so long, I'm beginning to wonder if it ever happened at all. I mean, when we were first married, Mark would tell me I was pretty or that a certain outfit looked nice when we'd get dressed up for one of his work functions. But in those final years of our marriage, I think he used up all of his compliments on other women and didn't have any left for me."

Straining his crystal blue eyes, Foster surprised her when he jutted a hand across the table and covered her own. "I find you very, very attractive, Camille. In fact, I'd find it hard to believe any man with a pulse wouldn't say the same. And you're a real kick to hang out with. You keep me laughing and you keep me on my toes, all of which I really like. I consider myself the luckiest man in this restaurant that I'm the one who gets to sit across from you right now."

Camille chortled with a roll of her eyes. "It's as though you've taken some sort of *All the Right Things to Say to a Woman* course."

"Really? I don't mean for it to sound rehearsed or trite. I'm just telling you what I feel."

"Don't get me wrong. I sort of love it. I'm just

wondering how many women you've used those particular lines on."

"As of this very moment, one."

"Man, Foster. You are good." Camille reached for her glass of merlot and took a generous sip. "I wish your daughter's future mother-in-law could see what a decent man you are."

"I hadn't realized she thought so little of me until you told me what you'd overheard. It worries me, though. Not that she doesn't like me, but that Becca will have to deal with such a difficult personality for the rest of her life. I know how challenging in-laws can be."

"You had bad ones?"

"Let's just say Darla's parents never wanted their daughter to be caught up with a guy who wore a hardhat for a living. The irony is that she ultimately ended up with someone who never worked an honest day in his life. But they weren't around to see the repercussions of Darla's bad choices. I suppose it's for the best that they died thinking their daughter had merely settled for a blue-collar worker, not a drug dealer."

"That's one way to look at it, I suppose. I was really lucky with my in-laws. Mark's parents were wonderful. Still are. Trudy still calls every now and again to check in and see how I'm doing. They had always wanted grandchildren, but Mark and I had such a struggle to get and stay pregnant. When Patrick was born, they were over the moon. Started a college fund for him and even decorated a small nursery in their home for when we'd come to visit. Sailboat themed. Of course, Patrick never saw the light of day outside of those hospital walls, so that nursery was never used." Camille gave a helpless shrug. "I bet Trudy's thrilled that she gets another chance to be a grandma."

"I wish things had been different for you, Camille. I wish you'd had the opportunity to raise Patrick. See him grow up and live the life you had planned out as a family. Even though I've only known you a short while, I can tell you have a lot of love to give."

The tear that collected in the corner of her eye took her by surprise. She shoved it away with the sleeve of her blouse. "Thank you for recognizing that, Foster. It means more than you know."

He squeezed and then released her hand. "I think Skip is going to be very lucky to have you. You're going to transform the energy of that place. I can feel it."

"And you? Are you up for transforming the look of it? As is, it'll be a challenge to get anyone out there," Camille said. "I'm just not quite sure where he plans to get the funds to do any of the renovations. It doesn't sound like he's in the best spot financially."

"I've actually been mulling that over in the back of my mind all night. You're right. I don't think he's got any extra cash lying around. I wish I was in a place to work for free, but unfortunately, that's not the case. But I do have an idea."

Camille's interest was piqued. "And what's that?"

"I'm wondering if Skip wants a partner of sorts. If I could put some sweat equity in and cash out when the two other houses sell. I think it would be a great investment opportunity."

"I think you could really be on to something, Foster. Definitely something worth running by Skip."

"I plan to," he said. He scooped up another handful of shrimp and dropped them onto his plate to be peeled. "But not right now. All I'm currently concerned with is making sure you're having a nice evening. And that I don't do or say something that makes this first date become our last."

Smiling, Camille flashed a quick wink when she answered, "I don't think that's something you need to worry about. In fact, I think you're on track to have many, many more nights just like this one. Especially if you end up doing the construction work for Skip. We could end up seeing a lot of each other."

"Well, that would be a win-win all around."

CHAPTER TWENTY-FIVE

*E*die squinted, wondering if the repeated zeroes in the text were some sort of illusion, like when you crossed your eyes and everything went double.

Cal said the potential client had talked big numbers, but she hadn't counted on a price tag this large. Imposter syndrome was in full force. Edie couldn't shake the notion that the client would be getting robbed if she accepted that figure. Her work wasn't worth anywhere close to their offer.

That's too much. She typed quickly and sent it off to Cal. It was her first communication with him since the dreadful meltdown at the country club. And though the words referred to the sale of the photographs, it could've summed up their relationship as well.

It was all too much. The passion. The speed with which things progressed between them. The lies. It was more than her heart and head had been able to process.

Within seconds, her phone buzzed in her palm.

Let's at least meet and talk about it before I give them a final answer. It would be foolish to pass up an opportunity like this. This could open a lot of doors and lead to many future sales.

Edie didn't need Cal telling her what was, and what wasn't, foolish. She was a grown woman who could make up her own mind about things, whether in life or in business. Cal's opinion held little weight in her life anymore.

She wasn't interested in opening any doors. And she certainly wasn't interested in re-opening a door when Cal stood on the other side.

You can go ahead and pass along to your client that I'm not the right fit for the job.

She placed the phone on her nightstand and picked up the novel she'd recently tried to immerse herself in. But the words on the page blurred together each time she opened it up, and the story struggled to hold her attention. She tossed the paperback to the empty side of the massive bed and yanked the duvet up to her chin with a sigh.

Admitting that she missed Cal didn't make her feel like the strong, independent woman she claimed to be, so Edie told herself that she merely missed the attention. The feeling of being desired. The rush of adrenaline when kissed with abandon. The way his hand in hers made the world feel like everything had finally slipped into place.

Those were things she could feel with any man, right? They weren't unique to Cal.

Another text had her phone skittering across the nightstand.

I understand that you don't want to see me, but if you're able to separate me from your business, then I think a meeting could be worthwhile. I'll be at Curly Joe's tomorrow at noon if you change your mind.

EDIE DID NOT plan on changing her mind. She went to bed resolute, firm in her decision to let this opportunity go. But those zeroes, they were a rich temptation she couldn't ignore. If she ever had hopes of getting her photography business off the ground, it would be a royally stupid move to turn this down.

She nearly chickened out when she glimpsed Cal through the coffeehouse windows, his hair irresistibly disheveled, that flicker of bold paint on his hands noticeable even from a distance. Something deep in her stomach ached like a pulse. Shoving it down, she reached for the door handle and entered the shop, shoulders back, head thrust high.

Cal saw her immediately and rose to stand as she made her way to his table. The strain of his brow creasing his forehead and the look of sheer anguish as he struggled to offer a handshake rather than a hug couldn't be ignored.

"You look good, Edie," he said, holding onto her hand for longer than a typical handshake required. It had only been days, yet the longing in his gaze made it seem like they hadn't been in one another's presence in months.

"You as well." Edie sat across from Cal. She steepled her hands in front of her, forcing the most professional demeanor she could muster.

"I wasn't sure you would show up," he admitted. "I really hoped you would."

"I wasn't sure I would, either. But those numbers were too tempting to ignore." She didn't add that he was just as tempting. That she couldn't look at his mouth without feeling the ghost of his supple lips on hers.

"Can I get you a coffee?"

"No, I'm fine. Thank you," she said. She sat up tall in her chair. "Let's talk about this opportunity. I saw the figure they're willing to pay for a series. I'm curious what they'd pay per individual print."

"That number isn't for the series, Edie. That *is* per individual print."

Edie could almost feel her face drain of all color, like a plug pulled from a sink. "My work isn't worth that."

"It absolutely is. I think it would be a real mistake to pass on this."

She'd made enough mistakes as of late. She wasn't

sure she wanted to endure another. No matter how badly she felt the need to nurse her injured pride, she had to relent. It was more money than she could grasp. If someone was really willing to pay it, who was she to deny them?

"I might be interested in a meeting." Edie folded her hands in her lap. "I'm assuming you'll want a commission on this?"

"I don't want anything from you, Edie." The false smile he'd worn earlier collapsed from his face. "I just want you."

"Cal—"

"I'm sorry, Edie. But that truth hasn't and won't change. Is it easy for you to sit across from me right now? Because it's killing me."

"It's not easy." She offered him that much. "But this is how it has to be. You're not who I thought you were."

"You keep saying that, but I'm still the same man you were falling in love with."

"I wasn't falling in love," she lied so quickly it felt like someone else spoke the words for her.

"Well, I was falling in love with you."

"Please, Cal. I can't do this. I'm interested in learning more about this opportunity with my work, but if our meetings are going to become this—declarations of one-sided love—then I'm out."

Cal breathed deeply, straightening in his chair with the lift of air. "I get it. This is a big opportunity, so I don't want you to drop out because I'm making you uncomfortable. I'll stop talking about my feelings for you, but I need you to know that just because I'm not saying them, doesn't mean they've gone away."

"At some point, they will have to." Edie slung her purse over her shoulder. "If you'd like to put me in touch with this possible buyer, I'd appreciate it. I can handle things on my own from here."

CHAPTER TWENTY-SIX

"*T*hanks for meeting me out here again, Tabs." Ben pulled his leg back and grabbed his shoe to stretch his quad. "You're the only one I know who's as committed to running as I am at the moment, and I really want to be consistent with my training. My goal is to not completely humiliate myself at that race in Nashville this summer."

"What about Donna? I thought you said she was a runner." Tabitha pulled her arm across her body and felt the muscles strain. "I assumed you two ran together quite often."

"Donna and I are…" He looked down as if he could find the words he needed written in the sand. "Complicated."

This friendship with her husband didn't feel *un*complicated, but she didn't mention that.

"I'm always up for a run." She dropped her arms

to her sides and shrugged. "Especially if it gets me out of hot yoga."

"Is that what the girls are up to today?"

"Yes, but normal temperature yoga sounds awful by itself. Hot yoga just feels like a whole new level of torture. Like Dante's inferno and the different circles of hell. Surely both regular yoga and hot yoga each have their own."

"That's funny, Tabs." Ben snickered, slightly shaking his head. "I never realized how funny you were. To be honest, I feel like I'm learning a lot of new things about you."

"That's probably enough stretching." Tabitha didn't acknowledge Ben's latest comment. "Ready?"

"Whenever you are."

THE WAIL just a few yards down the coastline made Tabitha's blood run cold.

"Did you hear that?" Ben slowed his pace, his feet planting in the sand.

"I did." Tabitha squinted. "Do you *see* that?"

Just beyond them, a young man waded through waist-high ocean water, struggling to cradle the body of a person of equal size in his arms. Blood spread out around the two men like a red, feathery dye. Staggering onto the shore, he dropped the limp body to the ground. Then he swung around and bent at the knees to wretch violently onto the sand.

Tabitha urged her legs into the fastest speed they'd ever carried her.

"Bring that surfboard over here!" she yelled. She jutted her chin toward the longboard leaning up against the VW bus parked illegally on the beach. "And gather whatever towels you have." Her eyes zeroed in on the red and white cooler wedged in the sand a few paces away. "Any chance you have alcohol in that ice chest?"

"Yeah. I just picked up a brand new bottle of vodka." The young man's voice was wrought with panic, his eyes wild with distress. "But we weren't drinking yet. I swear."

"I'm a surgeon, not the police. Get me that bottle. I can use it to disinfect the towels I'm going to apply to the wound. What's your name?"

"Tommy." The young man's voice shook. "And he's Carter."

Below Tabitha, the injured college student moaned, his eyes tumbling back in his head. "Stay with me, Carter. You're going to be just fine. Can you tell me how old you are?"

"Twenty-one," Carter murmured weakly in a voice barely above a whisper.

"There's so much blood," Ben groaned as he peered over Tabitha's shoulder. His face held about as much color as a blank sheet of paper.

Tabitha ignored her ex-husband's pallor and instructed him to call 911. She needed to focus on the patient at hand and not concern herself with the fact that Ben might very well pass out right next to her. "How far out is the ambulance?" she asked once he hung up.

"They said about five minutes."

Carter didn't have five minutes.

"There's an open fracture to his tibia—I can feel it." She ran her hand over his lower leg and scanned up, eyes moving to his swim shorts where the majority of the blood spurted from. She lifted the hem. "He has multiple lacerations." Tabitha pointed higher up Carter's thigh. "But that's the one I'm most concerned with. With this amount of blood, I'm worried it may have nicked his femoral artery." Tabitha had never talked in detail with Ben about anything medical, but the rounding of his eyes and the helpless look he gave showed he grasped exactly what that bleak statement meant.

Carter was going to bleed out.

"I brought everything I could find." Tommy returned in a rush with the requested supplies. He lowered the longboard onto the sand and the three gingerly moved Carter onto it, like they were transferring a fragile bomb about to detonate.

With a generous dousing of alcohol, Tabitha soaked the towels and then poured the liquid over her hands and arms, clear up to her elbows. She pressed down firmly on Carter's upper thigh, thankful for the board that offered some resistance. "Ben, I need you to monitor his pedal pulse for me. You're going to place two fingers on the top of his right foot. Can you do that?"

"Yeah. I can do that." Ben plunged his knees into the sand and picked up Carter's foot.

"Tommy, go up by Carter's head and hold his neck in a neutral position." She worried about a possible spinal cord injury, but didn't want to scare Tommy and Ben with that additional information. She needed their help and she needed them calm. "And keep him talking."

Ben pressed two fingers to Carter's clammy skin. "His pulse feels really weak."

"I know." Tabitha applied more pressure. "Tommy, can you tell me what you two were doing when this happened?"

"We were just goofing around on Pirate's Peak. All of a sudden, Carter fell to his knees. Started shaking. That's when he slipped off and landed at the base of the rock."

"He started shaking before he fell?"

"Yeah. I mean, I think so. I don't know. It's all kind of a blur. It happened so fast."

"Tommy, do you know if Carter has a history of seizures?"

Ben's gaze connected with his ex-wife's. "You think he had a seizure?"

"I think he might have. And if that's the case, we need to pray he doesn't seize again. And we need to keep him as still as possible. Another seizure will only make things that much more difficult to keep under control out here in the field."

Like a beacon in the distance, an ambulance charged through the mostly empty beach parking lot and bounded onto the sand, lights flashing red and siren wailing. It came to an abrupt halt next to the VW and the paramedic and EMT rushed from the vehicle.

"Dr. Parker." Nico Frazze, a paramedic Tabitha had met multiple times before in the Seascape Shores General emergency room, raced across the sand with both the gear and skills necessary to take over. "Tell me what we're looking at here."

"We have a possible seizure with a high level fall resulting in a major laceration in the groin area. Possible laceration to the femoral artery due to cooling off of the right extremity and decreased pedal pulses. He also has a tib fracture on the same side. I'm worried he might have suffered a concussion, as well. Tell the hospital to have a CT scanner on the ready, O neg on standby, and alert the OR." She rattled off the situation to Nico, feeling an odd, familiar thrill coursing through her. "I'll ride with you in the ambulance," she said, then turned to Ben. "You go with Tommy. We'll meet you back at the hospital."

THE HAND softly nudging her knee made Tabitha's spine pull taut against the waiting room chair. In any other situation, she would have waited in the break room or physician charting room, but this imposed sabbatical made Tabitha feel out of place within her own hospital. She hated that.

Eyes flashing open, she lifted her head from Ben's shoulder, a wave of nausea swooping through her stomach as though she hit the low dip on a roller-coaster.

"Sorry to wake you," Ben apologized in a soft tone as he patted her leg once more. "I think that's Carter's surgeon coming down the hall, yeah?"

Ben tipped his chin toward the waiting room door and the man now walking through it. The light blue scrubs did little to conceal the muscular build underneath and the black hair that peaked out from his surgical cap, falling just above caramel-colored eyes, made Tabitha take pause. It wasn't his undeniably striking appearance that tripped up her thoughts, though. It was the fact that—in all her years at the hospital—today was the first time she'd ever laid eyes on the man.

"Is there anyone here for a Carter Mason?" The handsome surgeon scanned the room.

Tabitha, Ben, and Tommy all jumped to their feet, and he nodded their direction in acknowledgment, then crooked his finger, indicating they follow him out into the hall.

Tommy looked like he was about to throw up, and the surgeon's first statement did little to dissuade that outcome.

"I'm Dr. Montes." The man didn't waste his time with the cordiality of a handshake. "Not going to lie," he started right in. "It was incredibly touch and go in there. But we did all that we could—"

"Did he make it?" Tommy hiccupped on a near cry. "He didn't die, did he? Please tell me he didn't die."

The surgeon lifted a hand and shut his eyes as though wincing. He breathed in sharply through his nostrils. "Yes, he made it. But this will go a lot more smoothly if you don't interrupt me. I need you to listen. There's a lot of information."

Tabitha wondered if she'd ever been so out of touch during her tenure at Seascape Shores General. If she'd bulldozed right through anxious family members' emotions while she delivered clinical news. Had she not recognized the expressions on their faces as true, justifiable fear? Had she been so eager to report her successes—and sometimes regrettably, her failures—that she couldn't pause long enough to acknowledge the sheer magnitude of their worry?

"Like I said," Dr. Montes continued after a drawn out pause that felt a lot like a scolding. "Connor lost a great deal of blood. Because of that, he required a transfusion. We also had to repair his tibia fracture by placing a rod and a couple of screws, so his journey toward healing is going to be a long one."

"How is *Carter*—that is his name, not Connor—tolerating the Keppra?" Tabitha spoke up. Dr. Montes' intimidating gaze narrowed in her direction like an arrow on a target. Confusion contorted his features.

"The reason I'm asking is that Carter had a seizure that caused the initial fall, so I assume you've given him an anticonvulsant. You would know that if you were even listening to Nico's report upon entry into the trauma bay. But from what I heard, you were too busy dragging him back into the OR as fast as possible."

"I saw nothing to indicate a seizure."

"But the way Tommy described the accident—"

"It's my job as an orthopedic surgeon to fix what is broken—"

Releasing her bottom lip from her teeth, Tabitha spat, "Oh, I am well aware of just what your job entails."

"Excuse me, ma'am."

"It's Dr. Parker."

Like he'd been doused with a bucket of ice water, the surgeon's eyes went wide. He rocked onto his heels as he half-laughed in the direction of the ceiling. "Dr. Parker." He rubbed his square jaw and smiled, a hint of devilry apparent in his smirk. Only after sizing Tabitha up for a brief moment did he extend his hand for an official shake. "It's nice to finally meet my competition."

"Your competition?" Reluctantly, she slipped her hand into his.

"For Chief of Surgery."

Ben coughed to clear his throat.

If Tommy had looked physically ill earlier, Tabitha figured she'd just one-upped him. Her tongue watered as though she'd just sucked on a sour candy, her mouth filling with bitter acid. "Chief of Surgery?"

"They told me you were no nonsense. Stiff competition. Now I see exactly what I'm dealing with." That smirk turned into a full-fledged grin when he added, "I must admit, this is going to be a lot more fun than I originally anticipated."

"I'm really trying not to interrupt again, but Carter's alive, right?" Tommy's voice squeaked. "That's what you're saying. He made it?"

"Yes. He made it. It'll be a few hours before he can have any visitors, but if you hang around, I'll send someone out for you when that time comes," Dr. Montes spoke to the worried young man before he swiveled closer to Tabitha and said, "You know? I'm *really* looking forward to this." He waved a hand back and forth in the distance between them. "It's been way too long since I've had anyone chase me up the ladder. But make no mistake, I plan to get to the top first."

CHAPTER TWENTY-SEVEN

"*Chief* Parker." Camille crossed her ankles on the stone ledge of the fire pit, far enough from the flames so she wouldn't singe her toes, but close enough to enjoy the emanating warmth that fanned out from the flickering blaze. "I like the sound of that."

"Really? I don't know." Tabitha plopped down next to her sister on the outdoor sofa and grabbed the jumbo marshmallow bag nearby. She shoved one onto her roasting stick.

"You're telling me you seriously had *no* idea this was in the cards?" Before Tabitha could place her marshmallow over the fire, Camille acted fast and swiped it from the rod, then popped the sugary treat into her mouth. She crinkled her nose like a child taunting a sibling. "You must've had *some* notion. You're a pretty smart cookie."

"I honestly didn't." Lifting her shoulders to her

ears in a shrug, Tabitha reached into the bag and fit another marshmallow onto her now empty stick. She switched hands and angled it far from her sister so she couldn't commandeer this one, too. "I thought this whole sabbatical was part of some process to strip me of my title, not offer me an entirely new one."

Behind them, Edie appeared through the sliding glass door and then wedged herself in the empty space next to Camille on the couch. She'd brought with her a thick teal quilt and handed one end to Tabitha to wrap around their shoulders. The sunset air was crisp with just enough ocean breeze to draw a shiver to bare arms. Now blanketed, the trio snuggled down under the weight of the fabric that cocooned them against the chill. "Is it a title you want?" Edie asked after settling in. "Chief of Surgery?"

Eyes squinted, Tabitha studied her marshmallow as orange flames threatened to char the gooey underside. "That's the thing. Part of me feels like I'd be a fool to pass up this opportunity." She rotated her wrist, turning over the portion that had yet to be charred. "But the other part of me wants to just get back to what I do best. And that's surgery. I don't know that I'm cut out for Chief. I like the nitty-gritty of it all, not the additional admin and organizational stuff. This morning, out on the beach with that kid...I felt that thrill again. The thrill of confidence in knowing exactly what to do in that precise moment. I don't think I'd have the same confidence when it comes to leading an entire surgical department."

"That's a decision only you can make." Camille rocked her shoulder into her sister's. "But whatever that decision is, I know it'll be the right one."

"You're giving me too much credit. I've made some pretty bad ones in the past." She pulled her eyes from the roasting marshmallow for a fleeting moment and that's all it took for the white puff of sugar to fully ignite. "Shoot!" Drawing it close and huffing against the fire that now engulfed the marshmallow, Tabitha groaned. "Well, look at that. Up in flames, just like so many other things in my life."

Camille and Edie locked eyes. "Are you referring to your marriage, Tab?" Edie inferred. "Because I don't think it exactly went up in flames."

"No, more like a slow, amicable extinguishing," Camille added. "And call me crazy, but is it fair to say that maybe there might even be some rekindling going on there?"

"Rekindling with Ben?" If she'd been told she'd suddenly grown a third eye, Tabitha's shock wouldn't have been any different. "That's ridiculous."

"Is it, though? Because you've been spending a lot of time with him lately. Running on the beach, saving lives and all. It's a bit of a one-eighty. To put things in perspective, I can count on one hand the number of times you even mentioned Ben's name during these last four years. Now you two are hanging out daily."

"You know how that goes," Tabitha started to defend. "Out of sight, out of mind. Unfortunately, I think that was the main struggle in our marriage, too.

We never saw one another, so we didn't really think about each other."

"And you're thinking of him now?" Camille inquired.

Tabitha flung the ruined marshmallow from her stick, sending the sticky glob careening into the sand just yards away. "Well, of course I'm thinking about him. You keep talking about him!"

"Just know that he's been thinking of you, too," Edie noted.

Camille waggled her eyebrows. "Okay, here's a fair question: if you had to choose between accepting the position as Chief or getting back together with Ben, what would it be?"

Tabitha grunted an incredulous laugh. "I'm not even going to dignify that question with a response."

"Oh, come on, Tab. It's just us. Your secrets are safe."

"I really can't answer that."

"Can't?" Camille challenged. "Or won't?"

Sighing, Tabitha reluctantly conceded, "Being with Ben is a known. Being Chief of Surgery is an unknown. For that reason and that reason *only*, I guess I'd choose Ben. But only because you're forcing me to make a decision." She wanted to ignore the telling smirks her confession produced on each woman's face, but they couldn't be overlooked. "Okay, so while we're at it, what about you, sis? If you had to choose between a future running The Getaway or a future with Foster, which would it be?"

"I don't have to choose," Camille said haughtily. "I get them both. He's likely going to be doing construction on Skip's place in exchange for a profit share, so I'll hopefully be seeing *a lot* of him in the near future. Lucky for me, my dreams are not mutually exclusive."

"Ben is not my dream!" Tabitha half-shouted, but Camille had already moved on.

"Edie. Your turn. Photography or Cal?"

"You both know I already made that choice."

Camille pulled a face. "But *did* you? Really?"

"Yes," Edie said. "I chose photography. Cal is nothing more than a month-long fling I had no business being involved with. It's over and done."

This time, it was Camille and Tabitha's turn to exchange knowing glances.

"Believe what you will," Edie said. "I'm over him."

"Alright, here's one." Offering her friend a little grace, Camille switched gears. "If you had to choose anyone in the world—famous or not—to be stuck at this Villa with for an entire month, who would it be?"

"I've already made that choice," Tabitha said as she burrowed into the comfort of the plush couch cushions. She tugged the quilt around her and pressed her side close to her sister's, dropping her head onto her shoulder like she used to do with their mother.

"You have?"

"Yep. Back when I asked you both to join me. There's nothing more important in my life than the two of you. I hope you know that. I couldn't ask for more than this once-in-a-lifetime opportunity to spend a month with two women I love, respect, and count as my life's truest gift."

"Well, maybe there's *one* more thing you could ask for," Camille offered with a playful gleam in her eye.

"What's that?"

"Some of those warm chocolate chip cookies from room service. I'm totally over our failed attempts at marshmallow roasting."

"Yes!" Edie giggled. "Those incredible cookies are a gift in and of themselves."

Laughing, Tabitha smiled. She couldn't say she disagreed with that one little bit.

THE GETAWAY HOUSE

Continue the journey with ***The Getaway House***,
book two in the Seascape Shores series, available for
preorder: https://lnk.to/SlBqCMrp

(And read on for an uncorrected sneak peek of
Chapter One.)

MEGAN SQUIRES

the Getaway House

A SEASCAPE
SHORES NOVEL

THE GETAWAY HOUSE: SEASCAPE SHORES BOOK TWO

(SNEAK PEAK: CHAPTER ONE)

"Stop that incessant cawing!"

"Technically, it's called mewing."

Camille Todd narrowed her eyes over her tepid cup of coffee, giving the old fisherman a disapproving look. It went utterly wasted. His focus was zeroed in on the Sunday edition of the Seascape Shores Tribune serving as a paper barricade between them, not on the bird that was about to drive Camille completely bonkers.

"Cawing. Mewing. Screeching like banshee. I don't care what the *technical* term for it is. I call it incredibly annoying!" She glowered out the big bay window at the seagull now perched on the deck railing just as it let out another squawk so shrill, it almost made her drop her mug.

Skip Hartley released the newspaper, lowering it to the breakfast table. His white, wiry brows pulled taut, then relaxed, softening over deep-set eyes that searched out his new housemate. "Camille, dear, why are you so concerned with the noises around here all of a sudden? Thought the familiar sounds of the sea were a comfort to you."

"Would you believe the Coastal Cove Inn received a one-star review because the waves crashed 'continuously against the shore' throughout the night and kept one of their guests awake?" She made air quotes around the ridiculous words. "A *one-star* review, Skip! That's horrible for business. We can't risk getting any of those. Certainly not on our opening weekend."

"Ah, I see." He nodded. "You're nervous about the arrival of our first guests."

"I'm not nervous. I just want to make sure things go off without a hitch. We have three guests checking in tomorrow afternoon. That is, unless they cancel once they find out this resident bird of ours doesn't shut up!" She angled another scowl toward the offending gull. "He's like a broken cuckoo clock!"

"I've always said you shouldn't pay any mind to the things out of your control. I do believe ocean waves and marine life fall into that category."

Camille thumbed her chin. "You have a big fishing net around here? Maybe if you distract him with some breadcrumbs tossed out onto the deck, I could swoop in and—"

"We're not trapping any birds," Skip interjected. "And I will not have you sit here all day listening and looking for more potential grievances. Everything is ready to go. You've worked hard to make sure of that.

I think you should take the afternoon off and splurge on something for yourself. Go to the beauty parlor or whatever is it that ladies do these days to feel special."

The hard edge of Camille's attitude sloughed off a bit from Skip's endearing words. Over the last month, they had formed an effortlessly easy camaraderie. In so many ways, he felt like a grandpa: equal parts curmudgeon and wise old sage. But the startling truth was that Camille's own parents wouldn't have been much younger than Skip, had they not perished in a sailing accident when she was just a little girl.

"Here." Skip rotated to withdraw his wallet from his back pocket. He fished out a twenty and slipped it between his fingers. "Take this and treat yourself—"

"I'm not taking a dime of your money. But I will take your advice and get out of here for a bit. I need to run into town to grab a few more toiletries for the bathrooms and I want to pick up some of those individually wrapped mints for the pillows, if I can find them. I think those would be a nice touch," Camille said. "Plus, I've got a meeting at that new bakery to nail down a menu for our guests. Can't have a bed-and-breakfast without the whole breakfast part. Goodness knows my culinary skills would have the negative reviews rolling in."

"You've thought of everything, Camille. Just like my sweet Gertie used to." A wistful gleam came to the old man's eyes. "Have I told you lately how grateful I am that you came to my rescue with this house?"

"Twice already just this morning," she answered,

patting him on the hand before rising from her chair. "But the feeling's mutual, Skip. I'm just as grateful for you as you are for me." Then, thrusting her pointer finger toward the window, she snorted, "But I'm not grateful for that bird. Not even one little bit!"

"Leave Gully to me. I'll see if I can talk him into quieting down while you're gone."

"You've named him?" Camille's hand flew to slap her forehead. "You can't go naming him. Now he'll never leave!"

"And I'm beginning to think you won't, either," Skip rallied. "Go on now and forget about this house and that bird for the afternoon. Scoot, scoot. Out you go."

Camille pursed her lips to button back further protest. Skip was right. She'd become so immersed in rolling things out for the grand re-opening of The Getaway House that she had spent very little time away from the property at all in recent weeks.

First, it was the renovation that garnered most of her attention. Thanks to her friend, Foster Spaulding, that daunting process went more smoothly than she ever could have hoped. Foster's construction crew not only brought the house up to date with building codes but in style and structure, too. Not that it took much to uncover the underlying beauty of the coastal home. After all, it had what Ben Parker, local real estate agent and Camille's ex-brother-in-law, referred to as "good bones." A knocked down wall here. A coat of paint there. Some crisp, white shiplap and new hardwood flooring throughout made the beach house feel like an entirely new dwelling, one Camille hoped people would pay good money to stay in.

That was the goal, after all: to breathe new life into The Getaway House and restore it to the marketable coastal destination it once was.

With her purse slung across her body and her sunglasses drawn low over her eyes, Camille set out to tackle her list of to-do's. Feelings of overwhelm threatened to take root when she scanned the lengthy sheet, but one emotion quickly smothered it all: *gratitude*.

Grateful that Foster's team was able to reroute the previously treacherous incline leading from the seaside home up to the parking lot, transforming the cliffy staircase to a sloping, meandering trail that no longer left her struggling for breath each time she ascended it. Grateful she didn't have to sit at an uncomfortable desk from nine to five, answering phone calls in a rehearsed cheery tone and writing down memos to hand off to her superiors. Grateful her best friend, Edie, was in escrow on the very beach house next to Skip's and that her sister, Tabitha, had purchased the one neighboring that.

She was grateful, alright. Somehow, the once scattered puzzle pieces of her life were now locking into place to create a more beautiful picture of her future than she could have ever fathomed.

For Camille Todd, life was good. That was just a simple, certifiable fact. ˙

The drive into town was quick. Windows rolled

down, she let the briny coastal air swirl about the cab, twisting her hair up in wayward, golden knots that didn't annoy her one bit. There were sacrifices to be made with coastal living and beach hair was one of them. She wasn't sure if she was willing to acquiesce when it came to unavoidable seagull noise, but there wasn't much she could do about that at the moment.

What she *could* do was start to check off the items on her list, and she set about that task with bubbling enthusiasm.

She found the most darling little apothecary shop on the main drag that had all sorts of handmade lotions, candles, and scrubs. With shopping basket in hand, she gathered glycerin soaps molded into starfish and shells, all in coastal hues. She picked up a few matching hand towels that had the phrase *Life is Better at the Beach* embroidered across the white terrycloth, and she even found a small soap dish in the shape of a sailboat on a nearby display. Little touches like these were sure to set The Getaway House apart, she just knew it.

At least, she hoped they would.

Camille couldn't hide the very real fact that she was completely new to the hospitality industry. It wasn't often that she even had the chance to travel. Apart from her recent month-long stay at the Seascape Shores Villas with Tabitha and Edie, she had very little experience as a vacationer. And to be frank, their Villa vacation wasn't the norm, of that she was fully aware. Pampering and indulging, relaxing and rejuvenating. It was an irrefutably unforgettable time, but not something Camille would ever be able to recreate for her guests at The Getaway House.

But that wasn't the goal. The Villas were a great, luxurious escape. A departure from reality.

She wanted Skip's place to feel like coming home.

It felt that way for Camille. As a child, she spent so many summers with her toes buried in the sand, her cheeks chapped with wind, and her skin kissed a freckly tan. She remembered youthful days sprawled out on their family sailboat under the protective bulk of a heavy quilt, the undulating waves swaying her to sleep more effectively than any rocking chair could.

Her parents loved the sea. It was the biggest part of their lives, and in a manner that felt tragically fitting, it had been the reason for their untimely deaths. For far too long, Camille's emotions rested in an uncomfortable space between anguish and awe each time she would look out at those relentless waves. Somehow, over the course of her adult life, that vacillation settled into what she could only label as profound respect. The ocean was an unmatchable force both in its beauty and its power, and it demanded an admiration Camille could finally fully give.

That she got to wake up each morning with those vast waters filling up the entirety of her bedroom window was a gift she would never take for granted. Seagulls and all, she supposed.

She laughed about that quietly under her breath as she paid for her items and then set back out onto Main Street to hunt down mints for her guests, a smile spread wide across her face. The fog had finally rolled out to sea and the sun—previously trapped behind its dense layering—now shone with bright abandon. It was all Camille could do to keep from closing her eyes and basking in the cozy warmth that caressed her bare shoulders and the tops of her sandaled feet.

Then she caught sight of something that warmed her far more than those morning rays ever could.

"Fancy seeing you here." Foster Spaulding had his hands shoved coolly into the pockets of his dark denim jeans as he paced the sidewalk toward her, coming nearer with each long stride. He pulled one hand free and took Camille's chin between his thumb and finger to draw her close, leaving a sweet kiss on her cheek that made her stomach go weightless.

"Well, hello there, Foster," she said, hoping she wasn't blushing, but knowing full well she was likely tomato red. "I was just shopping for some last-minute things before our first guests arrive." She held up the bag and gave it a little shake. "What are you up to?"

He stroked his well-past-five-o'clock shadow. That man made salt and pepper scruff look downright delectable. "Just heading to the tile shop to look at a few more samples before tomorrow's meeting with Edie. I think tomorrow is the day she's finally going to make a decision on tile for the bathrooms. Good thing, because my guys will be ready to install this week."

"Edie's making a decision? An accomplishment that should go down in the history books!"

Foster snickered. "It hasn't been that bad, honestly. Just a bit of a one-eighty from working with Tabitha."

"Tabitha is the ultimate decision maker, no question about that," Camille agreed. "Goes with the job territory."

As a trauma surgeon, Tabitha made life and death decisions daily. Selecting paint colors and tile patterns was a cakewalk. In the same vein, Edie's job as a photographer likely contributed to her lengthy decision-making process. She was always on the hunt for the perfect lighting, the best angle, the ideal subject. So it didn't surprise Camille one bit that her friend struggled to finalize the finishes of her new beach home.

"I've already offered a million and one times, but if Edie needs any help, I'm always happy to throw in my two cents."

"She knows that. Keeps saying she doesn't want too many cooks in the kitchen," Foster said. "And speaking of, I really hope we can nail down an evening for you to come over for dinner so I can finally cook for you. I know our schedules haven't allowed it lately, but I coming up on some free time. Can't think of anyone I'd rather spend it with."

Ships in the night. That's what they had become,

both busy with work that allowed little-to-no play. They'd met at the Villas and their attraction had been both mutual and instant, but a misunderstanding about Foster's past made Camille slam on the breaks initially. She'd been repeatedly burned by her ex-husband, and trust wasn't exactly something she handed out freely when it came to men.

But Foster proved to be everything she hoped he would be: trustworthy, caring, and fiercely loyal. It was that loyalty, in fact, that landed him behind bars when he was a young father. He'd been in an impossible situation and done what any man would do to protect his children. That reality—a testament to his true character—only made Camille's fondness for him grow.

She had hoped things would move quickly between them from there. At forty-six, she didn't feel the need to waste time on lengthy courtships or unnecessary wooing. She knew what she wanted, and she wanted Foster Spaulding. Plain and simple.

Unfortunately, nothing in life was ever all that simple. Least of all their schedules.

"You name the day and I'll make it work," Camille said, determined to get something on the calendar with the handsome man standing in front her.

"Tomorrow night. Five o'clock."

Her mouth thinned into a line.

"You've already got plans." Foster interpreted her dejected expression.

"It's just that our guests will be checking in after three, and I need to make sure I'm available in case we have any stragglers."

Foster waved his hands in understanding. "You don't need to explain it, Camille. I get it. This weekend is a big deal for you and Skip." He took her hands in his. "How about this? I'll be swinging by Tabitha's on Sunday afternoon to go over the issues the guys need to fix from the final walkthrough. What if I come by your place after? I'll bring a bottle of wine and a blanket. We can spend some time down at the beach. Watch the sunset."

Camille cut him off. "You had me at wine," she said. "But the sunset was a nice touch."

"It's a date then." He pressed another kiss to her cheek, leaving a fiery flush in its wake. "And if something comes up and you need to cancel, my feelings won't be hurt. I'm happy to wait until you have time, Camille."

"I'll *make* the time," she assured, a promise to both Foster and to herself.

Making time for her own happiness was priority number one for Camille.

Well, that and tracking down those silly pillow mints.

Order The Getaway House, book two in the Seascape Shores novels.

Also by Megan Squires

The Harmony Ridge Series
Love and Harmony (FREE Prequel)
Detour to Harmony (Book One)
In Sweet Harmony (Book Two)
Match Made in Harmony (Book Three)

A Winter Cabin Christmas
Christmas at Yuletide Farm
An Heirloom Christmas
A Lake House Holiday
In the Market for Love

Join Megan Squires' Reader Group!

Join my corner of Facebook where I share sneak
peeks, host giveaways, and get to know my readers
even better!

To stay up to date on new releases, please sign up for
Megan's newsletter:

http://subscribe.megansquiresauthor.com

ACKNOWLEDGMENTS

As with every novel I write, it is never a solitary endeavor. Like Camille, Edie, and Tabitha, I am so lucky to have such a wonderful tribe of women in my life who believe in me, encourage me, and make me a better person.

Amber Garza, you are so much more than just my writing bestie. You are someone I can always count on to listen to my worries, talk me down from the ledge, and let me know that I'm not crazy, even when I sometimes feel like it. You have been my cheerleader over the last decade of this writing career, and I honestly would not be where I am today without you. I love you more than words can say.

This particular book has been four years in the making, and a big reason for that is because—as you might have guessed—I'm not a trauma surgeon. Tabitha is a complex character, and I really wanted to get her right. Her personality, her passion, and her profession. Katie Shea, your input has been invaluable with this. You provided me with the medical and emotional details necessary to turn Tabitha into the talented surgeon I needed her to be. I cannot thank you enough for that.

And for my sister, Erin, and my mom, Norma: you two always get the first glimpse into my stories, and your excitement over this particular novel is what finally pushed me to publish. I hope my readers fall in love with Camille, Tabitha, and Edie as deeply as you did. Thank you for consistently encouraging me to put myself out there. I don't know about you, but I think a celebratory seascape retreat might be something to think about in our future!

ABOUT THE AUTHOR

 When Megan Squires isn't writing, thinking, or dreaming all things sweet romance, she's caring for the nearly sixty animals on her twelve-acre flower farm in Northern California. A UC Davis graduate, Megan worked in the political non-profit realm prior to becoming a stay-at-home mom. She then spent nearly ten years as an award winning photographer, with her work published in magazines such as Professional Photographer and Click.

In 2012, her creativity took a turn when she wrote and published her first young adult novel. Megan is both traditionally and self-published. She can't go a day without her family and farm animals, and a large McDonald's Diet Coke.

To keep up with Megan online, please visit:

facebook.com/MeganSquiresAuthor

twitter.com/MeganSquires

instagram.com/megansquiresauthor

bookbub.com/authors/megan-squires

Made in the USA
Middletown, DE
19 January 2023

22487601R00196